SHELTER FOR A SHIFTER

FOLK HAVEN
BOOK 4

LAUREN CONNOLLY

For Salem and Thackery Binx.

All Ame asks for is the right spell, a full moon, and a cooperative cat. She does *not* ask for a naked werewolf.

Ame Shelly has been searching through grimoires for years, hoping to find a way to save her cat companion. A feline she's ninety-six percent sure is a man stuck in the wrong form. When Ame and her sister start their own magical library in the small town of Folk Haven, the witch finally discovers an incantation that could free her friend. At least, she thinks Bee the cat is her friend. He hasn't run away from her since the night she discovered him injured in the woods. Plus, Bee doesn't growl at her the way he does with everyone else …

Bee wants revenge.

Bee is not a cat, his name is not Bee, and he is *not* happy.

ISBN-13: 978-1-949794-24-3

NEWSLETTER SIGN UP

Get another Folk Haven romance for FREE! Sign up for my newsletter to receive *A Selkie's Secret,* a novella that tells the story of Isla, a selkie, and Finn, the human she refuses to fall in love with...

CONTENT WARNINGS

This book contains scenes with self-mutilation for magic, sexual harassment, captivity, blood and gore, and a violent death.

This book contains scenes discussing neglectful and abusive parents and kidnapping.

Extra warning: this book is darker than the first few in the series, just FYI.

PROLOGUE

AME

Three Years Ago

AN URGE, not entirely my own, demands I press the brake
pedal.

Now.

Stop now.

NOW.

NOW!

The RV shudders at the abrupt halt, and I hear a loud
thunk and a yelp from behind me that I hope was my sister
toppling out of bed and not a pile of books falling over.

She would prefer that outcome.

"Amethyst Shelly," Morgana snaps, appearing next to me in
her matching flannel sleep set, her hair a bedhead tangle, the
red curls muted in the glow of the dashboard. "Why in all the
gods' names are you Tokyo drifting in the middle of the night?"

"Drifting would require going around a corner," I point out.

"Do we need to watch the movies again?" Action movie marathons are one of my favorite pastimes.

"No. I promise to never improperly reference a Vin Diesel film again if you promise never to make me watch them."

"Technically, he wasn't in that movie. Not more than a few seconds anyway."

"Ame," my sister groans as she stares past the wide dashboard, studying the section of road visible in the beams of our headlights. "Enough with the movie. Why did you stop? Was it a deer?"

"Sorry, no." I pause, trying to explain the sudden urgency to halt our massive vehicle in the middle of the night on a back road in Maine. Trees press in from all sides, giving this stretch of lane an ominous air in the moonless night. "Do you ... feel that?"

There's *something*. A tugging. A necessity in the air. A drive to pay attention.

But that doesn't make sense.

"I don't feel anything." My sister watches me, confusion crinkling her brows.

"I'm sorry. I must be tired. Maybe I should find a rest stop. I don't know why I offered to drive through the night."

It's not like we're in a hurry. Morgana and I have destinations, but no deadlines. We form our schedules how we want.

Well, how *she* wants. But I don't mind.

Still, even as I say one thing, my body does another. I slip the gearshift into park and unbuckle my seat belt. I reach for a heavy-duty flashlight behind the passenger seat and pop open the door, letting in a gust of chilly fall air.

"Ame! What in all the hell dimensions? Where are you going?"

"Outside." I hop down from the cab, belatedly remembering I prefer to drive barefoot. The frigid asphalt shocks the bare soles of my feet as the loose gravel pricks like needles. "Ouch. Crap. Bad idea."

Still, I sidle forward, swaying the beam of my flashlight back and forth over the road. The entire world looms dark around me, as if I were drifting off into outer space, the RV a space station representing safety I willingly left behind.

The tug grows, guiding me toward the woods. I follow the urge, disregarding my sister's voice behind me.

On one pass of my light, two reflective discs shine back at me.

Not discs ...

Eyes.

They sit low to the ground, staring at me with the terror of an animal. But scared animals normally run.

"Hey there, little one. Are you friendly?" I whisper my question. *Please don't be a pissed off skunk,* I silently pray to The Dark One. Though I'm not sure the goddess—creator of all magic, witches included—cares much if I get sprayed.

Crouching low, I shuffle closer.

It's a cat. A tiny black beast, panting hard with fear. When I take another step, it lurches to the side, trying to escape, and that's when I see the gash on its backside.

Without thought, I reach out with my magic, meaning to persuade the animal to calm down. To trust me. I come from a line of witches born with emotion-centered magic. My specialty is desire, which means with a little mystical push, I can get someone to want what I tell them to. Animals are always easier than humans with their simpler urges and thoughts.

But my powers collide with a more intricate tangle of feeling than I've ever experienced when using my powers on an animal. The emotions are almost ... human.

But not.

"What are you?" Curiosity disappears, replaced with concern when the feline jerks again at the sound of my voice.

"Ame!" Footsteps approach along with my sister's scolding. "You can't run off into the dark. I couldn't—"

"Wait." I keep my command quiet but firm.

The cat, who grew agitated at Morgana's approach, stills again. My sister also does as I said, more likely from shock at my order than from the urge to obey me.

"There's a cat. It's hurt. Could you go grab a blanket?"

"Oh."

After a pause, I hear her retreat. Morgana isn't what I'd call an animal lover, but she's not about to let one suffer.

Alone again, I sink to the ground, crossing my legs and setting the flashlight aside.

"Hi. My name is Amethyst. Friends call me Ame." Not that I have a lot of those. "I'm going to try to help you. I swear I'm not dangerous. Not to you anyway."

Maybe this animal understands me; maybe it doesn't. What can telling it my plan hurt?

"I'm not a healing witch by trade, but we found a grimoire a few weeks ago, full of medical spells." As I speak, I keep my tone level and extend a hand, resting it on the grass between us.

The cat doesn't move toward me, but it also doesn't try to retreat again.

Morgana returns, her approach quieter this time, and she hands me one of her knit blankets. "What else do you need?" She keeps her voice low.

"The healing poultices. Water. Food. I'll come back to the camper when I have him." And in that moment, I realize this cat is a *him*, and I know that without checking between his legs.

"The spells weren't meant for animals."

"I think they could work on him."

My sister leaves without another word, likely thinking it's a waste of potion supplies but willing to humor me.

Keeping my attention on the cat, I drape the blanket over both of my hands. "I'm going to wrap this around you. And then I'm going to carry you to my home." The urge that drew me here has me wanting to speak to the animal as if I were talking to a human. "Then, I'll try my best to make the pain go away."

Slowly, I lean forward and use my blanket-covered arms to gently bundle up the injured creature.

He growls, the sound lower than I thought feline vocal cords could go, but he doesn't fight me. Once he's in my arms, the urgency that had me stopping in the middle of nowhere eases.

"Hello, buddy," I murmur to him as I ignore my cold, aching feet on the walk back to the camper. "Seems The Dark One wanted me to find you. I wonder why."

His only response is another growl.

1

AME

Present Day

MY BATHROOM GETS perfect southern exposure, which means I have to eject a man from the windowsill every time I shower.

"We've discussed this close to, possibly more than, one hundred times, Bee. I'm not letting you stay here."

To help with my scolding, I prop my fists on my hips and attempt my best glare at the black cat refusing to vacate the bathroom. He merely blinks at me, the slow gesture full of insolence.

But what did I expect? I'm no good at glaring. Never have been and was never willing to put in the effort required to learn.

"I'd like to think that I'm an open-minded witch," I tell him with a sigh. "But I refuse to shower in front of you when you're likely a human man."

Bee yawns in response, then finds a way to sprawl in even more of a furry puddle in the warmth of the afternoon sun spilling through the stained glass window. Every bathroom in this old Victorian house has a stained glass window, which I find odd but endearing. Each has a different bird scene; this one sports a blue heron.

We see plenty of the birds standing on their stilt-like legs on the banks of Lake Galen, the great watery expanse that this house sits next to. Sometimes, I catch sight of a heron in a beautiful, smooth glide over the calm water.

Then, the bird lets out a noise like a prehistoric monster and ruins the calm of their presence.

Just like I'm about to ruin Bee's relaxing afternoon nap.

But I need a shower. I've been reorganizing old books all day, and I'm wearing a second layer over my overalls that's fashioned from condensed dust.

Is there such an ailment as a gray lung? If so, I have it.

"Fair warning: I'm about to touch you. You know I don't like manhandling you like this, but you've left me no choice."

That's not exactly true. I could go ask my sister to use her bathroom. But she loves strongly scented body wash and hair products that always make me sneeze, even when I'm not using them. Like the floral scents have melded with the tiles in her shower.

I want to use *my* bathroom now that I finally have my own.

Morgana and I spent years in close quarters, traveling around the country in an RV, stopping at every used bookstore we came across to search for discarded grimoires and texts that discussed mythical creatures. My older sister had a dream of establishing a library to house the books, where our kind could access the information and develop a greater understanding of ourselves.

When she asked me to come along, I saw an opportunity to

help the sister who had raised me fulfill her life's passion. I couldn't say no.

But I was more than a little relieved when we heard of Folk Haven—a town in Georgia, rumored to be a safe place for mythics—and Morgana claimed it was the perfect place to settle. Getting permission to buy this lakeside Victorian, previously owned by a dragon, wasn't easy, but we're here now, and one of the many benefits of moving out of the RV and into this house is the new space I get to myself. Including my own bathroom. But apparently, Bee wants to share.

I could use my magic on him, make him *want* to leave. But I've never magically manipulated him, and I refuse to start now. Especially when I'm ninety-six percent sure he's a man, trapped in a cat's body.

Luxuriously soft fur tickles my palm as I slide a hand under his prone body. The cat knows what my goal is, and I watch him go totally boneless—his normal defense against me removing him from the bathroom. Maybe he thinks, one day, I'll be too tired to shift him and decide to leave him in peace.

Not going to happen. No matter how many heavy volumes of books I sorted through today, I still have enough strength to move the obstinate creature.

He hangs limp in my arms, a solid black rag-doll cat, letting out his *you're ruining my day* growl. Bee has an entire catalog of growls I've learned over the years.

The *pet me and lose your hand* growl.

The *you're boring, and I'm leaving* growl.

The *I don't care if you think I'm human; stop trying to feed me Brussels sprouts* growl.

And his all-time favorite ... *if you look at me one more time, I'm going to fuck you up* growl.

Lucky me, I'm almost never on the bad end of the violent growls. I think Bee likes me as much as he's willing to like a person. We've established a truce.

But not enough of one where he gets to leisurely watch me strip naked.

"Here. There's sunshine on your ottoman."

When I lay the heavy, protesting feline on his normal sleep spot under a window in my bedroom, he grumbles in a way that *has* to be human. I don't know how anyone could doubt Bee is something more than an ordinary house cat. But whenever I express my above ninety percent surety that my friend is meant to be a man, the person I'm telling gives me a skeptical look and asks if I'm feeling lonely. When I assure them I'm not making up his manly attributes out of a need for companionship, the person usually recommends attempting to communicate with words to prove my theory.

As if I haven't tried. Less than a week after finding him, I bought a poster board, wrote out the alphabet, and tried to ask the cat questions.

It didn't go well.

The first I tried was, "What is your name?"

His feline eyes went unfocused as they flicked between me and the board. After an extended pause, he pounced on the letter *B*. Then, he sat there, unmoving.

Since there was an endless list of names that start with B, I decided calling him Bee would have to do. That was as far as we got. All other questions resulted in him wandering in a directionless manner over the board until he eventually started shredding the poster in agitation.

Morgana pointed out the animalistic behavior indicated he was *not* a man.

But I wasn't so easily dissuaded. So, the board didn't work. Over the years, we've found other ways to communicate. Or, at the very least, I've learned how to interpret Bee's collection of growls.

For now, that works. We can have plenty of long conversations once I discover how to change him back to a man.

"I'm going to lock the door because I don't trust you. At least, not as far as the bathroom is concerned."

Bee lets out another grumble as he stretches on his new perch. Despite the dismissiveness of the move, I feel his attention on me as I head to the shower and even after I close the door.

As the water warms up, I unbraid my hair, the red shade muted with dust. In the mirror, I can barely make out my freckles through the grime. When I step under the spray, I let out a sigh of relief as the grime washes away. The odd thing is, I feel dirtier, covered in dust, than I do when I'm coated in actual dirt. I'd rather roll around in mud than sort items on a shelf in a dimly lit room.

But Morgana needs my help. And more importantly, walking through the forest won't bring me closer to finding a solution for Bee's curse. The answer has to be in one of the spell books we've collected over the years.

Even if I've already searched through all of them.

You have a possibility. It could work. Maybe tonight is the end of the hunt.

As I massage a subtle-scented mint shampoo into my scalp, I list off the ingredients I'll need to gather before I head out this evening.

"Four sage candles. Extra matches. White roses. Chalk ..."

The list goes on—one I memorized after months of repetition.

Will tonight's spell finally give me the answer I want?

That's all I've searched for since the night I found Bee on the side of the road.

Answers.

Why was he there?

Who or what had hurt him?

How did I feel him needing help?

What do I need to do to change him back to whoever he used to be?

Three years later, all these queries still pinch at my mind.

But tonight ... maybe I'll start getting answers.

2

———————

AME

BEE GLARES at me from across the clearing.

"There's no reason for that look," I tell him. "I can't make the moon rise any faster."

But maybe he's not glaring. Maybe he's just watching and he has no idea what this spell is.

And maybe he's just a cat.

No. I'm ninety-six percent sure he's a man.

And I'm one hundred percent sure I will never stop trying to find a way to change Bee back to his original shape. Whether it was The Dark One's plans, a trick of fate, or a mere accident, that night I found Bee wounded on the side of the road, I claimed him as one of mine. I don't have many of *mine*, and those I do have, I'll do anything for them.

If he is a man, I will get his body back for him.

Trees loom tall around this small clearing, but despite the dense foliage, I can still hear the gentle lap of waves from Lake Galen, which is only a short walk away. This waterside forest thrums with a subtle magic, stronger tonight than most others.

In a few weeks, on the autumnal equinox, this power will thicken the air even more so.

But more magic isn't always the answer to making a spell work. The grimoire I found this incantation in specifically stated a full moon was recommended to complete the spell. Something to do with a light to see the truth.

I'm not attempting to transform Bee back into a man tonight. Two years ago, I came across a set of instructions in a book from a family of truth-teller witches. The author claimed if a witch followed the steps, the spell would reveal if casting another—more dangerous—incantation would end in success or disaster. This truth-revealing spell is simple—other than requiring the light of a full moon—but vitally important.

Ever since learning the charm, I've used it to test every transformation spell I've discovered, hoping for results that indicate it'll work on Bee. A mystical peer review of sorts. A necessary one.

The witches who originally wrote the grimoire could probably cast this spell anytime of the month and get a result as good as I will tonight. That's the difference between using spells within and outside of your specialty. As an emotions witch, I can manipulate desires whenever I want with just the press of my hand and a touch of red powder. But a truth-teller witch wanting to do the same would need to set up a special altar, use certain crystals for a power source, have the proper incantation ...

It's a whole thing.

Which is why I need this full moon to get her shiny white ass in the sky.

If I try to change Bee with the wrong spell, novice that I still am, I could leave him in worse shape than a mere cat.

I could kill him.

All I want is a cosmic thumbs-up.

I lean over my electronic tablet, eyeing the document

where I typed the instructions so I wouldn't have to expose a priceless artifact to damp grass and red clay dirt. Even though I've performed this magic twenty times or more, I mutter the steps to myself while mentally checking them off. If I get this wrong, we'll need to wait another month before I can try again.

"I have high hopes for this spell."

Bee can't talk back, but I still converse with him regularly. If I were transformed into an animal, I would prefer if people continued to treat me with dignity and respect. So, following the Golden Rule, I include him in my conversations.

"The grimoire had a whole section on shapeshifter anatomy. I figure knowing all that would help transformation spells."

Silently, I hope the witches who wrote all these incantations down—however many hundreds of years ago—came by the information honestly. Mythics might not always get along with each other, but we don't use one another to gain power.

That toxic magic is the way of sorcerers.

Sorcerers are the bane of mythic existence. They are humans who steal the life force from mythics in order to cast spells.

Aka a bunch of creepy motherfuckers.

As the full moon creeps higher in the sky, blotting out the hint of stars, I finish lighting the candles surrounding my spell casting space and the book—this grimoire I *did* bring with me —containing the incantation which will hopefully work on Bee.

The clearing glows brightly under the milky light of the moon. Though I can hear the buzz of insects, they stay away from the candle flames, either driven off by the fragrant herbs in the wax or the aura of power already gathering.

"It's time. Stay where you are."

Bee doesn't normally take orders well, hence the almost-constant, forceful removal from my bathroom. This time, he obeys, sitting stoically in the shadows between two trees.

I step out of the circle, kneeling with my back to the south, a hint of Lake Galen glittering through the leaves on my left. From one pocket, I pull out a piece of notebook paper, and from another, I remove a stick of charcoal that stains my fingers black.

Will this spell help my friend, who I call Bee, regain his true form?

The original text emphasized clarity when writing the request. I can't write *will this spell change my cat into a man* because what if there's another cat wandering by or what if it would make him a man, but the wrong man?

And I can't write *will this spell turn Bee into his true form* because Bee is a name I gave him, which might mislead the spell again. This is as clear as I think I can get it.

After a hopeful, deep breath, I hold the paper to the flame of the candle sitting directly in front of me. A wind stirs through the circle, yet the candles don't flicker, and the white rose petals I scattered over the ground don't move.

The paper in my hand flares to life, burning higher and brighter than it should, yet giving off no heat.

And somehow, the color is vibrant despite its shade.

Black.

A onyx flame consumes my question.

"No," I sigh the answer in defeat, glancing over to Bee in time to watch as my feline friend turns his back and lopes into the woods.

As the black flame eats the rest of the paper, I let it drop into a copper bowl beside me.

"I'm sorry," I say to him in the empty night. "I'll keep looking."

But he's too far gone to hear me.

3

——————

AME

I HOLD the door of Coffee & Claws open for Bee to make sure his tail doesn't catch when it swings shut. He immediately abandons me to go greet Gigabyte, an anxious dog that peers out the top of his carrier under a table near the window. Delta, Gigabyte's owner, smiles at my cat companion, then at me. Then, she goes back to typing on her computer, her nails—or more accurately, claws—filling the café with pleasant, repetitive clicking.

Would like another academic article. Her subtle desire slips into my mind, riding a current of my magic that brushed against the dragon, who is also a professor.

Despite the innocent nature of the want, I attempt to ignore the magical message by focusing on the stacks of colorful mugs behind the counter.

The red one with the yellow leaf design is pretty. How many leaves? One, two, three ...

The thoughts might be childishly simple, but I've found focusing on random objects, digging into every little detail about them, distracts my mind from hearing the desires of everyone around me. An unfortunate side effect of my magical specialty. My siblings have learned to shield themselves, but everyone else unknowingly shouts their secret cravings the moment I'm within hearing distance.

As I keep my gaze on the mugs, I approach the counter and tug my phone out of my pocket, swiping open the Notes app. My sister is a creature of habit in many ways, but she constantly experiments with coffee. Every day, it's something new, which means I have no hope of rattling off a memorized order.

"*Iced coconut latte with almond milk and cinnamon on top,*" I read off to the barista. Belatedly, I remember to make eye contact—actually staring at a freckle on the bridge of her nose —smile, and add, "Please."

Please don't accidentally share any dark desires with me.

"Hi, Ame. That sounds yummy. Another Morgana experiment?" Sonya, the woman behind the counter and co-owner of the shop, gives me a smile that creases the copper skin around her eyes, reassuring me I haven't offended her with my distracted delivery.

Want to stretch my wings. The siren's silent longing is a quiet whisper I can easily ignore, like an overheard conversation.

"Hello, Sonya." I slide my phone back into the pocket of my overalls. The clothing piece isn't exactly flattering, but the depth of the pockets is worth the shapeless form. "Yes. She said she wanted her drink to taste like summer turning into fall."

With her so fully entrenched in the library, I was surprised that my sister knew we were approaching a change of seasons. Morgana only realized it was midsummer when I built a bonfire in our backyard.

"That's genius." Sonya raps her knuckles on the counter. "I might steal that and make it the drink of the week leading up to the equinox. I'll give your sister credit, of course."

I imagine it—the chalkboard sign outside this staple of Folk

Haven, proclaiming the specialty drink was invented by a Shelly witch.

"Morgana would like that, I think."

My sister doesn't seek out notoriety—coffee-related or any other kind—but she might like the subtle approval of Coffee & Claws. After living in this small town for a year, she's shared her frustration with how we're both still seen as outsiders. I never expected to be an insider. People don't like when I get too close to their insides, worried what I'll do to them with my magic.

Can't imagine how they'd feel if they found out I knew their secret desires too.

But I see Morgana's point about fitting in when she wants to run a well-trafficked magical library.

Currently, the Folk Haven Public Mythic Library is only meagerly trafficked.

"You let her know my plan," Sonya says. "She can object if she wants."

"Will do." I pass over the cash for the coffee, then drop the change in the tip jar before I wander toward the pickup end of the counter.

As I peer around the shop, searching for Bee, my eyes catch on a blue set that holds my gaze in place.

The intensity is uncomfortable, more so when I recognize the stare's owner. And eye contact always opens a direct path into ...

Want to bend her over a table, spank her ass. Fist her red hair. Have her moan and call me daddy.

I tear my gaze away, drop it to the floor, and trace the grain of the oak hardwood. Anything to clear the man's craving from my mind.

"Amethyst. I was hoping to run into you." Hamish strolls up to me, his hands in his pockets and a wide smile on his broad mouth, no idea that I glimpsed his fantasy, starring me.

I don't blame him for being attracted to me or making a

mental porno. Honestly, I've seen much more explicit desires than his. But it's particularly uncomfortable because I see Hamish so often, as he's one of the few frequent visitors to the library.

The selkie is a handsome mythic by many standards with his strong jaw, wavy and dark hair, and muscular build. Plus, there's the Scottish lilt in his voice, which hints at a life lived on a different continent.

But he's never inspired a hint of lust in me. He'll have to find another partner to bend over a table.

"Hi, Hamish." I give him a polite smile and examine the dark metal light fixtures on the ceiling to avoid hearing any more of his imaginary dirty talk.

The smell of freshly baked pastries is another pleasant distraction, and I glance toward the kitchen, wondering if Heath—the baker and other co-owner of Coffee & Claws— might be on the verge of bringing out some tasty creations. I never drink coffee—I've found caffeine makes me anxious— but I wouldn't deny myself a scone.

"It's been too long since I came by the library," Hamish says, still intent on speaking to me.

"Not too long," I murmur. "You came last week." And I might have snuck out the back door after seeing his car from my bedroom window.

From the corner of my eye, I see the selkie grin as he continues to watch me.

"Keeping track of my visits? I'm flattered." *Take me in her mouth.* "Why don't you let me buy you a treat to go with your coffee?" *Watch her suck me.* "We can grab a table and get to know each other better." The selkie gestures to the empty seats in the café as his imagination has me on my knees.

Normally, I don't mind lingering in Coffee & Claws, especially if it means I can sit on the floor near Delta's table and say hello to Gigabyte. Even though I can manipulate what animals want, I never seem to sense them the same way I do with humans and mythics. They're a relief to be around.

But I don't have any urge to spend my afternoon with Hamish, dodging his desires. Luckily, I have a ready-made excuse.

"I'm here to get coffee for Morgana. To go. Need to get back to the house before the ice in her drink melts."

"Here you go, Ame. Tell your sister I said hi." Sonya slides my cup to me across the counter with perfect timing.

"Sure thing." I turn to find my path blocked by the selkie.

"You're eager to get back to that library of yours." He smiles down at me.

Thinking of all the texts that still need reviewing and sorting and translating, I wrinkle my nose, as if preparing for the future sneezing that comes with the work I do. No matter how many times I run a microfiber cloth over the lot, the dust returns. Dust loves old books.

I—please never tell my sister this or else she might perish on the spot—do not.

Leather spines, cracked with age. Yellowed pages with preservation spells wearing off. Plus, witches have terrible handwriting, making their scrawled spells uneven and almost illegible on the parchment.

Give me an eBook any day.

"In a way," I say. The way that going there gets me away from minds that can't help broadcasting into mine.

He laughs, as if I said something witty. "You know, I've only ever seen the lower level. I'd enjoy a look around. Maybe you could show me what you all are hiding upstairs in that old house."

I frown and wonder if the wetness on my palm is condensation from Morgana's drink or sweat.

"There're just bedrooms upstairs."

Hamish grins. "Even better." He steps close, bringing the scent of seaweed with him.

In the coastal town I grew up in, there was a sea witch who would create a cracker-like snack out of the slimy green foliage and would gift batches of them to families around town. One night, I was hungry for dinner, but Morgana was at a friend's house, my brothers were at the movies, and my parents were doing what they often did—working on spells that required zero distraction. The only food in the house were those crackers, so I ate the lot. Turned out, that much salt on an empty stomach didn't settle right, and an hour later, I puked all over my favorite blanket. No washing machine or cleaning spell was strong enough to eradicate that level of stomach acid and half-digested algae. Morgana had to throw my blankie away.

The memory and the smell have my stomach churning now.

"What do you say, Amethyst? Want to give me a private tour?" Hamish leans toward me, his eyes a deep ocean blue as they try to snag mine. *Tie her up—*

A growl rips into the space between the selkie and me, followed closely by a small black body. Bee leaps onto my shoulder, rudely hooking his claws into my T-shirt to hold his perch. Somehow, the feline-man manages not to pierce my skin.

"Gods," Hamish barks, stumbling back a step as his searching gaze connects with Bee's dark, menacing glare.

The cat continues to emit a noise he shouldn't be able to make.

I don't know that I've ever heard *this* growl before. Or if I have, not enough times to assign a specific meaning to it.

Normally, I try to correct Bee when he's overly aggressive. I assume being a man, stuck in the body of a cat, has him in a perpetual stage of confusion that makes it hard to distinguish friend or foe, so he makes it easy on himself by assuming everyone is foe.

This time though, I'm silently grateful for his intervention. The salty scent lingers in the back of my nose, coaxing a queasiness in my stomach.

"You are free to visit the downstairs part of the library. Because it is public," I tell the selkie as I step around him without letting his eyes snag on mine again. "Bye."

If Hamish has anything else to say to me, he chooses not to.

Bee's unbroken growling would have made the words hard to hear anyway.

4

BEE

WATER MAN SMELLS of fish and lust.
He wants my witch.
I will tear his face off.

5

——————

AME

"AME?" Morgana calls out to me just as I walk in the door.

No doubt my emotional vibrations, as subtle as they are, alerted her to my arrival.

Our whole family—my parents, my sister, my two brothers, and me—has magical focus in some way related to the internal workings of those around us.

Morgana has a connection to emotional spectrums, able to read the intricate tangle in others' minds. Her power could make it easy to deal with those around her, having an understanding of the currents below their surface and the ability to subtly shift the flow.

But she tries not to peek unless pressed to, claiming people deserve privacy.

She says that like she has a choice in the matter. I don't.

I'm constantly working to ignore my ability to hear the desires of those near me, but I've had mixed results. Most often, I unintentionally learn about the odd wishes of the people I encounter.

There was the woman who wanted to tell her boss to stop wearing corduroy pants.

The siren who imagined stuffing her dresses into a suitcase and sinking them to the bottom of Lake Galen.

A merman who wanted to pierce his nipples with shark teeth.

Plus the werewolf who fantasized about getting pleasured on an active pinball machine ...

And that was only a fraction of what I picked up in my first week after moving to Folk Haven.

My magic tells me *what* people want, but not *why* they want it. Kinks come up a lot. I could create an entire library out of others' sexual desires.

But I'd rather distance myself from that aspect of my power and stick with only one library—my sister's—in my life.

"I have your coffee," I call out to her, trying to pinpoint what room in this massive house her voice came from.

The old Victorian used to belong to Delta—the dragon with the cute dog in Coffee & Claws—and, before that, her father. He'd bought it and moved to Folk Haven years ago.

Poor man. After the loss of his wife, his natural inclination toward hoarding grew toxic, to the point that almost every spare inch of this house was full of dangerous scrap metal. When he passed away, Delta had to clean out the entire mess. She seemed eager to sell this place to us once it was ready for the market.

However, the sale didn't go through quickly. Morgana and I needed to petition the Folk Haven Mythic Council. The town founders—a group of mythical creatures themselves—had put restrictions in place about what type of mythic could live where. The divide seemed arbitrary to Morgana, especially because she specifically wanted a house previously owned by a dragon.

When a dragon makes a hoard, they instinctively set up

magical defenses to protect their precious items. Those protections linger even if the dragon leaves or, like Delta's father, passes away.

Since my sister's collection is full of precious texts, Morgana wanted as many safety measures in place as possible.

Despite The Council's reluctance, we struck a deal.

Morgana got the house.

And the town got me.

I pause in my search for my sister, pulling in a series of deep breaths, all aimed at dispelling my sudden anxiety.

Whenever The Council feels Folk Haven has an unsavory character in town limits who needs a magical shove, they call me. The desire witch, who can make the road out of town look like the most appealing thing in the world. Problem is, I'm not overjoyed by my job as the town's newest tool to keep humans from discovering Folk Haven's secrets. Not because I don't care about the townsfolk's safety.

But because I don't like forcefully manipulating people. Especially because the ones who need that emotional tinkering usually have gross brains I'd rather not delve into. Dark desires that make me want to step out of my own skin. Luckily, The Council has only asked me to step in once, a year ago.

Hopefully, I'll never be called again.

Hopefully, word of what I can do won't spread far past The Council. People in town already think I'm a bit weird because I never make eye contact and I'm always distracted.

I can't imagine how they'd react if they knew I could warp their wills on a whim.

Another few breaths, and I'm able to push away my disquiet enough that I don't think Morgana will detect any anomaly. With her also reining in her powers, she should only notice if there's a major spike in my mood.

Bee, tired of waiting, strolls ahead of me, heading toward the back of the house. I follow and find him and my sister in what we've dubbed The Study. At least, it's where we've been studying all the books in the collection before deciding which section and shelf they belong in.

Morgana has her curly red hair—the same shade as mine—gathered in a messy bun on the top of her head, a few errant strands sneaking out. Dust streaks her pale cheeks, and stray bits of paper cling to her T-shirt.

She glances up at my arrival, a distracted smile on her face. "Coffee. Thank the gods. Will you go through this box while I drink?"

Morgana hurries around the table to accept the cup. She leans against the wall as she sips, always insisting food and beverages maintain a minimum of four feet distance from the books.

This is not a library for snackers.

"Is this one of ours?" I take her place at the table, pulling back the flaps of an unfamiliar, small cardboard box.

Morgana invested in uniform-sized plastic containers to store the texts we'd collected over the years. I don't remember storing any of the books in cardboard. Too high a risk of damage.

Plus, I thought we'd finished unpacking our seemingly endless collection. Took months, but every book we bought over our years of journeying now sits on a shelf.

Will they remain in their original spot? Doubtful. Morgana has already begun a cataloging project that will likely result in the mass of volumes shifting to new spots.

I try not to frown at the thought.

At least I was able to convince her to use a computer and not a physical card catalog.

"Broderick sent that, if you can believe it." She names one of our brothers. Broderick and Anthony, the other two Shelly siblings.

"Broderick is easier to believe than Anthony."

Morgana grimaces, no doubt replaying one of Anthony's many speeches condemning magic. Our one brother has sworn off all things mystical, and while he's happy to lecture us on the benefits of a purely human life, he's never divulged his reason for forgoing magic entirely.

Bee hops up onto the table, and I'm about to tilt the box his way so he can see the old book inside when he plops down in a sunny spot and immediately falls asleep.

To be fair, the book isn't too exciting. Many grimoires are ornate, meant to represent the prestige of the witch family. This one's leather cover is faded with a barely discernible emblem that involves a five-pointed star surrounding a dragon. The image of the mythical creature doesn't mean these witches necessarily *associated* with dragons. They might have had magic specialties that coincided with dragon powers or simply wanted to convey their line was as strong and long-lasting as dragons tended to be.

But if that were the truth, they'd still have living descendants in possession of this book of spells.

A note sits, tucked into the side of the box. I slip the sheet out to read it.

Hello, sisters.

I happened upon this at an estate sale. It might look worn, but it's sturdy. And the magic is strong. I wasn't even looking, but I felt it. Hopefully, it will be a credit to your collection.

I'm working on Anthony. Once I get him to crack, we'll both come for a visit.

Best,

Broderick

"Why didn't he text us to tell us he was sending it?" I ask as I set the handwritten note aside.

Morgana waves her hand in a dismissal. "You know he loves the look of his own handwriting. So, what is it? Can you tell?"

Despite Broderick's assurance of its sturdiness, I reach for a nearby box and pull out a set of latex gloves. When my hands are properly covered, I carefully lift the book from its packaging and set it on the tabletop.

Though the brass latch keeping the grimoire shut appears rusty, nothing flakes off when I press it open.

"Family name is Slattery," I murmur, finding the mention inside the cover in a beautifully written witch language.

As is common with grimoires, there's a family tree in the beginning, marking the generations. This one ends in the 1950s. No names added past that point.

"Slattery ... Slattery ..." Morgana sifts through her mental library as she sips her coffee. While my sister doesn't have a photographic memory, she does have an impressive ability to recall information. "I believe there was a mention of them in a grimoire from a German coven. I'll check later. Are the spells labeled?"

"Not clearly." I read through the steps of the first few I come across.

That's the difficult thing about found grimoires; they were never meant to be used by anyone outside of the original witch family. New generations would be taught the mysteries and meanings of the spells. No need for titles and evenly spaced bullet points.

But Morgana and I have spent years finding the clues to decipher these texts. Her archival degree helps, and mass exposure leads to more hands-on learning.

"What's your guess?" she prods, eagerness in the way she shifts from foot to foot.

"The first line of this one says: *To tear the earth.* Battle witches maybe?"

Hundreds of years ago, witches often used their powers for defense and fighting. Humans who knew about their power were either terrified or bought their spells for protection.

"Battle has never been established as a specialty. Merely a common practice. Must be something else," Morgana presses.

I flip through a few more pages, seeking out words that hint at spell results. "*Causing a slow separation ... prepare for the glass to shatter ... severing the binds ... will then break the—*" I stutter when my eyes find the next word.

"What is it?" Morgana, having finished her coffee, sets the cup to the side and moves to read over my shoulder.

I place a finger, one that quivers slightly, under the line I was reading. "*Will then break the enchantment.*"

"Of course," Morgana murmurs, reaching for her laptop and opening a blank entry in the archival software I pressed her to buy. "They must be a family of *sunder* witches." She names the subset of magic that focuses on breaking. They are the witches that can rend, tear, and crack with barely more than a thought and a gesture.

Break the enchantment.

Too set in the mind of a cataloger, my sister doesn't make the connection I did. Morgana sees an item to be sorted and shelved. Not a spell to be used.

But I do.

When I glance to the end of the table, I find Bee's eyes are open.

Watching me.

6

AME

One Month Later

As I've been doing daily—more like hourly—since opening the grimoire my brother sent last month, I berate myself for the obvious error I made.

A sunder spell. *Of course* I need a sunder spell.

My mind got stuck in a single way of thinking, and I forgot to explore other possible solutions.

Bee is a man stuck in the form of a cat. I thought the answer had to be a transformation spell, so that was what I was searching for all this time. Something to change him. To morph him back to the correct form.

It never crossed my mind to *break* the original enchantment. I was too focused on the physical adjustment to consider what this curse truly was.

He didn't just shift to another form.

He's bound to it.

And all I need to do is break the binding.

Theoretically.

The sunder grimoire and the spells contained within are all I've thought about for the past weeks. Because, yet again, I've had to wait for another full moon. I refuse to rush something like this even though there's a pressure in my gut, an urging for me to *go, go, go.*

Finally, I've found it. The answer.

At least, I think I have.

"Stay where you are," I tell Bee.

The black not-really-a-cat perches on a low tree branch, watching me set up another testing spell, like I did twenty-eight nights ago.

I've spent the time not only continuously bemoaning my lack of creative thinking, but also memorizing the breaking enchantment spell and gathering all the needed ingredients. The final item only got delivered two days ago, so one could argue waiting for another full moon was necessary anyway. Witches don't tend to sell legit ingredients on Amazon, which means no two-day shipping.

Still, when the autumnal equinox came and went, the influx of power on Mabon seemed to taunt me.

Free him today, the force in the air whispered.

But I held off.

I need to be sure.

There's a chilly breeze tonight, proving that fall does in fact come to Georgia. Still, I push up the sleeves of my sweatshirt as I get ready to feed my question to the candle.

Once again—hopefully for the last time—I scrawl the query.

Will this spell help my friend, who I call Bee, regain his true form?

Like I've done every time before, I hold the paper to the

flame, waiting for it to catch. Waiting to see the black flame tell me I've got the wrong spell yet again.

The flame burns blue.

I blink, slow at first, then rapidly, trying to make sure I'm not imagining the change in color.

The paper continues to burn a lovely aqua.

"Bee," I whisper, then louder, "Bee!"

A brush of fur against my arm, and I realize he abandoned his perch and is now at my side. I drop the burning paper into the copper bowl, waiting as the entire question ignites and burns, making sure the color never shifts to black.

The blue remains.

"This is it." I face Bee, finding his dark eyes on my face. "I don't know if you can understand me, but I think you can. And I'm telling you, this"—I point to the grimoire lying on a silk cloth, open to the page with the sunder spell—"is it. We can break your enchantment. Tonight."

Because, with my desperate optimism, I gathered all the needed ingredients for it too. With a whole month to prepare, why not?

Excitement and panic battle under my rib cage while I clean up the leavings of my truth-teller spell. I need a clear space. I'm starting from scratch.

When I have the intricate witch language symbols drawn in white chalk on the grass, following the diagram on the aged page, I move on to the fires. I need four—and not just candles. These require stone circles and logs.

As I move around the space, building up the flames, tall figures lurk through a break in the trees. My spell clearing sits beside a larger swatch of grass. One that holds a collection of metal statues I learned had been sculpted by Delta's father before his mental decline. Morgana doesn't like to go near the place. She claims dark emotions cling to the creations.

Seeing as how they were all made by a dragon who had lost his mate, I'm not surprised.

Tonight, they seem more like an audience than ever before.

With full fires burning—thank the gods the forest fire risk is low—and the proper herbs added to each, the air grows pungent with smoky scents.

The preparation takes two hours. I follow every step outlined in the book. The author might not have clearly labeled the spell, but the instructions are thorough.

Tonight is the hunter's moon, with any luck marking the end of my hunt for Bee's cure. With each step complete, a pressure grows, like the moon knows I'm calling on her power. That I'll need her weight to assist my forceful magical blow. The one I hope is strong enough to break Bee's curse.

The cat, who is actually a man, prowls around the edge of my casting area. His dark eyes watch every move I make.

Does he know this is for him? To bring about the end of his prison?

"Almost done," I tell him, my voice tight with anticipation and nerves. "Please don't run off."

He stays.

Meticulously, I review each step, making sure I haven't missed anything. The ground before me matches the diagram in the grimoire faithfully.

Everything is as it should be.

Now for the final words. And the final sacrifice.

"Bee? Could you sit here?" I crouch low and point to a character I sketched on the lush grass.

The cat paces a moment longer, then comes forward and settles where I asked.

"Stay there, please."

I'm not sure what will happen if he moves, but I can't stand the idea of pinning him to the spot in any way. Bee's already had enough forced on him, assuming he didn't choose to become a feline.

I kneel in the middle of my configuration and arrange the grimoire before me. Then, I reach into my pocket and pull out the silver knife I blessed on Mabon, doing what I could to bottle the power of the holiday.

Bee's eyes fixate on my hands, the empty one and the one that holds the weapon, as I start to chant the commanding words of the spell. I hope he's not worried that I might hurt him. There will be no stabbing of cats today.

Only stabbing of me.

Well, not stabbing exactly. *Slicing* is more accurate.

When I reach the part of the spell that requires sacrifice, I do my best to dissociate from the coming pain.

"Take of my body. My blood to break."

With a swift move, I swipe the sharp blade across my palm, making sure not to cut too deep and sever anything important.

Still, it hurts like a hell dimension.

Bee lets out a ferocious growl I've never heard from him before, and I watch as he attempts to leap forward, toward me. But in the end, he doesn't move.

And I don't think it's his choice.

As blood wells and drips from my palm onto the chalk-covered grass, the symbols I drew begin to glow a dark red color. The light pulses, the beat growing rapid, and I realize the pace matches my pulse.

I am connected to this spell. In charge of it.

Time for me to make the power do what I want.

"A curse before me." I speak in witch tongue, a language I was born knowing, as all witches are. "Break it." I say the words and watch as a shiver travels over Bee's body, his fur puffing out until he appears twice his normal size.

"Break it," I repeat.

The light grows brighter, bathing the tree trunks and metal

figures in an eerie crimson glow while still holding rhythm with my pulse. The cut on my hand stings.

Aches.

Burns.

The pain increases with each beat, the blood spilling from me a heated fire.

"Break it," I hiss through grinding teeth, doing my best not to whimper as I cradle my hand.

Bee lets out a long, low yowl, a shudder overtaking his small body.

Is he changing?

Something seems different about his form, but maybe the distortion comes from my tears of pain.

"Break it. Break it. Break it," I chant, a stab of agony in my palm with each repetition.

Needles prick my quivering muscles, sweat beads on my skin, and black dots flood the edge of my vision.

This is not your specialty, a doubtful thought hisses in the back of my mind. *You are no sunder witch.*

No matter the pain, I refuse to stop. I've found the solution, and I *will* get Bee's body back.

Besides, I learned how to handle pain long ago.

With a growl of my own, I scoop up the dagger and score my palm a second time, leaving a bloody X on my pale skin.

"Break it. Break it! BREAK IT!" The last is a scream of unrelenting demand and torment.

A flood of red light fills the circle I drew, too bright for me to see my cat companion or the woods surrounding us or even my own bleeding hand.

I close my eyes against the glare, continuing to mutter the demand. "Break it. Break it. Break it."

All at once, the pain vanishes. At least the supernatural pain. What's left is a more manageable yet still uncomfortable stinging ache in my palm. The crimson pressing against my eyelids winks out.

Panting, I lift my chin and blink my eyes open, searching for Bee, praying to The Dark One that the enchanted light didn't hurt him. That the spell didn't misfire and consume him.

There's no sign of a small body covered in black fur.

Bee is gone.

Where my cat was held in place by magic sits another form. A much larger body, crouched and curved in on itself. A head of shaggy, dark hair is bowed low to the ground, and I watch a set of ribs expand and contract on heavy breaths.

The head jerks up, and I gasp when I meet his eyes.

Bee's eyes.

Make her mine.

"Finally," the man growls, lunging forward.

I don't have time to retreat or defend myself before he catches me in an unforgiving hold, clutching me tight against his *very* naked body.

"Bee?" I manage the single-worded question before I can't ask anything else.

Before he claims my mouth in a searing kiss.

7

JACK

As my mouth fuses to hers, I breathe in deep.

She smells so fucking good.

My woman carries the scents of earth and candle flames and mint. She smells like mine. Finally, I can claim this woman who was always so close yet impossible to reach.

Now, I have arms to hold her, and I never plan on letting her go.

She tastes of pleasure and salty cheese crackers.

Delicious.

I stroke my tongue along the seam of her mouth, craving more. Eager for everything.

Open for me.

There's a sharp burn on my lower lip, and I realize my woman is biting me. So gentle yet so fierce. I groan deep in my throat and break the kiss, so I can admire her pouty frown before diving back in.

Only to meet an obstruction.

My little witch stares up at me, hand over her mouth, her green eyes as round as the full moon above us yet so much more enchanting. Even now, the glow in the night sky calls to my bones, but I hold off.

I've been a beast for too long. Now, I need to be a man. For her.

If only she'd clear the way for me to claim her.

"Move your hand," I demand.

Her freckled nose wrinkles as her eyes squint. "Are you going to start kissing me again?" she asks from behind her fingers.

"Yes. Immediately."

"Then, I think I should keep my hand where it is."

"Little witch." I rumble the endearment, coaxing her to reveal those lovely lips.

"You don't know my name?" She doesn't remove her palm as she asks the question, and I ache to see how her mouth shapes words.

"I know that you're mine." I lean in, nudging my nose against her knuckles. "One more taste."

"My name is not *mine*. Are you Bee?"

"My name is not Bee," I growl.

Her spine stiffens. "You're not the cat?"

"I was trapped in that ridiculous feline body, yes." Despite my dark tone, her tension eases. "But I am *not* a cat, and my name is *not* Bee."

"Oh. Sorry. If I'd known your real name, I would've called you by it. I'm Amethyst Shelly." The witch draws up the hand not guarding her mouth and shoves it between us, palm open, as if expecting a handshake. "Friends and family call me Ame."

Fine. I guess if I don't want to be considered an animal, I should stop acting like one. Reluctantly, I loosen my hold, giving the witch space to step away. She doesn't run from me, which I find promising. She merely waits for my grip.

I take her hand, loving the drag of her calluses on my palm. My fingers feel clumsy and overly long. It's been a while since I had them.

"Ame." The sound is familiar. I've heard it, I know. But things sounded odd to me when I was in that cursed body. My human understanding was muted, and I largely ran on instinct. And those urges didn't care much for language. "I'm Jack Lim."

"Jacklyn?" She says my two names as if they were one and the last letter is different.

Not the first person to do so. Now, I'm just glad that someone is speaking it.

That *Ame* is saying it.

"First name Jack. Last name Lim, with an *M*."

Under my skin, my bones thrum, responding to the song of the moon. I won't be able to hold on to this body for much longer. It's only my craving for this woman that keeps me on two legs.

"Jack," Ame repeats. "Jack," she says again, this time with a half-laugh, her hand dropping away to reveal a smile so glorious that I lean closer to soak up the warmth.

Her eyes narrow, and she raises her hand to cut off my view again. The movement brings an intoxicating wave of her earthy, minty scent to my nose, but that's not all. The iron smell of blood permeates the air, mixing with her natural heavenly fragrance. I blanch at the crimson stream dripping from the palm she holds over her face.

"You're injured." Carefully, I grasp her wrist, drawing Ame in close and rotating her hand so I can examine the gruesome gashes. A vague memory returns to me—of her wielding a knife just before my eyes drowned in red light. "You did this for the spell? For me?"

"Stronger spells usually need some blood," she explains, her voice almost cheery. "I brought bandages in my bag." She points to a green backpack sitting under a nearby tree.

Change, the moon whispers to me.

"Not yet," I growl back.

"What?" Ame stares up at me in confusion.

"I was talking to the moon."

Releasing her, I stalk over to the bag and tug the zipper open, my movements embarrassingly clumsy. I need more human practice. Still, I manage to find the first aid kit, and when I turn, Ame is already at my side.

"I'm sorry," she says as I spray disinfectant on her palm, then press gauze to the wound.

She's sorry? Doesn't she know what she did for me?

"There will never be a time in our lives when you need to apologize to me." My eyes meet and hold hers.

Ame blinks at me, her eyes swiping away, then back to mine. She doesn't flinch as I wrap a thick bandage around her wound.

She hurt herself for me. She has done everything *in the world for me.*

I've been loved before, but this level of unwavering devotion …

The little witch is a gift I will never earn but refuse to relinquish.

"I *am* sorry though. I didn't bring you any clothes."

Her gaze trails over me, and I revel in her attention.

Take me in, every inch that is man.

Not cat.

"I don't mind you seeing me naked." After tying off the bandage, I step back. "Look your fill."

The little witch blushes a deep red but still takes advantage of the offer. Ame eyes me from the top of my unkempt hair, over my face, across my shoulders, and down my abdomen. As if aware her sight lingers between my legs, my cock rises to meet her. I can't help the reaction of my body. I've wanted this woman since the night she set me a place at the table and served me chunks of raw steak.

Where the rest of the world saw an odd, angry cat, Ame saw a tormented, trapped man.

And despite the erratic nature of my memory, I know one thing: she never gave up on me.

"Well, now, I can at least say I'm one hundred percent sure."

Ame's emerald-green gaze flits up to mine, and a rueful smile tilts her mouth to the side. I study that angle, wanting to map the exact curve with my tongue.

Her bandaged hand blocks the view again.

"I wasn't going to kiss you," I mutter, grumpy at losing the sight of her lips and the reminder of her injury. Plus, the moon is shouting in my brain about the change.

I'm not ready. I need another moment with her.

Ame drops her hand. "If your name is Jack, why did you sit on the *B*? And why did you tear up the letter board?"

Remembering that time is like sinking into a cloud of rage. I'd rather not let the fury consume me. Not at the moment anyway. There will be a time and place to allow my temper free rein.

"Things were confusing. Most of the time, I was functioning little better than an animal, only with a vague knowledge that what I was wasn't right. Being around you clarified the world, but not nearly enough. If I tried to read, my head felt like splitting open."

Ame nods, as if the strange description of my fractured mental state makes sense to her. "It was a curse then. Not a choice?"

"Never," I growl. "I would never choose that."

Her gaze trails over me again, and I bask in the attention, even as my muscles twitch and tense to shift.

"You're human then? A human man?"

I scoff. "No, little witch. I'm much more than that." I step back, directly into a beam of moonlight, and finally allow the glowing celestial orb to have what she wants.

The world around me softens like smoke, and I stalk from the cloud, an animal once more.

8

———

AME

A werewolf.

Some sadistic person trapped a werewolf in the body of a cat for *years*. Now that I think back, Bee was always in a foul mood the day leading up to the full moon, and he would often go off on his own at night. I figured he left because of disappointment over my testing spells. But maybe he was just sad he couldn't take on his canine form.

Or he was in pain.

There's a terrible sensation in my stomach. Sort of like the time I ate sushi from a gas station in Kansas. Only this roiling twist grows tighter and catches fire, burning my nerve endings until I wonder if I shake or glow with the power of the emotion.

This is ... fury.

I am terribly, horrendously furious.

All on behalf of Bee. Of Jack.

Someone forced my friend into a body he never should have been in and would have had to keep living in if I'd never found the solution.

But I *did* find the answer.

As the majestic gray wolf steps toward me, my anger subsides. I will revisit the sensation on another day. For now, I admire the beauty of Jack's thick coat and long, proud snout. He gives me a canine grin, and I marvel at the sharp white teeth.

Should I be scared of this shifter?

One glance at the bandage on my hand, and I dismiss the possibility. Jack isn't a danger to me. But for all I know, the world is hazardous to him. Since he no longer has a voice, I can't question him about his past and if the magic wielder who cursed him is searching for their victim.

Breaking the enchantment might not solve everything. Jack's my responsibility for a while longer. A trickle of relief seeps through me, but I save that emotion for later as well.

"You're a beautiful werewolf," I tell him.

The beast lets out a huff that sounds like a scoff, and yet he stands up straighter. Preening.

He's handsome in his two-legged form too. Not like the rugged, bearded men Hollywood usually gets to play their fictional werewolf characters. Instead, this shifter—with the sloping planes of his face and smoldering eyes with folded lids —could star in his own fantasy K-drama.

I would be lying if I said his demanding kiss didn't affect me. And those desires ...

Make her mine.

Taste her lips.

Stroke her hair.

Keep her safe.

Make her pain go away.

Each one had a simple, pure nature that I found oddly soothing. They weaved together into a more bearable hum of wanting, and I realized meeting his eyes was pleasant instead of overwhelming.

Jack isn't the first person to desire me, but I don't have the urge to distance myself from him.

"Let's go back to the house. It's late, and once this adrenaline wears off, I'm going to pass out. I'd like to be near a bed when that happens." As I talk, I kick dirt onto the flickering coals of the fires and pack up the spell supplies, shoving everything haphazardly into my bag. But I handle the grimoire carefully. Some of the books almost seem sentient, and I don't want to wake up, cursed like Jack, because I bent the corner of a page. "It's probably better that you're a wolf. No risk of you flashing anyone. Although all animals are usually naked, so I guess we're constantly getting flashed by them." The best way to tell I'm tired is when my mind takes trips down nonsensical roads.

I pull the strap of my bag over my shoulder, tuck the book under my arm, and weave through the metal sculpture garden on the way toward the house, spying the roof of the Victorian peeking over the treetops in the glow of the full moon. I don't hear Jack follow, but when I glance back, he is only a step or two behind me. His paws make no sound as they land.

A light is on in the kitchen when I step through the front door. Jack follows behind me, somehow avoiding the creaky floorboards, his entry silent despite him being twice my size.

Lacking the energy to explain the events of the night, I wave for Jack to wait in the hall. If my nonverbal command bothers him, he doesn't show it. I set my bag and book on a side table in the entryway, then tuck my hands into my pockets to hide my bandaged palm before heading to the kitchen. Morgana is sitting at the table with a cup of tea and an old, ragged book open before her.

"Is that a grimoire?" I ask.

She doesn't glance up from her reading. "No. A history of water mythical creatures. According to this, mermaids enjoy the taste of human flesh." She flicks her eyes to me, then back to the page. "I'm wondering how best to ask them if the text is accurate."

"Cover yourself in butter and see if they start to drool?" I offer.

Morgana smirks as her eyes continue to roam the page. Tonight, I'm glad she's thoroughly distracted as I head to the refrigerator and pull out some leftover takeout fried chicken and mashed potatoes. With the container in hand, I move to leave.

"Late-night snack?" My sister continues to focus on her book, but I get the sense most of her attention is on me. Not so distracted after all.

"Kind of," I sigh, disliking even the hint of a lie that misdirection is. "I have a lot to tell you, but not enough energy to say it all. Tomorrow, over breakfast?"

Morgana meets my gaze now and holds it. "Nothing pressing?"

"It can wait," I assure her.

She takes me at my word. "Good night then. I look forward to breakfast."

"Night."

Leaving the kitchen, I find Jack where I left him, standing in the hallway. His nose flares, dark eyes dropping to the container in my hand.

"Upstairs," I murmur, leading the way.

Once in my bedroom, with the door closed, I open the Tupperware and set it on the floor. "I figured you would be hungry. Careful. Chicken bones are bad for dogs because they splinter. Or so I've read."

Jack lets out one of his wolfy scoffs and licks up the mound of potatoes with one swipe of his tongue. I leave him to figure out the chicken on his own, grabbing pajamas and locking myself in my bathroom.

Not that I'm scared of the werewolf. But after years spent with Bee, I know the cat version of him doesn't respect bathroom boundaries. Hopefully, the man and wolf will be more courteous, but for now, I'll take precautions.

Not up for a full shower, I use a wet washcloth to wipe off the sweat caused by stress and pain. No blood has seeped through the bandage, so that's a plus. The spells took a lot out of me, and my fingers quiver with exhaustion as I tug on my sleep shorts and T-shirt, then brush my teeth.

When I reach for the door handle, I pause.

What if he's a cat again?

Sometimes, I get so lost in my imagination that I need a moment to drag myself back to reality.

Is that what this night was? Maybe my mind played out a scenario where I finally found a solution for Bee's problem, but in fact, it wasn't real, and on the other side of this door, I'll simply find my grumpy cat, curled up on his ottoman.

With a quick tug, I jerk open the door.

And there sits a wolf.

"Thank the goddess," I murmur.

Jack tilts his head in the exact way that Bee always used to, and the gesture makes me smile, but it also causes a sharp jab in my chest area.

"I was wondering if I dreamed everything," I explain to him as I duck back in the bathroom and come out with an offering. The short, floral cotton robe is the only one I own because it's the only one I've ever liked.

I also think it's the only piece of my wardrobe that will fit Jack's human body.

"If you'd like to shift at some point, you can wear this." I lay it on the top of my dresser.

Although with the full moon still high in the sky, I suspect he'll stay in animal form until morning at least. All the texts I've skimmed about werewolves agreed that they change for the whole of the full moon.

Immediately, Jack proves the books wrong.

The air in the room grows heavier, and I turn to find a dark cloud condensing around the wolf. Something else I've learned —mainly from reading—is that different shifters move through their shapes in different ways.

Sirens unfurl their wings from magical hidden pockets in their backs.

Selkies put on and remove a cloak—or second skin.

With animal shifters, it seems to vary family to family. Looks like Jack's magic has a mass of shadows clinging to him, obscuring him completely. When they drift away, a naked man remains. He strolls to my dresser, plucks the robe up, and slides the garment onto his body.

It fits, but only in the loosest definition of the word.

Still, he doesn't object to wearing it even though the bottom barely covers his intimate parts and the sleeves don't pass his elbows.

"Snug," he says. Then, he lifts his arm and sniffs the sleeve.

"Sorry. I wouldn't say it's dirty exactly. I've worn it a couple of times since I last washed it. But I was straight out of the shower."

"You wear this when you're naked and wet." That isn't a question, and the way he strokes his hands over the lapels gives me the sense he's imagining the scenario of when I wear the robe. Then, he hums a satisfied noise deep in his throat.

His kiss replays through my mind, sending tingles through my body. I try my best to soothe them.

He's a man who's been trapped as a cat for years. He's probably starved for a lot of things. If my magic wasn't drained, I could pick out what those individual desires are.

But I'm tapped out, and like in the clearing, his cravings are blending into a general urge of *want*. Whether or not he's feeling horned up, I still trust that he won't do anything about the urges.

Jack is Bee, and I trust Bee.

9

JACK

THIS ROOM LOOKS ODD, but that's probably because I'm taking it in close to six feet higher than I'm used to. It smells the same though. Like earth and mint and Ame.

Ame Shelly. Mine.

Or more like I am hers.

How long until I can claim her? My odd little witch.

I take my time, studying her. *Seeing* her. As a feline, I half-understood the perfection in front of me. Her fiery hair is tamed against her skull in two long braids that fall past her shoulders. The loose clothes she wears make her arms appear thin where they stick out of the large sleeves, but I know she has muscle. I've seen her heft endless cardboard boxes full of books. In the dim light of her bedroom, my sharp eyes make out a flush on her skin. Embarrassment? Or ... no ... the *sun.* She's burnt, and the discoloration has me scowling.

Did sunscreen disappear while I was a cat? My witch needs a high SPF with that paper-pale skin.

I vow to buy a supply and rub the protective cream onto every inch of her delicate skin multiple times a day.

As I make my plans, Ame stares at an ottoman underneath the window. A perch I often frequented when it was size appropriate.

She'd better not expect me to curl up on that tonight. Or ever again.

Her delicious scent amplifies, mixing with salt, and I spy watery tracks trailing down her freckled cheeks.

My woman is crying?

I will murder whoever made her sad.

"What's wrong?" A growl weaves into my voice.

"Oh. Crap. Am I crying?" She roughly rubs the back of her hand under each eye. "Sorry. I was just having a selfish, self-pitying moment."

"Explain." I need to know every thought in her brain. Especially the ones that make her sad.

She huffs a sigh. "It's just that I realized I'll never see Bee again." More tears fall, and her misery guts me.

"I'm right in front of you." Stepping closer, I try to take up her entire field of vision. "I'm here. There's no need to miss me."

"Yes, I know." My witch gives me a watery smile. "But I meant, my grumpy cat partner. You were a very cute cat. And I realize it's horrible to miss you being in a form you obviously loathed, but I can't seem to help it."

I grunt, reluctantly understanding her point, but also hating the idea that she'd prefer me any other way than I am now.

"I promise you'll like me better as a man." With a hunter's caution, I slip closer. Into her space.

"You want to be a man, so I already like you better this way." Ame pats my chest, appearing unaffected by my looming presence. Stepping around me, she walks over to a wooden chest and opens it to reveal a collection of blankets. "But you might have been more comfortable, staying a wolf. These floorboards aren't exactly soft, and I don't have an air mattress."

"It won't be an issue," I assure her.

Because I have no plans to sleep on the ground.

Not when there's going to be a bed full of a lovely witch.

10

AME

WHEN I TURN toward Jack with an armful of blankets, I find him watching me with hungry eyes. None of the other werewolves in town stare at me in the same way, so I have to assume it is a Jack quirk.

I want to know more of his mannerisms. More of his thoughts and his background and his everything. I spent years living with Bee, not knowing the truth. But here is the answer.

"How did you end up as a cat?"

The hunger in his gaze dims, and Jack shifts to stare out the dark window at my back.

"It's not a good bedtime story," he eventually says as he stretches out his arms to accept the blankets.

When I pass them over, his hands brush mine. At the touch of his warm skin, I realize it's been a long time since I last had human contact. I'm not much of a hugger or even a handshaker. Those kinds of touches amplify my magic, so I don't seek out skin-to-skin contact. But it's nice to be reminded of the sensation.

And Jack's unsortable thrum of desires is pleasant.

"I wasn't looking for a way to be soothed to sleep. Can you tell me the basics? Are you in danger?" Despite the seriousness of my question, I can't fight off a jaw-cracking yawn. It's late, and I worked multiple big spells tonight.

Jack tosses the blankets on the foot of my bed, then walks around to the side with my nightstand. There, he pulls back the covers, creating a pocket in the bed I neatly made this morning.

"Lie down," he commands. "And I'll tell you."

"I should have known you'd be bossy. All that growling." Still, I do as I was told.

He steps back to give me space, and I neatly slide under my covers like I do each night. One of the reasons I'm glad Morgana and I finally stopped living out of a camper is this. A nice, large mattress that doesn't sway because my sister is driving while I'm trying to doze or because we parked in a particularly windy campground. Here, I can snuggle into the expansive cushion and sleep through the night.

But I don't want to fall asleep yet.

Leaning back against a mound of pillows, I meet Jack's familiar eyes. They're the same dark shade as when he was a cat.

"I did what you asked."

"Yes, you did." He smiles and takes a seat on the edge of my bed, the mattress dipping enough that I partly roll into him. "Now, my story." He sets a hand on my blanket-covered hip, keeping me in place when I would move away. "What year is it?"

When I tell him, a grimace twists his lips.

"Six years," he says.

Without thought, I reach out to clasp his hand. *He's been in the wrong form for more than half a decade?*

"I grew up in California," he says, voice low and soothing, as if this really were a bedtime story. "When I was in college, I fell in with a group of werewolves. They turned out to be a bad sort and sold me to a sorcerer."

He gives a tight nod in response to my widening eyes. Our kind—mythics—avoid sorcerers because the twisted humans only get their powers by stealing the magic from mythical beings. To make a deal with one—and worse, to *sell* one of our kind to them—it's horrendous.

Jack continues his tragic story in a clipped tone. "I almost broke free of him once, so he transformed me into a cat. Both as an insult and to better manage me. He moved around a lot at first, then settled in a place. I'm not sure where, only that it was colder than I was used to."

"We found you in Maine three years ago." *How close were we to the sorcerer that night on the road?*

"*You* found me." Jack leans closer, his eyes boring into mine.

When his approach doesn't end, I place a staying hand on his chest. Right over his heart, where my insufficient robe gapes open to reveal his golden chest. Half of my palm is on cotton, but my fingers rest on bare, hot skin.

The steady beating of his heart comforts me. He was so close to death that night.

"I never would have been on that road," I say, "if Mor hadn't wanted to scour the country for mythical texts. She gets partial credit for your rescue."

Jack keeps his weight pressed against my hand, not forcing himself forward, but not retreating either. He tilts his head, the gesture so wolflike that I find myself smiling despite the somber topic.

"Is that what you all have been doing? I never really understood."

I nod. "But that's my story. You promised me yours. How did you get free of the sorcerer?"

Jack straightens suddenly, and I curl my fingers to guard against the chill from the loss of him.

"I *tricked* him." The way he snarls that one word conveys his disgust for whatever he had to do to deceive the sorcerer. "When I saw my chance, I escaped. Ran into the woods and kept going as fast as I could. For days. I was too exhausted to defend myself when a coyote tried to make me his dinner. Got away though."

"That's why you were wounded." A memory rises to the surface—of blood on my hands and blankets as I worked healing magic I'd never tried before that night.

He nods, jaw tight. "I thought I was going to die," Jack admits, voice low. The sound a hollow torment. "Free of him, but still trapped in that cursed form. Alone in the woods." When he gazes at me now, there's too much going on behind his eyes for me to sort it all out. "Then, your voice came. And I wasn't alone anymore."

We sit on my bed, staring at each other, and I try to get my exhausted brain to come up with the next steps as an internal voice begs for me to pull Jack close, hold him tight, and keep anything bad from ever happening to him again.

"Do I scare you?" The werewolf narrows his eyes, studying me.

Now, it's my turn to tilt my head and study the stranger—yet not a stranger—before me. "No."

"How do you feel about me then?"

That's the question, isn't it?

"I'm trying to figure that out. I know and *don't* know you. We're close, but not." Well, right now, we are *very* close. "It's like when Anthony and Broderick visit. We're important to each other, and I know them, but I rarely see them. There are changes they go through when they're away that make them less recognizable."

"Who are Anthony and Broderick?" The wolf reaches out, slow, as if I might get frightened, and picks up my bandaged hand.

"You must really not have understood a lot of what I said when you were in that cat form."

Jack shakes his head as he runs his fingers over my palm, tracing the creases with his thumb. "Some things were as clear as this conversation. Some were like a foreign language." He cradles my injured hand in both of his. "Who are they?"

"My brothers."

His head jerks back. "You think of me like a brother?"

The horror in his voice amuses me.

"Is that a bad thing?"

"Yes." His dark brows dip in a glare, which he directs at the bedding. "I'm not your brother."

"I know that." I curl my fingers around his thumb, a small embrace. "But you're someone who I thought I knew a lot about, but I really only know a sliver. Still, I trust you." Because I trusted Bee.

"It's late, and we're going to have to talk a lot more about this tomorrow with Morgana. We'd better sleep. Are those enough blankets?" I gesture with my free hand toward the pile at the foot of my bed.

My sister knit the one on top, and it's the same pattern as the one I wrapped around Bee all those nights ago when I found him on the side of the road.

"I'll be plenty warm." Jack lets me slide from his grip as he rises from the bed.

I settle on my side, watching him move around my room. The werewolf turns off the light, but the glow from the full moon sneaks through my lace curtains.

"Don't you have to be in wolf form on the full moon?"

"She calls to me," Jack admits, approaching the bed from the opposite side and grabbing the top blanket. "But I've never needed to spend a full night as a wolf. Tonight, I have reason to stay as a man."

"What reason?" I ask, watching over my shoulder as he unfurls the blanket.

"To talk to my little witch."

After that announcement, Jack climbs into my bed. And he doesn't simply spread out on the few feet of free space. No, the presumptuous shifter stays but slides close, slings an arm around my waist, and pulls me into the spoon of his body.

Bee never started off in the bed with me. He would begin the night on his ottoman, sound asleep as far as I could tell. The sight of him relaxed that way was a comfort. To know he trusted me enough to be unconscious around me.

Then, I would go to bed myself, sliding under the covers. At some point during the night, Bee would relocate, and by the time I woke up, he would be beside me, curled up in the bend of my knees.

The same notch that Jack fits his knees into now. And just like the cat, he stays on top of the covers while I nestle beneath them. But he takes up much more space than Bee ever did.

"Jack?"

"Shh." He pulls my back tighter against his chest. "You're just cuddling with your cat."

The logic doesn't track, but I'm too cozy and sleepy to protest.

11

———————

JACK

FOR THE FIRST time in years, I wake up in a body that belongs to me. I didn't want to fall asleep last night in case the spell was a dream.

In case *she* was a desperate fantasy.

Ame Shelly.

The little witch still sleeps in my arms, her crimson hair a tangle on the floral pillowcase, sun-kissed face slack as she breathes a steady, deep rhythm. Every fifth breath catches at the hint of a snore.

My savior.

The woman I swore myself to, even when I barely had a grasp on my mind.

She only knows me as a cat, I remind myself. *She's like a doe. If I move toward her too fast, she'll startle and run.*

I'll lose her.

Insisting on sleeping in the same bed with her, draping my body around hers, like I've done it nightly for years, was moving too fast. She'll wake up and push me away. She'll insist on distance between us. In the past, I was a better hunter than this. I knew how to take my time.

But *my* time has been taken, and I'm left with this rabid wanting.

I want Ame to fall for me and accept me as her mate *now*.

Then, I want to find my old pack mate and tear out her throat.

Next, I'll visit the pack leader and remove his heart from his chest with my claws.

And finally, I want to locate the sorcerer and rip off his head, staring into his panicked eyes as his life fades from them.

So, yeah, I have a lot on my to-do list.

But Ame is at the top. I savor this moment of getting to hold her, filling my lungs with her addictive earth and mint scent while I memorize the exact temperature of her warm body against mine.

Once she wakes up, I don't know when I'll have her close again. No doubt she'll try to send me on my way to a past life that has no place for me anymore.

But I'm not going anywhere without her.

She is my home now.

Her vibrant green eyes blink open a moment before her hands fly to my face. "Bee?"

"Jack," I correct her but gently. Because that's how she's cupping my cheeks. Tenderly. And that's how she spoke the name she's known me by. With care.

I'm not nothing to her. But I want to be *more*.

Ame lets her hands drop to her chest with a thunk, but she continues to gaze up at me. "Jack. It's weird how I see you and think *Bee* even though you don't look like you did when you were Bee. I would've thought it would be easy to call you by the right name since you look like someone I just met." Her pupils adjust to the glow of the rising sun casting rays through her parted curtains as she talks.

"Why do you still think of me as Bee?"

The little witch reaches up again, but this time, she sets her palm against my chest. With the borrowed robe gaping, we're skin to skin, my heart pounding harder, as if driving to pummel its way out of my rib cage to get to her.

"Because you feel the same, I think. Like ... your soul has always been you. And I guess I named your soul Bee." A twitch at the corner of her mouth has me struggling not to dip down for a kiss. "Sorry."

"Never," I growl, my throat clogged with emotion. "You *never* need to apologize to me."

"You said that last night." Ame props herself on her elbows, bringing her face close to mine until I could extend my tongue and stroke her bottom lip. "But I'm not perfect. And you don't owe me anything." Her head tilts, as if angling for a kiss, crimson hair spilling over her shoulder. "Except for my robe. I'm going to want that back. I've never been able to find another I like."

Then, my sneaky prey rolls out of my arms and out of the bed while I'm still drunk on her delicious scent. Ame strides to the bathroom, closing the door behind her. After a pause, there's the definitive click of the lock, which has me snorting.

One of these days, I'll earn my way into that room while she's in there.

Muttering curses at the gods for putting such a delectable woman within reach but not letting me grab her, I climb from the bed and straighten the covers in the way I've seen her make the bed every morning. I don't know why that detail is clear to me and others aren't. It must be something to do with the evil son of a bitch's spell.

Not only did he transform me into a cat, but he also fogged

my ability to communicate using any kind of language or interpretive movements. Even understanding speech was difficult, though not impossible. Like everything was said with a lag. If I wanted to pay attention to words, I lost track of the present moment I existed in, which could be dangerous for an animal.

Ame always seemed to understand though. If she said something to me, she'd often wait a stretch to see if I'd respond in any way.

One more reason I'm fucking gone over her.

As my highly attuned hearing picks up the sound of bristles against teeth, I wander around the bedroom and catalog the similarities and difference of viewing this space with my normal eyes. Everything is smaller from this perspective, but not in a way that stifles. Ame has made her room into a cozy space.

I'm using my reacquired opposable thumbs to open a dresser drawer when Ame emerges from the bathroom.

"Are you snooping?" she asks without heat.

"I'm ..." I struggle for a way to explain. "Moving." My fingers flex on their own to emphasize the point.

"Hmm." Ame nods. "I guess even a werewolf would want to shed his paws every so often."

She understands. I've been an animal for so long. Too long.

I need to reorient myself to a human body.

Ame comes to my side and pulls a lower drawer open, revealing neatly folded clothes. She sifts through the bundles of cotton until she finds a faded gray T-shirt I've seen her sleep in.

"This used to be Broderick's. I think it'll fit you. And I have an idea for pants. I'll be right back."

Before I can ask about this pants plan, the witch slips out of the room. My natural urge is to follow her, make sure she doesn't disappear forever. But I trust she'll come back.

Ame has never abandoned me before.

While she's gone, I take my turn in the bathroom.

"Jack?" Ame speaks my name on the other side of the door at a normal volume, as if she knows I have no trouble hearing her. "I found you bottoms."

When I open the door, she offers a black bundle. "Leggings. Morgana is a few sizes larger than me, and these are stretchy."

"Morgana is ..."

"My older sister. Sorry. I keep assuming you know these things."

I nod, not bothered. "Does your sister know you're giving her pants away?"

Ame extends her hand further. "She has more than twenty of the same pair. Easily replaceable."

I accept the offering, unable to hide my smirk. "These won't leave much to the imagination."

The little witch glances to just below the robe belt, then quickly back to my face.

I want to know where her thoughts went.

"Well, it's the best we've got. After breakfast, we can go into town and buy you some better-fitting things." Ame carefully closes the bathroom door—a clear instruction to get changed so we can start my first full day in six years of living in man form.

The leggings are more comfortable than I expected, and the T-shirt smells like Ame. Overall, one of the best outfits I've ever worn. Who cares if the faded gray cotton has a small hole in the armpit and if the bottoms have a smear of purple paint near the knee?

For all I want to be naked with Ame, I've got to admit, I've missed a comfortable set of clothes. I learned later in life that werewolves tend to lack modesty, but that wasn't how I had been raised. It's only the little witch that brings out the urge in me. The one that begs me to strip us both down and show her exactly how grateful I am for all her tireless work.

She's my hero, and I want to make her come on my tongue.

Patience, I remind myself. *Take time on the hunt.*

When I leave the bathroom, I find Ame near the window, staring through the glass as she braids her hair. The russet strands fall halfway down her torso and beg for a set of fingers to drag through them.

"Am I presentable?"

At the sound of my question, she turns. Her eyes slide over me, slowing as they drop to the skintight pants.

"I don't think you'll get arrested for indecent exposure," she says. "But if you do, I'll get you out. The police owe me." Her tone refuses to give away if she's joking or not, but her words send me back to a half-understood memory.

My muscles tense, and I hope I'm wrong. "We were at a police station once, weren't we?"

Ame blinks, then nods slowly.

Fuck. Tell me she didn't do what I think she did.

"You talked to a tall white woman. And a man. Black hair and tan."

"Samantha Reedsy, the police chief, and Levi Abadi. He's on the Folk Haven Mythic Council. You remember that?"

I close my eyes as I throw my mind backward into that moment. "Your hands ... they were red. And you grabbed that man behind the bars ..." The faces drift into focus, Ame's more than the others'. "You were scared. And sad." I blink my eyes open and search Ame's out, capturing the green. "You wanted to leave, but you didn't."

I don't care how long ago this occurred; I'll kill anyone who frightened her.

"They needed me. Needed my magic." She holds up her hands. "Do you know what I can do?"

I shake my head, suddenly wary. I know witches and

sorcerers are not the same thing. But they both work magic, and I'm not entirely comfortable with the idea.

This is Ame though. I'll never make her feel bad about a part of herself.

"I can sense desires. That's my natural ability. Certain mixtures amplify my power. That's what you saw on my hands."

She steps around me, moving to her dresser. She opens a wooden box, which I assume contains jewelry, only to reveal red powder. Now that I see the contents, I can recall times when Ame scooped a spoonful into a smaller container that fit in her pocket.

"This is a family recipe. Morgana has some too, for whenever she needs to work big magic. With it, I can manipulate someone. Make them want things. That night, I used it with my magic to convince that man you saw me grab—a human—to never come back to Folk Haven. He was going to cause the town trouble. The Council needed him gone, and I knew I could get it done."

The other times when Ame smeared red powder on her palms and touched a person come back to me. Like that dark night when she climbed into the backseat of a stranger's car.

"Why?" The question comes out ragged as I realize how close to danger she was when I didn't know any better. When I couldn't protect her. "Why is this your job?"

Ame's eyes flick around, taking in the room. "Morgana wasn't going to be allowed to buy this house. The founders of this town had created territory lines, and this isn't where witches live. But she wanted *this* house."

Disbelief and anger duel in my chest.

"You offered yourself in exchange for a *house*?"

Ame frowns. "Not myself. They don't own me. I'm like ... a contractor. They can call on me for the next two years."

"And after that?"

"After that, I'll charge a service rate."

"You're not getting *paid*?" I barely keep myself from shouting.

She sighs a big, heavy gust, like this topic is so inconsequential that it's boring. "No, I'm not. That's the deal. No one forced me to sign off on it. I was the one who came up with it. Besides, they've only called me in once."

"Yeah, I remember." I grind out the words through my teeth as I recall the way she shivered in discomfort or maybe fear the moment before she enthralled him.

There's no doubt she's powerful. But that means more people will want to use her.

I have to protect her.

The overwhelming urge brings up a thought I don't even want to contemplate. But I have to ask.

"Have you ever used your magic on me? Affected my desires?"

The little witch vigorously shakes her head. "Oh, no. I swear on The Dark One, I haven't. When I first found you, I tried. I most often use the magic on animals. Their desires are simpler, relatively easy to adjust without any assists. I wanted you to trust me, so you wouldn't be scared. But when I encountered your emotional grid, it was more intricate than any animal. I knew you were different, so I stopped, and I've never tried again."

"And will you?" I ask.

Ame chews her lip, big green eyes meeting mine. "I won't say never, but it's unlikely. I'll use it to protect myself. You would have to suddenly become dangerous to me or my family, and I can't fathom that happening."

"You can't fathom it?" I step closer, looming over her. Not because I want Ame to fear me, but because I want her to realize how fragile she is. To take her safety more seriously.

To comprehend how easily she puts herself into dangerous situations.

She has a strange werewolf in her bedroom, and she's acting like I'm a harmless poodle.

But Ame doesn't waver under my looming. Her emerald gaze adheres to mine until I feel like we're of equal height.

"No, Jack," she says, "I can't."

12

—————

AME

If I didn't trust Jack, I wouldn't have brought him into my home. I wouldn't have slept in his arms.

I won't be doing that second one again for separate reasons.

But Jack has no desire to hurt me.

If he meant me any harm, no doubt I would have lain awake all night, listening to the violent craving scraping at my mind. Instead, I easily fell asleep to the soothing loop of his protective and physical desires.

No one has ever calmed me with their silent cravings before. My family intentionally learned how to block my magic, so being around them is simply silence. But with Jack, it's different.

The way he wants me is a song I can listen to or let play in the background.

I think I'll miss it when he's gone.

"Don't you know how dangerous werewolves are?" Jack asks, staring down at me, his voice insistent.

Does he want me to fear him?

"Of course. I bet one could tear my throat out without transforming."

"Exactly."

"But *you* won't hurt me."

Maybe Jack is unsure of himself. Living in the wrong body has to leave behind trauma. Wanting to reassure him, I reach out and rub a pacifying circle on his chest. The wolf dips his chin to watch my hand.

"You're going to get yourself killed." Jack's declaration rumbles out on a growl in the exact same cadence as a Bee growl.

The familiarity has me grinning. Which has him frowning deeper, the expression digging creases into his cheeks. Suddenly, his hands cup my face, cradling me, determination dipping his brow.

"I won't let anyone hurt you, little witch."

His words warm me, paired beautifully with his desire.

Protect.

Protect.

Protect.

"I'm not in any danger. But thanks." I wrap my fingers around his wrists, a small embrace. "I won't let anyone hurt you either."

Jack's head jerks back, as if I'd snapped at him.

Poor, skittish wolf.

I run gentle thumbs over the pulse beating in his wrists as I carefully remove his hold from my face. He still has a strong urge to kiss me.

I pull away because I want that kiss. But it's a bad idea.

Jack has been trapped for years, and I'm the person who saved him. An averagely attractive woman. It's no surprise he'd want to fuck first, ask questions later.

But I ... can't. He means too much to me to have a fling. Sharing that intimacy with him, then watching him leave would hurt all the more.

"Time for food. And for Morgana."

Thoughts of my sister distract me. Normally, I have a decent idea of how she'll react to news.

But presenting her with a werewolf first thing in the morning isn't a common occurrence.

"Ame."

I pause at the door, turning back to meet Jack's intense stare. "Yes?"

"I'll answer all her questions, but she can't send me away. Only you can do that. And I won't go far."

"Of course." When I pull open the door, I extend my hand to him. I've never been much for touching other people because of my magic, but with Jack, I don't mind. I enjoy the brush of his skin against mine. "Just because the curse is broken doesn't mean I'm going to abandon you."

He tilts his head, studying me, and I let him while trying not to glance lower than his waist. It'd be rude to stare at how the stretchy cotton clings to his legs and ... other things.

Jack takes a deep inhale, his nostrils flaring. A moment later, he's at my side, hand in mine, so close that he looms over me.

"A decent man would leave you alone." He leans down until his mouth is next to my ear. "I'm not that man." The words and his hot breath have me covered in goose bumps.

Make her mine.

He'll get over that urge soon. Once he gets to know me better, he'll leave.

"Let's get you some bacon." I pull him toward the stairs.

Bee was extra grumbly in the morning before he got meat in his belly. My bet is, Jack is just the same.

When we enter the kitchen, Morgana is sitting at the table again, reading the same book from last night. The only indication that she's moved is the different set of clothes she's wearing and the bowl of cereal in front of her. She pauses, a spoonful of Cheerios halfway to her mouth.

"Good morning," I say as I pull out a chair at the table and indicate that Jack should sit.

He stays standing. "I'll help you with the food."

"You don't have to. You're a guest."

"I'm a freeloader. Besides, you hate cooking the bacon."

I sputter, "What are you talking about?"

"You always make a face when you take the package out. You think it's gross."

Huh. His memories must be returning.

"I'm used to it by now."

"No, you're not. I'll make the bacon. You make the toast."

"Are you going to eat the toast now?" Bee never wanted toast.

"Yes. I'll have fruit too."

"Oh, good idea. Mor, you didn't finish the gala apples, did you?"

When I look to my sister, I find her spoon hasn't moved, and she's flicking her eyes between Jack and me at a rapid rate that can't be healthy for her optic nerves.

Oh yeah. We're supposed to talk.

"Sorry. I forgot introductions. Jack, this is my sister, Morgana Shelly. You might remember her from...before."

He nods, keeping his dark gaze on her face as he dips his chin. "I appreciate your help when I was hurt."

My sister's brows rise so high that they almost disappear into her hairline.

"Mor, this is Jack. His last name is Lim, with an *M*. He's a werewolf, and he's also formerly Bee, the cat."

Her spoon clatters into the bowl, sending droplets of milk splattering over the table.

"What?" She whispers the word in harsh disbelief.

As Jack and I go about making our breakfast, I tell her about the past failed spells, the successful sunder spell, and what happened last night under the full moon. My sister knew I was trying to help Bee, but from her flabbergasted expression, I guess she either didn't realize the extent or she didn't believe me all the times I insisted he was more than a feline.

"And so I brought Jack home last night and figured this morning would be better for your questions. After some sleep. And finding him clothes. Before you ask, yes, Jack is wearing a pair of your leggings. I promise to wash them after we get him some clothes of his own today."

Jack grunts in agreement from his place at the stove, where he's moving sizzling bacon around in a cast iron pan. He was right; I don't like the raw bacon. Any raw meat really. Handling it tickles my gag reflex. I find it fascinating he noticed, even as a cat.

"You ..." Morgana shoves up from her chair, eyes wider than when we first walked in. "You're Bee? Bee, the cat. The cat that ..."

If anything, my explanation seems to have confused her more. There's a frantic, frazzled element to her breaths.

"Mor? Are you okay?" I watch my sister, combing my eyes over her, and wonder what I can say to ease her concern.

I hoped she'd treat this like finding a new, fascinating book. Ask some probing questions, explore the pages with curiosity.

Suddenly, Morgana is around the table, shoving herself in between me and Jack, forming a wall with her body. My sister stands a handful of inches taller than me with broader shoulders that make it easy for her to blot out the werewolf from my view.

The loss causes a tight panic in my chest. I'm suddenly worried I'll step out from behind her to find he's gone.

That's silly. I don't need to keep my eyes on him at all times.

Still, Morgana's not having the best reaction.

"You've been sleeping in my sister's bed? Creeping on her when she's alone in her room? What the fuck?"

"Mor!" I slide out from behind her to find the two of them in a glare battle. "I told you for years that he was a man. You never said anything then. You *cannot* get mad at him now."

Ignoring my sound argument, she flings out an arm, as if she thinks he's about to lunge at me. My face heats, and I worry how Jack might feel at the blatant hostility. He's already gone through enough.

Plus, he hasn't eaten his bacon yet.

"You're right," Jack says, seething stare locked on hers. He doesn't sound apologetic. "I did do those things. And I kept a closer watch on her than *you* ever did."

Morgana flinches but holds her ground, face a thundercloud.

Jack isn't done. "Ame told you I was a man, but you thought she was being silly. You're lucky I care about her safety. That I didn't want her hurt. Even as a cat, I could have killed her a hundred times over."

"You—" she gasps.

"*Me*," he growls. A Bee growl. A *don't fuck with me* growl. "I was with her when she went into the police station to use her magic on that disgusting human. The one who had tried to assault the siren. *I* was the one who went with her to find that vile man slinking around this town, smelling of twisted magic. *I* watched her get into a car with him. Alone." He looms over my sister, rage burning in his gaze. "*I* was beside her as she ran through the woods, terrified of what she saw in his head. And *I* was next to her when she first walked into this house. The house *you* wanted and only got because of what she had risked.

You're right. I, a useless cat, was at her side the whole time. But *I* was there. Not you."

As he makes his horrible list, I watch the blood drain from my sister's face and the guilt fill her eyes.

I can't stand it.

"Jack!" I snap. "Get out."

13

———

JACK

The floating dock sways beneath me, but the rocking does nothing to soothe my furious, pounding pulse.

"Get out."

The little witch growled the words at me, and I was simultaneously proud of her fierceness and devastated by the hurt on her face. A pain that I'd put there.

More and more memories come back to me from my time in that hateful form, all of them meaning more now that I have better mental capacity to understand what was going on.

And all I can see are the ways Ame put herself in danger. Like I said to Morgana, I was there. But I was also a cat with little comprehension for the situations. I was functioning on instinct, making my dislike of people known, but never realizing how much more help Ame needed.

Gods, she's been around multiple people who could have—and would have liked to—hurt her. Only her quick-working magic kept her safe.

Still, Morgana thinks *I'm* the issue?

I gaze out across the water, watching as a bird with broad wings soars low over the gentle waves and the occasional fish breaches the surface to snap bugs from the air. In the distance, rounded mountain peaks rise above the trees. I'm more familiar with the Rocky Mountains, which pierce the sky with steep, jagged slopes. The Appalachians are older, worn smooth by time.

Still, I'd like to run to them. Become a wolf and disappear into the wild. My animal rages within me, trapped for so long in the wrong form and unsatisfied with the brief transformation the night before.

But I can't go. Not until I'm sure Ame will wait for me to come back.

"Get out," she commanded. But because my little witch is neither cruel nor a liar, she clarified. "Wait outside. On the porch or the dock. Please. Just ... give us a moment."

Despite the hunger in my stomach and the conviction that I was right, I still went. Because even though I'm an asshole, I swore to her I would go if she asked me.

But never far.

The wind shifts, and on the breeze, I catch the earthy, minty scent of her and know she approaches. I stay still so as not to spook her. The dock dips as Ame steps on the worn wood. A moment later, she's beside me, a spot of warmth on the cool fall day. And she smells of meat.

"Here. You must be hungry." Ame sinks to her knees beside me and holds out a plate, piled high with bacon, pieces of toast, and slices of apple.

"Thank you." I accept the plate and try to figure out a way to apologize for saying something I'm not sorry for. "I—"

"Mor has done a lot for me," Ame cuts me off, and I click my teeth shut as I meet her intense stare. Her green eyes don't hold anger. But there is a burning within the irises. "She and my brothers raised me when my parents couldn't be bothered.

She's given up a lot for me, and I owe her. Now that I'm an adult, I can take care of myself and make my own choices. Some of them might be dangerous, but they're mine to make. Morgana protected me when I was young and I needed her to, but that's not her job anymore. Please don't try to make her feel bad for decisions *I* make about *my* life."

Ame's words wash through me, and I mull over what she said. I have to acknowledge, there are years of history between the two witches I'm not privy to even if I organize all my cat memories. They lived a life together before I stumbled into it.

And Ame is right that her protection is no longer her sister's job.

Now, it's mine.

"I'm sorry," I say, not lying. I *am* sorry that I upset her.

"Apology accepted. I just need you to know, whatever your feelings about my sister are, I won't stand by while you or anyone tries to make her feel bad."

Yet another reason why Ame Shelly is perfection. Her loyalty.

"Understood."

I'll keep my mouth shut, but my mind hasn't been swayed. Morgana might not do it intentionally, but she takes advantage of her sister's giving nature. If I can't call the older witch out on it, then I'll have to make sure I'm the buffer between Ame and a world that takes too much from her.

"Good. Time to eat your food, and then I'll take you exploring."

She plucks a piece of bacon off my plate and holds the crispy strip in front of my mouth. Leaning forward, I snap it up in one bite, which earns me the start of a smile.

"We'll get you some clothes first. Or maybe shoes." Her eyes drop to my bare feet. "Sorry, I don't think we have anything in the house that'll fit you."

"I don't mind going barefoot." I have been for years now.

She nods and fiddles with her earlobe as she thinks, and I shove toast in my mouth to keep from trying to kiss her.

"You'll need ..." Ame's eyes go wide. "A phone. Oh goddess. Your *life*. You had a life. Damn The Dark One's plans, I don't know why I didn't think of it. I'm so sorry, Jack."

Ame stands abruptly, aiming for the house, and I mourn the end of our short time on the dock. It's peaceful by the water.

But my mouth is too full of bacon to protest, so I rise and follow her, chewing fast, intent on calming my suddenly anxious witch.

"I can't imagine. The people who care about you must be worried. You've been missing for years. We can call them. Right now."

"Ame," I say after a large, painful swallow, "there's no one to call."

I made sure of that.

The witch pauses, one foot on the dock, one foot on land. "No one?" she asks, not looking at me.

"No one who would want to hear my voice." I manage not to sound full of self-loathing, which I count as a plus. "Let's stick with your first plan. Shopping. Can I use your computer to check if my bank accounts are still intact?"

Please don't let them have declared me dead.

The witch turns back to me, her head tilted at a curious angle. "Of course you can. But are you sure there's no one wondering where you are?"

"That sorcerer might be." But he won't have to wonder for long. Because I'm going to find him and knit him a sweater with his own guts.

"I mean, family or friends."

Ame faces me fully now, and I focus on my breakfast to avoid seeing pity in her gaze.

Not ready to dig into that shadowed part of my past, I give a simple, accurate answer. "My pack was supposed to be my family. And you already know how that turned out."

Sold to a sorcerer like an object. I was only an item with a price tag.

There's a cringeworthy scraping noise, and I realize my claws have extended, scratching the surface of the porcelain plate. Forcefully, I rein in my temper and sheathe my claws.

"Jack?"

Every time Ame says my name, I think one of my internal wounds heals. And I can't avoid her eyes anymore, but when I look up, I don't see sad sympathy. The witch appears curious with a touch of earnestness.

"Yes?"

"Do you believe me when I say I'm your friend?"

"I do."

"And that I'm here for you? Whatever you need."

Too much. She gives too much of herself, and I'm greedy enough to take more than I deserve. But unlike others in her life, I plan to give back tenfold.

"I believe you."

Ame offers a distracted nod, her mind half somewhere else. But that doesn't bother me. With her attention divided, she's less likely to notice I'm obsessed with her.

No doubt she'd want more space between us if she knew.

"I won't abandon you, Jack. Even when you go back to your life, we'll still be friends."

Go back to my life?

I keep my mouth shut and nod because if I make a noise now, it'll be a scoff. Or a laugh. Maybe a growl.

Because what this witch hasn't grasped yet is, my past existence is gone.

She is my life now.

14

AME

In a small town like Folk Haven, clothing shops are limited. I drive us to the outdoor supply shop, owned by a siren named Cassandra. She smiles at the two of us from behind a counter decorated with paper bats and rubber spiders for the upcoming holiday. Only a few weeks until Halloween. The winged mythic points us to the back corner of the store, where we find a few promising racks. Ten minutes later, we're at the register with a stack of shirts and pants, plus socks and a set of boots. The beginnings of Jack's new wardrobe.

"I'll pay you back," he promises when I swipe my credit card.

"I know."

After the awkward breakfast, I lent Jack my laptop to check his accounts, and he found all his money intact. I'm glad the pack that had betrayed him didn't also steal from him too.

Unfortunately, without ID or a debit card, there's no way for him to access his money. All of that is back in California.

I know he needs to go back. Return to his home to rebuild

the life he once had. I've offered to drive him, figuring if we take the RV, we could have a decently comfortable ride.

And I won't let the ache in my chest rise to the surface at the thought of losing my friend.

It's not really losing him, I remind myself, *since he'll still be alive*. Just ... all his grumpiness will be on the other side of the country. I'll have to call him to hear his growls.

Now, I watch as Jack sits on a bench to pull on his new socks and boots. Every move he makes, even the subtle ones, have a certain grace to them. But not catlike. Even when Jack was a cat, he never moved like one.

He's always been canine.

His brown hair hangs shaggy around his dark eyes, and I'm wondering if I should offer a trip to the barber shop next when a deep voice calls my name.

With my focus on him, I notice how Jack goes tense.

"Ame." Hamish repeats my name as he strolls up to my side.

The selkie smiles at me as if I'm something special to him, and I try not to fidget under his intense focus.

"Hey, Hamish."

"Why don't you walk with me?" The selkie gestures down the street, as if there were something on the next block that might interest me.

"Walk with you where?" Not that I plan on going with him. My day is full of Jack. But I ask the question as a courtesy and because I'm half-distracted by a sudden realization.

I don't sense the selkie's desires.

I've never been this close to Hamish without an involuntary glimpse into one of his sexual fantasies, starring me.

Come to think of it, I didn't hear any desires from Cassandra either.

"Oh, I don't know. Just for a stroll. Maybe we could meander to the lake." He offers a grin full of straight white teeth.

Bracing myself, I meet his blue eyes directly.

Still nothing. All I sense is …

Protect her.

Make her mine.

Hold her hand.

Buy her lunch.

Kill the salty motherfucker.

"She's not going anywhere with you." That growl comes from the bench. Comes from Jack.

His desire is overwhelming Hamish's.

My friend rises to his feet, another inch taller because of the boot soles. Hamish frowns but doesn't back away from what I have to admit is an intimidating display of dislike.

I can't imagine where the animosity is coming from.

"Who are you?" Hamish asks.

Instead of answering the question, Jack's lips curl. "You smell like canned tuna."

Hamish scowls, and I get the urge to correct Jack. The selkie smells like seaweed, and again, the smell reminds me of spending hours bent over a toilet.

But Jack is a werewolf with a much keener nose than mine. So, maybe Hamish *does* smell like tuna fish as well as water plants. The thought does nothing to ease the queasiness in my stomach.

The selkie steps closer to me, and that doesn't help either.

"I don't know who you think you are, and I really don't care. I was talking to Amethyst." Hamish turns fully to me then, trying to maneuver himself in between Jack and me.

But the werewolf is too fast, placing himself at my side. "I'm Ame's protector. Whatever you have to say to her can go through me."

I want to protest, but I'm also trying to hold my breath before the smell of seaweed makes me lose my morning bacon.

"I'm an important person in this town," Hamish snaps. "Not a threat. As a matter of fact, *you're* the stranger here. I might have to swing by the police station and let them know a suspicious man is lingering about."

Jack's grin goes wolfish, which is probably natural for him. "Try it."

"I'm going to vomit," I announce, then let out an impressive gag.

Hamish's face blanches, and he stumbles a step back. Meanwhile, Jack whirls toward me, hooking an arm around my waist and guiding me to a nearby trash can.

He presses a warm hand to my forehead, searching for a fever. "How long have you felt sick? Is it just your stomach?" He slides his touch to the back of my neck and gathers my hair in a gentle fist, holding the braid away from my face. "If you need to puke, go for it."

"Feel better," Hamish calls as he strides away. "We'll catch up another time."

Jack mutters something that sounds like *pathetic* under his breath.

I suck in a lungful of fresh air, tinged with the scent of Jack —crisp breeze and pine needles—and my stomach immediately calms. "I'm better now."

"Are you sure? Where's the doctor in this town?"

"I don't need a doctor." I meet his dark gaze, trying not to shiver at the teasing caress of his repetitious desires. "Are you done arguing with strangers?"

Jack's hold in my hair eases as he glances away. "Yes," he grumbles.

But I still pick up a darker urge in the melody of his cravings. Jack *wants* to be violent.

"You're really angry, aren't you?" Extending my uninjured hand, I let my palm hover barely an inch away from his chest, where I envision the rage and resentment at what was done to him eating away at his heart. "It's festering inside you."

Jack's eyes narrow. "Yes. I'm mad. Mad at the sorcerer who

caged me. Mad at the pack who betrayed me. And mad at the pompous asshole who makes you queasy."

Being mad at Hamish for his smell—that only I seem to have a problem with—is nitpicky and drives my next question.

"Are you going to hurt me?"

The wolf flinches, dark eyes wide with horror. "No. Never."

I can tell he believes what he's saying, but that doesn't mean it's the full truth.

"You seem angry, like a bomb," I explain. "There's always a radius to rage, and if I stay close to you, I might get hurt. Even if you don't mean to."

His mouth drops open, maybe to deny my claim. But he almost immediately snaps his jaw shut, clenching his teeth so tight that I'm worried he might crack them.

"Jack—"

"Are you done with me then?" His tone is terse, so sharp that it almost severs off the question mark, as if he already knows the answer.

But he doesn't.

"*Done* implies a finishing point. You're my friend, first as Bee and now as Jack. Fur or flesh doesn't matter. There's no end to us." Letting my hand drop down, I find his and slide my bandage-free palm against his, making sure I have a good grip on the unpredictable werewolf as I lead him down the street. "I have an idea. For how we can defuse some of this excess violence."

Jack doesn't protest, and when we reach a familiar storefront, I glance back to see he has his focus on our joined hands. I can't tell if my hold bothers him, but when I loosen my fingers, he tightens his. Retaining the connection.

"Do you remember this place?" I nod toward the window. The normally clear glass has a beautiful mural of autumn leaves, colorful gourds, and a scarecrow holding a coffee cup.

Jack lifts his gaze, running dark eyes over the sign hanging above the door.

"Coffee & Claws," he murmurs. "We've been here before. Many times. You drink ... tea. And you eat pastries."

"Bingo." Keeping hold of him, I push through the door, setting a small bell to ring.

In a rare turn of events, a burly, bearded man stands behind the counter. Heath is more often in the kitchen, baking all the pastries, including their famous bear claws. Well, famous in Folk Haven anyway. I'm not sure how far word has spread.

I'm glad for this change in routine because he's exactly the bear shifter I wanted to find.

"Hey, Amethyst." His greeting is gruff yet friendly, which is normally how Heath communicates. "What can I get you?"

"A fight."

15

———————

JACK

I can smell bear on the man the moment we step into the shop. A shifter no doubt. But unlike the selkie from a moment ago, this mythic doesn't reek of lust.

"Hey, Amethyst. What can I get you?"

"A fight."

I expected her to name a type of tea, so I need an extra second to mentally process her answer.

A ... fight?

WARNING! My witch is challenging a bear shifter to a duel!

Quickly, I slide in front of her and stare down the burly man. "She didn't mean that. She's not going to fight you."

The shifter seems as confused by her request as I am, which keeps me from upping my level of aggression. But just barely. No one in this town—in this world—is going to hurt Ame Shelly while I'm living. I will rip their throat out with my teeth if they so much as try.

"Not me." Ame presses her hand against my waist, trying to move me out of the way. When I don't budge, she simply continues to communicate, even with my body as the obstruction. "I meant, a fight for you."

Her finger taps my back, right on my spine, and I struggle not to close my eyes in pleasure at the touch.

"Heath, this is my friend, Jack. He's Of the Claw, and he's had a lot of life stress lately. I thought you might like to have a wrestling match. Work out some aggression."

Some of the tension eases from my shoulders when I realize my witch isn't throwing herself in the path of danger yet again. With new eyes, I examine the barista, and he does the same with me.

We're the same height, but he's easily twice as broad. Under normal circumstances, that would give him the advantage. But this bear shifter, in his pumpkin-patterned apron, has been living the easy life, baking cakes and pastries in a quiet town.

Meanwhile, I've been sold, enslaved, and forced into the wrong body for years.

Ame is right. I'm suddenly eager for a chance to pound on someone. *Anyone.*

"Yeah, sure," Heath says with a shrug and half a smile. "Shop closes at six today."

A short time later, my witch and I are back on the street—her with a steaming cup of ginger tea and a pumpkin spice muffin and me with a slip of paper that has an address for my brawl with a bear this evening.

I can't wait.

Literally. My body is suddenly vibrating with the excess energy, as if knowing I'll have somewhere to siphon it off. It's all pooled just under the surface of my skin, ready for the release.

But the match isn't for *hours.*

"Abstaining from coffee was a good choice," Ame says as her gaze runs over me, noting how I'm bouncing on the balls of my feet and curling my hands into fists.

"Hmm." That random noise is all the response I can

manage when my body is telling me to find an enemy and rip them to shreds.

No. I won't leave Ame for my hunt. Not until she is mine.

"Let's walk." She wraps her fingers around my wrist and starts down the street. This isn't the same as walking with hands clasped. There's an element of tugging or being led. But I also like Ame's grip on me.

A lot.

"What did you miss most when you were stuck in cat form?" she asks.

That's easy.

"Sex."

Ame keeps walking but throws me a narrow-eyed stare over her shoulder, and I give her a smoldering smile.

Doesn't work.

"Noted. What else?"

Clearing away the idea of peeling off Ame's clothes, I recall my life before my pack betrayed me. What things, big or small, brought me joy.

My mom.

Hanging with my best friend Niko.

Former best friend and a mother who wants nothing to do with me.

Don't think about them. They're better off without me.

Something simpler then.

"Driving."

Moving fast in general, but yeah, sitting behind the wheel of my car—an old Camaro—and rushing down the highway as the engine rumbled, that was almost as good as sprinting through the mountains on a full moon.

"Good. I can give you that." The answer implies she can't give me the other thing. Or won't.

I would never force her. The idea disgusts me. That any

person would take something that should be all mutual pleasure.

But I also know there's something between Ame and me. Potential.

"You don't still think of me as some cuddly cat, do you?" I ask as we approach her car.

Ame presses the keys into my palm but doesn't immediately let go. Instead, she holds my gaze, a smile playing around her sweet mouth. "I never thought of you as a cat. Not really."

"But you never thought of me as a man either. Not really." Not the way my infrequent bouts of lucidity had me realizing she was a woman. A glorious, adorable, irresistible woman.

She grows thoughtful. "You're right. You were a … consciousness. It wouldn't have been right to imagine you as a man because I didn't know what you looked like, and so it wouldn't have been *you*. I would have been one more person assigning you a wrong body."

The weight of her words shudders through me. Even in her mind, Ame tried her hardest not to betray me as others in my life had. The urge to kiss her threatens to overwhelm me, and I find myself leaning forward.

"Jack, you do know …"

"Yes?" I can scent the mint of her shampoo, recall the taste of her on my tongue from that one stolen kiss.

"You were *never* cuddly." The witch grins wide, her freckled nose wrinkling, and she steps away from me, leaving the keys in my palm but taking my heart in her hand.

Her playful side threatens to unman me.

"I will cuddle you *so* hard, Ame Shelly," I promise her.

16

───────────

AME

JACK DRIVES WITH AN INTENSE JOY. I directed him to the back roads of Folk Haven. The ones that lead to monster territory and see less travel. There, he pushes my compact car as fast as it will go. Briefly, I worry he'll do permanent damage to the engine with the way it revs and whines like I've never made it do before.

But when I see the eager light in his eyes, on his face that is more often scowling, I decide a trip to the mechanic shop will be worth it. Air streams in through the open windows, smelling crisp with the start of a Southern fall. Some of the leaves on the trees still struggle to hold on to their green while, up north, I'm sure half already coat the ground.

I'm grateful for the gentle season change because it means I can watch wind ruffle Jack's dark brown hair and flush his cheeks red. On a particularly winding road, one that has us close to the Smoky Mountains, he lets out a triumphant laugh, navigating the curves with skill.

"You're good at this." I shout the compliment over the roar of the wind and engine.

Eyes almost black with passion clash with mine, and the werewolf reaches over to snatch my hand from where it lies lax in my lap.

Make her mine.

Go faster.

Touch her.

Hold her.

Taste her.

Thank her.

That last desire catches on my consciousness like a discordant note.

He's *grateful* for me. That's what this is and no more.

"Want to know what else I'm good at?" Jack's focus returns to the road as he steers one-handed.

I get the sense he doesn't expect an answer or plan to give one. But his grin grows wider, and I can feel the stretch against my knuckles because, suddenly, he's pressing the backs of my fingers against his mouth.

Lips against skin. But no suggestive lick or bite. Jack simply presses me to him. Holding me in place as he races along the two-lane road through the Chattahoochee National Forest.

When the road becomes too rough to go fast, Jack pulls a U-turn and shoots us toward town again. We have a couple of hours until meeting up with Heath, so I point him south, toward Mary Jo's bagel truck. I figure it's best to keep a werewolf well fed throughout the day, especially when he hasn't worked off his aggression.

Jack frowns when I hand over my credit card to the smiling nymph. "I'll pay you back."

"You already said that. I trust you." I sign the receipt. "We'll check on the camper tomorrow and head out the day after.

You'll be in California in no time." *Don't think about the good-bye. Don't think about the pain of no more Jack.* "You can find your secret cash stash and all your IDs, then go to the bank and fill your pockets with even more money, and make it rain all you want. I expect you to pay me back with a thick stack of ones in a briefcase, which you will arrogantly slide to me across a table in the office of an abandoned warehouse and say, 'You can count it if you don't trust me.' " I smirk to hide my sadness at the thought of parting. "If you're not planning on paying me back that way, don't even bother."

"Smart-ass," he grumbles, even as the corner of his mouth ticks up.

While Mary Jo makes our food, we settle at a picnic table, the wood warm from the sun. Jack sits on the same side as me, close enough that our thighs brush, and I remember reading a passage in one of Mor's books that werewolves are physically affectionate with people they trust.

A werewolf pack lives in town, but I've never made friends with any. We never seem to end up in the same spaces. Although I did once have a conversation with a bartender at Local Brew, who I was *pretty* sure was a werewolf. That's another odd thing about Folk Haven. There are enough oblivious humans wandering around that we can't go spouting off mythical knowledge left and right. But even if we could, what's the polite way to ask someone what mythical designation they are?

And what if they're a monster? Plenty of our kind dislike the idea of mythical beasts mixing magical DNA to create mystery creatures. There's judgment and scorn, and insisting someone deal with that just so you can properly catalog them in your head is unfair.

All this to say, most of my werewolf knowledge has come from the texts in our library, and there are only a few wolves in town I'm sure of.

"How old were you when you first shifted?" I ask, wanting to know more about Jack and his mysterious past.

Jack stiffens beside me, and I feel his heavy stare on the side of my face. When I tilt my chin to meet his eyes, he holds me in his thrall.

"Fourteen." He presses his shoulder against mine, as if seeking comfort. "Before that, I thought werewolves were fictional."

The obvious question lingers in the humid air between us. *What happened?*

No doubt the story is sad or scary, and it seems unfair to demand more from this man who's had so much taken from him already.

Instead, I choose to give of myself.

"My family has always had emotion-related magic. But a witch never knows exactly how their power will manifest. Most magic—spells and the like—we need incantations, ingredients, timing to make it work. But all of us have one thing that comes naturally. And it can pop up whenever."

"Your connection to desire." There's no judgment in his voice, but plenty of curiosity. Jack leans closer, as if he wants to delve into my head and suss out all the information in my past. Maybe that's the hunter in him.

I nod. "When I was ten, my brother Anthony was being bossy. I can't remember about what, but I just wanted to be left alone. So, I shoved him and told him to go jump off a bridge."

That day is burned into my mind. The way his body tensed against my touch before he strode away from me, as if he was in a trance. When I glanced down at my hands, I saw a red glow. I ran after him, but his legs were longer than mine. He didn't turn when I called him.

We're both lucky that the closest bridge was over a creek, barely six feet above the surface of the water. Still, I was terrified when Anthony heaved himself over the railing without hesitation. Once he hit the water, my compulsion was done, and he shook the dirty droplets from his eyes and stared up at me in horror.

I don't think that incident is the sole reason my brother has sworn off magic, but it certainly didn't help.

"Did he?"

At Jack's question, I realize I played out the past silently in my mind instead of continuing my morbid story.

"Yes. A small bridge and not too high, so he wasn't injured." Mentally though, emotionally, that's a different story. "Still, I hurt him."

My brother has never looked at me the same way after that day. No matter how many times I swore it was an accident and I didn't really mean it. He believed me, but it's hard to relax around someone who can bend your will to theirs.

That's the day I learned what it was like to be feared.

My hands lie flat on the tabletop, and I curl them into gentle fists, as if my magic is at risk of spilling out now. But my power is stabler than when I was ten, and most times, I can't manipulate desires without the red powder assist.

That day was an anomaly. A terrifying occurrence that could have been avoided if …

I shake my head, not wanting to think about my parents and what they did to me.

"Have I met your brothers?" Jack asks, his face scrunched in thought.

"No. Last we were in the same space together was a few days before we found you. They're both in England right now, but Broderick is trying to visit soon. Hopefully, Anthony will come too."

"Does he still blame you?" There's a growl in Jack's voice, which is almost enough to bring a smile to my face.

"I don't think so. But he's sworn off magic. I don't think a town full of mythics appeals to him."

Mary Jo—a forest nymph with ombre-green hair—strolls up to us with a tray of our food, giving us a break from the morbid conversation. The whole time she's laying our meals on the table, asking if we need anything else, then strolling away, I wait to hear some random secret craving.

Nothing.

Just Jack's string of desires for me.

The wolf takes a bite of his bagel, eyes thoughtful as he chews. I follow his lead, preferring eating delicious food to talking about the strained relationship between Anthony and me.

"I shifted in our kitchen. That first time." Jack wipes his hands and mouth with a napkin, keeping his voice steady. "I was confused. The world looked different. Then, my mom started waving a knife at me and screaming."

I can imagine. Even if humans knew werewolves existed, having one show up unexpectedly in your house would be terrifying.

"Everything would have gone to hell if my friend Niko"—Jack's voice catches on the name, and I store that fact away for another time—"hadn't been on his way over. He burst in the door, saw what was going on, and stepped between us. But he had his back to me, spreading his arms wide. Protecting *me* from my mother." The wolf's voice has gone as rough as gravel. "He knew what had happened. What I was."

"Niko was a werewolf too?" I guess.

Jack shakes his head. "Another type of mythic. A kappa."

The mythic name sounds vaguely familiar. There may have been a chapter about them in one of the books in our collection. All I can recall is they're considered Of the Fin, like selkies and merpeople, but they tend to live in East Asia. Still, like people, plenty of mythics have moved across borders over the centuries.

I would like to meet a kappa one day.

"Niko knew about my kind even if he didn't realize I was one until that moment," Jack says. "He got his parents—they were kappas too—to come over and talk to my mom. They were friends. And he sat with me in my room and explained the best he could. He told me about mythical creatures living hidden in our world. How werewolves need to shift on the full moon and have advanced reflexes and senses." Jack grimaces. "But he didn't have all the answers I wanted. Which is why ..."

His jaw tenses, and I can almost hear his teeth grinding.

And I know he's thinking about the pack that betrayed him.

"If I never knew another witch"—I tear off small pieces of my bagel and toss them to a daring squirrel that's ventured close to our table—"I would be excited to find someone like me. Someone who understood and could teach me everything I didn't know."

Jack's eyes bore into mine. "Yes." He rasps the answer.

But what did that pack teach him other than lies? Did he ever get the answers he wanted?

And where are Niko and his mother now?

Jack said no one is expecting to hear from him.

Not wanting to bring up every painful piece of his past on the first day of his freedom, I keep my curious questions to myself.

"Thank you for telling me." Copying his earlier move, I press my shoulder against his, leaning into his hard body that's somehow still comforting.

"I ..." Jack trails off, staring down at me.

His face is as unreadable as when he was a feline. I almost wish he would growl. Those sounds I at least knew how to distinguish.

The streams of desires flowing from him are bundled together, so tightly packed that they're currently indistinguishable.

"How's your bagel?" I ask when the silence has stretched long enough that I don't think he'll finish his thought.

"It's fucking amazing." He holds my eyes as he takes a large bite.

17

───────

JACK

RESISTING the urge to kiss Ame takes all my willpower, leaving nothing left over to rein in my temper, spurred hotter by thoughts of my old pack. Good thing I'm about to go a few rounds with a bear.

My witch lets me drive us to the address as she gives the directions. Apparently, navigation technology gets glitchy in Folk Haven, making it easy for new arrivals to get lost. I look forward to memorizing all the roads. And then I want to learn more about the way magic and tech interact in this one-of-a-kind community. Before that, I'll need to catch up on all the tech advances made while I lacked opposable thumbs. I'd just started my career as a programmer when my life went to shit, and now, I'm years behind.

What number iPhone are we on now?

Figuring all that out will have to wait until my mind is clear. When I have enough control to think and reason and not act like an animal with even the smallest provocation. There was a time in my life when I could easily ignore my werewolf heritage. Back when I was focused on college classes and building a future for myself.

Now, the beast constantly shifts and growls under my skin, demanding acknowledgment. Not even Ame can distract me from the itch.

My witch pulls a folding camping chair out of her trunk and settles beside a group of people—mythics by the smell of them—who've gathered on the grassy expanse. We're on a farm, it looks like, with a barn off in the distance and a wide swatch of cleared land. There's the subtle scent of horse and manure in the air, but faded—as if they were here once, but not anymore. On the ride over, Ame told me this land belongs to Heath's cousin, a bear shifter named Mahon.

"Hope you don't mind, but I put the word out." Heath gestures at the crowd and grins.

He's already shirtless, where he stands in front of me. If the man had told me he was a mammoth shifter, I would have believed him. He's that huge.

And I can't fucking wait to take a chunk out of him.

I didn't used to be this bloodthirsty.

Yeah, well, the mild-mannered Jack got betrayed and enslaved. Better I err on the side of a grumpy asshole and save myself another round of that shit show.

If that hadn't happened, I wouldn't have met Ame.

The thought is an odd one and has me glancing her way again. When our eyes meet, she smiles and waves, then holds up her electronic tablet, the one she was typing on earlier in the car.

Go, Jack! flashes on the screen.

It's all I can do to stay in the makeshift fighting ring instead of striding over to her, dragging her against my chest, and claiming her delicious mouth.

I would have found her. If I hadn't been thrust into the little witch's path, somehow, I would have found Amethyst Shelly and made her mine.

"*Do* you mind?"

The rumbled question pulls my gaze from her freckled face, and I spy the shifter frowning at me because I never answered his question.

"No." I shrug. "More people to watch you eat dirt, the better."

He booms out a laugh, his barrel chest shaking with the noise. "You got spirit. I like it."

"Okay, here I am." A redheaded white man, almost as large as Heath and also smelling like bear, jogs up to us, grinning wide. "I'm Mahon, and I'm gonna be today's referee. Fight is happening within town limits, so there're some rules."

"Rules?" I scoff.

The ginger giant doesn't stop smiling as he looks me over. "Yeah, buddy. You must be new. Folk Haven has rules. You follow them, you live in peace in our little slice of Georgia. You break them, you're out of here. Council's orders."

My muscles tense in anger. The Council. Of course. And who would they send after me if I decided to break one of their precious rules?

Ame?

My eyes sneak her way again, this time involuntarily. She offers me a thumbs-up.

I give zero shits if everyone in this town hates me and wants me gone. Nothing new there. But Ame would care. Especially if she was tasked with being the one to drive me out of town. I could hear the pain in her voice earlier when she told me about the time she accidentally spelled her brother. She considers me her friend—though if things go my way, we'll be more—and manipulating my mind would distress her. That is, if she agreed to follow The Council's demands. But her refusal would start an entirely new string of issues.

I won't make trouble for her. And I won't let anything come between us.

"Fine," I growl. "What are these rules?"

"First—obvious one—no killing. This is a wrestling match, not a duel to the death."

"Got it." I don't have the inclination to kill the bear anyway. Those fatal urges are directed at villains outside of Folk Haven.

"Second, no permanent maiming. Let's leave with the same number of limbs as we arrived with, cool?"

"Fine." I can get out plenty of aggression without tearing one of the guy's arms off.

Now, if I were fighting another wolf, I might not be able to make the same promise. Not when I know just how shitty my kind are. Bears though will get a pass—for now.

"Third, no weapons but those naturally yours."

I nod, feeling the pressure of claws lingering in the root of my nail beds. "What else?"

"That's it!" The redheaded referee sounds remarkably cheerful.

"Really?" I expected more. No killing, maiming, or using weapons? Simple enough.

"Yep. Fight on three?"

We give our assent, and Mahon backs away, counting slowly as he goes. "Three ... two ... one ... FIGHT!"

I expect a moment or two of circling. Feeling each other out to identify weaknesses.

But Heath barrels toward me, grinning all the while and letting out a whoop. I don't know if it's strategy or chaos, but either way, I refuse to let him take me down.

He hits me like a train from a hell dimension. My ribs groan in protest, and my toes almost leave the ground. But I kicked off my new shoes before this bout, and I let my claws extend, digging them into the dirt to anchor me. Still, an embarrassingly loud *oof* shoots out of my chest at the impact.

Luckily, there's plenty of noises from those gathered that mine likely goes unnoticed.

As the bear wraps his arms around my waist, I know what technique he's going for. Some combination of a chest-crushing lift, probably followed by a move to slam me on the ground once my feet are out from under me.

This was the takedown that Finnick liked best too. My former pack leader was a beefy guy, just like Heath, and he relied on those muscles. Too much. At least I got plenty of bouts in with that asshole before he drugged me and sold me.

A flash of that night comes back to me. Finnick insisted we go on an extended hunt together, months in our wolf form, living in nature. He told me every werewolf had to go through a wild trial before they were considered part of the pack.

I had to leave my job behind.

My friends.

My family.

Give myself over to the pack fully. And I believed him. I trusted him as he handed me a flask and told me to drink deep.

Then, I woke up in a cage in time to see my pack leader accepting payment from a stranger before driving away. Leaving me in the hands of evil.

Fury fuels my muscles. With relish, I let Heath grip me hard around the torso. Then, I slam my elbow into the base of his skull, ringing his bell. He groans but doesn't let go. Not that it matters.

I become smoke.

I utilize the moment between shifting, where I'm not fully corporeal, and I slip from his hold. Finnick could never use this during a brawl because his shift was different than mine. All solid, no smoke. He tried to get me to stop, claiming it was cheating. But before I realized I was a werewolf, I had just been a scrawny kid in public school and had plenty of run-ins with bullies who taught me to use any weapon at my disposal to win.

That was how I almost got free of the sorcerer the first time.

He hadn't thought I'd be willing to break my own wrists to get out of the manacles. He was wrong. But chains were just the first part of my prison, and a spell caught me up before I made it out.

The next time, I had to use different techniques—ones that are truly shameful—to get away.

But now, I'm my own man—my own wolf—with the perfect little witch watching as I'm about to hand this bear his ass while still following all of their precious rules.

These thoughts flow through my misty mind in half a second, which is how long I'm made of shadow. I don't consider the dark cloud one of my forms because I can't hold on to it. It's a transitional state to claim my third and final form.

The hybrid.

"How hard did he hit me?" Heath mutters, rubbing the back of his head and blinking as he stares at my now seven foot height. "I'm seeing a wolf man."

I snarl a laugh, wondering if he forgot who he was fighting when I tapped his skull.

There's a rising wave of noise from the spectators, but I ignore them as I launch myself at my opponent. He dodges to the side, narrowly avoiding my snapping teeth. Twisting in the air, I land on all fours even though I can stand perfectly well on my hind legs. But low to the ground, I gather more power for another lunge, launching myself at the baker. This time, he doesn't move out of my way. I expect to collide with flesh, but instead, I grasp fur.

Heath shifted so fast that I barely registered the alteration. We tangle and tumble to the ground, evenly matched once more. Or maybe I'm overmatched again, what with Heath's bear being the size of a tool shed.

But he doesn't have my speed. And he doesn't have my rage.

The world around us fades away as we clash, twining

together and falling apart. Blood from shallow cuts sprays over the ground, but at some point, I stop trying to wound him, preferring the burn of muscle to the sting of a laceration—a thought he seems to share.

When we're both breathing heavy, thoroughly worn, and the physical exertion has dulled the sharp edges of my anger, I figure it's time to end things.

With a feint to the right, I dodge a swiping paw the size of a serving platter, and I land and leap onto the bear's back. There, I close my jaw around his neck, not biting down, but letting my fangs sink deep enough so we both know I could sever his spine in a killing blow if I wanted.

Heath stops moving, and then after a heavy sigh, he slaps the ground in the universal sign for tapping out.

I won.

After releasing him, I shake off the residual tingles of fight aggression, then search the spectators for my witch. The crowd grew while we were fighting, and suddenly, I'm anxious to be by her side, if only to know she's okay.

At the edge of the gathering, still in her chair, Ame waves at me, her red hair glinting in the setting sun. I bound toward her, sliding to a stop at the last moment and crouching so my snout is level with her wide-eyed face. I want to reach out and stroke Ame's freckled cheek, push the mussed russet strands out of her eyes, but I worry my razor-sharp claws might nick her delicate skin. Instead, I rest my fur-coated forearms on my canine-shaped thighs and allow my panting to even out with deep, controlled breaths.

With the successful fight and her in my eyeline, I begin to feel a measure of peace.

"Jack?"

At the question in her tone, I cock my head. Does she not recognize me? She knew me in my wolf form. Why would my hybrid shape be any different?

She doesn't know many wolves, I remember.

Maybe she's never seen one in hybrid shape before. I find perverse pleasure that I'm her first.

Ame pushes out of her chair to land on her knees, inching closer to me with the move. Her hands rise, as if to cup my face, but she pauses. "Can I?"

I extend my neck and huff in pleasure as her curious fingers dive into my ruff.

"You have three forms?" Again, the questioning tone.

I dip my nose, then give in to the urge to let my tongue sneak out and lick her wrist.

"Jack," she scolds me with her tone, "just because you have the face of a German shepherd doesn't mean you can act like one."

"Why not?" I growl the words from deep in my chest, my vocal cords stretched after relocating during the change.

Ame blinks in surprise. "You can talk in this form?"

"Yes." But there's a straining discomfort, like I'm trying to utilize a muscle I rarely use. "Not easy."

"Do you know what he is?"

A husky, feminine voice has me glancing to the side.

A beautiful woman with tan skin and midnight hair stands nearby but with intentional distance between us, her eyes on me. The expression on her face has my hackles rising.

Fascination.

"A werewolf," Ame replies to the stranger as the wind shifts, and on the breeze, I catch a whiff of a wolf at the same time my witch says, "Like you."

Werewolf. The information tears through me, and suddenly, I have Ame clutched to my chest, careful of my claws, my fangs bared at the woman as a terrorizing snarl rolls out of me.

Her eyes widen, and she rocks back on her heels. But she doesn't retreat.

If she comes for me or my woman, I will gut her.

"No," she says, and for a moment, I think she's responding to my aggressive warning, but then I realize the word was for Ame. "He is *not* like me."

"What do you mean?" Ame doesn't let my protective hold stifle her curious nature.

The stranger shakes her head. "I'm going to have to tell my father about him."

"Okay," Ame says. "But Jack is just visiting."

My insides, previously heated with anger, grow cold at her words.

I am not leaving.

"Still ..." The woman doesn't elaborate further. She gives me another searching look before turning to a gathering of cars.

Others watch us as she retreats. They watch me, as if I'm somehow captivating.

Was it really that impressive that I beat Heath? Is he some kind of reigning champ?

"Jack?" A gentle hand on my chest has me glancing down into Ame's freckled face. "You can let me go. And it might be best if you change back to human shape."

My animal instincts protest, wanting to keep her close, especially with another werewolf nearby.

I learned—too late—the selfish, violent nature of my kind.

For now, I ease my grip on Ame, but I know I'll never truly let her go.

Because like all werewolves, at my core, I'm a greedy, self-serving asshole.

18

AME

THE METAL DOOR of the garage bay groans and clatters as it rises and reveals the RV that used to be my house on wheels. As far as motorhomes go, Morgana sprang for a luxury option. Not that the Winnebago looked like a five-star ride by the end of our voyage. After years of scouring used bookstores for mythic-related texts, every surface and cubby had old books tucked into the spare space.

Now though, the books have been relocated, and the massive vehicle sits quietly in this rented storage space behind the selkie-owned mechanic shop on the edge of town.

Morgana originally planned to sell the RV, but we both realized that would be a bad idea.

After storing strong magical artifacts in one spot for a long stretch of time, some of the power is bound to seep out. There's no telling what a normal human family would have experienced in our subtly altered camper.

"Looks smaller than I remember." Jack circles the Winnebago, examining it from all sides.

"*You* were smaller." I pull the keys from the back pocket of my jeans and unlock the driver's door.

When I climb into the familiar seat, a sense of melancholy overwhelms me.

This is where I was sitting when I first sensed Jack, some magical force demanding I stop and search the shadowy sides of the road.

Now, I'm about to embark on another trip, one I doubt he'll come back from.

Jack insisted he only wants to go to his old home in California to collect his personal documents, then come back to Folk Haven. But when he says nothing is waiting for him on the opposite side of the country, his emotions spike. A flare of desire.

Go see her.

Go see him.

Hold them close.

There's someone—some*ones*—in California that he wants. Badly.

Maybe something from his time in captivity convinced the shifter that he can't have what he wants. But once we reach his hometown, Jack will likely seek out the people from his past.

Is he in love?

The thought makes me queasier than Hamish's scent.

Why?

As I sit quietly behind the wheel—a place I've spent many meditative moments over the years—I examine my own emotions. Not magically, just with an objective eye.

I'm upset because ... I want Jack.

I blink at the revelation, at the possessive nature of the longing. But it's true.

Even though I bought and set up an air mattress for him in a spare room, he came to my bed again last night. Snuggled with me in a way Bee never had.

And I want to grab hold of the wolf and never let him go.

That is the last thing Jack needs.

He deserves to be free, not owned or restrained by anyone. Still, I dig deeper, explore the urge further.

I want Jack. And not just because he was Bee. I want Jack because ... he's Jack.

I like the grumpy werewolf. A lot.

A sigh gushes out of my throat as I accept the truth. The man is appealing despite—or maybe because of—his wild intensity. From the moment the enchantment broke, my body and heart have responded to his physical affection. But the way he is with me is nothing more than simple desire.

My front row seat to the world's cravings have taught me how fleeting desires truly are.

Jack appreciates me, and he wants to sleep with me—figuratively and literally—but that will fade with time as he reacclimates to the world. Once he finally accepts who I am—a witch with the power to make him do anything I want.

No one wants to be around *that* kind of witch.

Jack may not think he minds now, but the fear will set in eventually.

When I press my hand against my chest, I realize I'm trying to ease away a sharp ache, the pain of knowing he'll leave. That the more likely outcome of this trip to California is, he'll make amends with the people in his past and choose to stay behind.

Out loud, I'll encourage him when that happens.

But inside? Curse The Dark One's plans, I'll miss him.

"What are you thinking so hard about?"

Jack's voice surprises me, and I jerk in the seat. He climbs up the step at my side, leaning into the cab, looming over me.

"Tell me your thoughts." His dark eyes bore into mine.

I can't. Not all of them at least. He'll be uncomfortable, knowing I want to claim him.

So, I go with another—more important—thought I had.

"Is there anything in Folk Haven you're particularly attached to? If there is, we should bring it in case you decide you want to stay in California."

Jack's frown digs deep grooves into his face. "I'm not staying in California."

"Still—"

"And I'll have everything I care about with me." He stares at me, our gazes locked.

Kiss her.

Touch her.

Hold her.

Make her mine.

His desires pulse like a heartbeat.

They'll change, I remind myself. *They'll fade.*

"That's good," I murmur. "Just in case."

His eyes shut, and he mutters something, but the words are tangled with a growl, so I don't make out what he says.

"Can you unlock the back?" he eventually asks, clear enough for me to understand.

"Sure." I slip out from under his intense scrutiny and walk to the door that leads directly to the living space of the RV.

When I unhook the latch and pop the door open, Jack has already circled around to meet me. I shuffle backward as he stalks up the stairs and peers around the space.

"It should be more comfortable to travel this time. More space." I wave at the clean interior, recalling how our belongings used to make the inside of the camper claustrophobic.

Jack doesn't respond as he walks deeper into the trailer, past the small kitchen and living area, reaching the first set of beds. They're single-sized mattresses, stacked like bunk beds in the wall.

"I'll sleep in one of those." I follow and place my palm on the thin mattress I don't miss. "And you can take the bed in the rear." I point past the bathroom to the only official bedroom in the RV. "It's a queen."

"You and Morgana didn't use that bed." Jack says the fact slowly with a hint of question, as if he's drawing out a memory. Sifting through the facts that lurk in the foggy time of him living as Bee.

"Most of the space was book storage by the end. We each took a bunk bed instead. That worked fine for us. But we're both shorter than you." Me more so than my sister. "Since we're not hauling books, you can use the big bed."

Jack faces me, his stare forceful once again. His desires meld into that solid mass of indistinguishable noise I find soothing. I breathe easier under the comforting pressure.

"Also, I'm sorry," I say. "I know you like to drive, but I think I should be the one behind the wheel for the trip out. Since you don't have your license. I know that'll stretch the length of the trip, but we should still be able to make it to San Francisco by Thursday."

"Five days." Jack states the number without inflection in his voice, and his eyes drift over my shoulder toward the windshield, as if he could already see the road. Already see the coast on the other side of the country.

Five days until good-bye.

19

JACK

I PLAN to learn every detail I can about Ame and use each one to find a way to make her fall in love with me.

The hunt has begun.

"Tell me about your family." I lounge in the passenger seat of the RV, eyes on Ame as she guides us down a busy highway.

Her arms look delicate compared to the large steering wheel, but when I offered to drive, she repeated the issue of my lack of a license. Even the one I have hidden away in California is probably expired by now.

As much as I hate giving up control, she has a point. If we got pulled over and I had no form of identification, things could get bad. I'd rather keep as far away from law enforcement's radar as I can.

Especially when I'm plotting multiple homicides.

Date TBD.

The order though, that's set.

First will be Veronica, who hailed me down on one of my jogs around campus. The one who sniffed out my wolf and realized what I was. The one who invited me to join that gods-forsaken pack with a smile on her face, as if I had nothing to worry about.

Next will be Finnick, alpha of the San Francisco pack and the asshole who sold me off like a rat to be tested on. The one who turned my dream of a werewolf family into a nightmare.

The rest of the pack members can live as long as they don't get in my way. If they do, then I'll pick them off one by one. My mercy has limits.

The last life I want to rip into bloody pieces is the sorcerer's.

I don't even know the fucker's name. Hopefully, it's buried in my memories. If not, this is going to be a long hunt.

Three deaths. Not too many in the grand scheme of things, but plenty enough to get a man arrested.

"You already know Mor, and then I told you about my brothers, Anthony and Broderick. They're twins, and they both live in England right now. Broderick because he got a job at a university there and Anthony because … well, I don't think he had any other plans. He's pretty go with the flow. At least with everything that isn't magic-related. *That* he's rigid about."

"How so?"

Her eyes flick to me, then back to the road. "He hates it. Or is scared of it. Maybe both. Whatever it is, he won't practice it and tries to stay far away from it. We don't push him. If he'd rather live a human life, then that's up to him."

I get the sense things aren't as easy as that, but I leave the topic alone for now.

"What about your parents?"

Ame's shoulders tense and creep toward her ears. "Both witches. They live in Maine."

The different way she talks about her siblings versus her parents is telling. Even her brother Anthony got a rueful half-smile.

Now, her tone is almost fearful.

"Were you visiting them when you found me?"

Ame bobbles her head. "We were visiting another witch who lives in the same town they do. She let us store some books on her property. We'd visit every so often to lighten the load. Sometimes, we'd see them when we were there. You were there the last time."

I frown, trying to sift through my blurry feline memories to a time when I might've encountered her parents.

An image comes to mind—of a man wrapping my witch in a loose-armed hug. He was white, average height, with messy golden-gray hair and green eyes that stared at me.

"A man, you say? Fascinating."

When he approached, I growled but found I couldn't move away.

A woman, her red hair shot through with white, knelt before me. "You just stay in the stone circle, pretty kitty."

Her long finger tapped a smooth stone in front of my paws. I crouched low to the ground, snarling when I saw the rocks surrounding me on all sides.

"She's not sure," another voice—Morgana's, I know now—said, and the tension in the witch's voice strummed my anger higher.

"We will know." The man reached toward me, as if he had every right.

"We can't stay." A foot scattered the stones, and a set of familiar arms scooped me up.

The scent of earth and mint alerted me to the carrier, and I restrained myself from biting Ame.

"You'll stay for a little while," the older woman argued, her eyes on me. "We'll take a look. It'll be fun."

The memory sends a dreaded chill down my spine. The way the woman said *fun*, as if I were a game to be played.

Ame left without another word to them, only speaking to me. *"Don't worry,"* I remember her whispering against my neck as she held me close to her chest and walked with stiff limbs back to the RV. *"I won't let them touch you. I'll keep you safe."*

"They tried to hurt me."

At my words, Ame flinches.

"But you got me away from them."

"I don't know that they were going to hurt you." Her mouth tightens as her eyes stay on the road. "But they might have. My parents enjoy studying magical oddities. They don't stop to consider safety measures or if their experimenting might cause pain." At this, Ame unconsciously rubs her collarbone, and I wonder what she's thinking about.

What she's remembering.

Did they hurt my witch?

Fury is a slow-spreading toxin in my veins.

How would she feel if I added two more names to my murder list?

"I'm sorry."

There she goes, apologizing to me again.

"You have nothing to be sorry for."

"I never should have let them see you. They scared you. But they're both very powerful, and I never asked if they might know how to turn you back to a human. I worried over their methods."

"You figured it out on your own."

"Not my own. Not entirely. Broderick sent me the grimoire, where I found the sunder spell. He's the one you'll want to thank."

"I will," I promise.

But her brother isn't the one who made sure I survived. He didn't ensure I had everything I needed and a safe place to lay my head. The male witch might have stumbled upon the right book, but he's not the one who scoured hundreds of texts, searching for an answer. He did not sit under the full moon, testing magic for me, month after month.

Ame did. My little witch is the reason I'm here. I owe her everything.

And I want to be *her* everything.

The topic of her family has her curling in on herself, knuckles white on the steering wheel. The protective posture has me cursing my pushing. I'll work out the rest of her family history over time, in smaller bites to avoid upsetting her.

"Tell me about our travels. Help me remember. Am I the only animal you found?"

This question earns me a small smile at the corner of her mouth, and as Ame tells me stories about stray dogs and cats they took to shelters—how I'd growled at all of them—along with sightings of moose and bears and other wildlife from around the country, she relaxes back in her seat.

We drive all day like this—Ame talking and me asking her questions. Sometimes, the events she describes come back to me in an altered perspective. Our visit to the Grand Canyon, massive burnt-orange cliffs I backed away from. The time we explored a cave full of bats in Kentucky and I kept my gaze on the shifting ceiling. The time the RV's back wheels got stuck after a massive rainstorm at a campground and Ame had to magic them out while covered in mud.

I apologize for staying in the warm, dry trailer during that last one, and she chuckles a sweet sound that I want to record.

We make occasional stops for gas, where I note the amount spent, and make good time to the first RV park on our route. Once situated in our assigned spot, Ame demonstrates how to level the RV, then hook up the electric, water, and sewer. She moves through the process with ease, having done the same for years before she and Morgana settled in Folk Haven.

I can't tell how she feels about being in the mobile home

again. Does she miss it, or would she rather be in the lakeside library?

Dinner is foil-packed meals over a campfire, and I recall hazy memories of sitting beside open flames while the scent of smoke mingled with the earthy fragrance of my witch. I had a green plastic plate. Ame would cook me pieces of meat. We would sit side by side as we ate our meals—a woman and a cat that she always treated like a man.

When I ask questions, Ame answers them, but she doesn't ask any in return.

Half of me is glad she's not digging. But another selfish part wants her to be curious. Craves her interest and attention.

Especially when it's time to sleep. Ame uses the bathroom first, and when I finish my turn, I try not to grind my teeth at the state I find her in.

She's curled on her side in the bottom bunk, facing the wall of the RV. The mattress is too small for me to settle on next to her even if I transformed into my wolf shape. I glare at the tiny bed, then scowl at the spacious mattress in the back of the camper.

We'd both fit there perfectly.

A patient hunter would go to bed by himself, knowing more chances will arise in the future. But I'm not as patient as I thought. I can't fathom spending a night apart from her when she's *right here.*

"Ame." My voice is a gruff whisper.

The little witch rolls over, green eyes wide as she takes in my proximity. If she had a wolf's ears or nose, she would have known I was standing here, watching her with pent-up lust and longing.

"Do you want to cuddle?" I can't help the harsh note in my voice. The one that says, *Why aren't you always in my arms with my mouth on your skin and your gasps in my ears?*

Ame lets silence fall between us, her expression unreadable as she considers my question.

I start to brainstorm ways to woo her.

"I do," she admits.

Triumph flares in my chest, and I don't wait to slip my arms underneath her warm, soft body, carrying her to the bed she should have started in.

With us both under the covers, I drag her against my chest, only to feel her palms press in a staying manner. I want to growl in protest, but I freeze.

If she doesn't like how I cuddle, she'll leave. Then, I won't have my witch.

"Let me get comfortable," she says, and I relax.

Ame reaches for a pillow, fluffing the white rectangle before laying the cushion in the cradle of my armpit. She lies down, her head featherlight now that there's padding between us. I'm regretting the loss of her hot breath caressing my neck when she distracts me by stretching out an arm across my abdomen. I'm shirtless, her forearm resting against my skin, the callous pads of her fingers cupping my hip. She uses the embrace to drag herself closer, the front of her plush body pressing against my side.

"Can I put my leg over yours?" she asks.

I don't know if I should laugh or groan at the ridiculous question.

"Yes," I rumble.

When she slings her freckled leg over my thigh, my blood rushes south. The dim light in the camper hides the stirring below my waistband. I don't plan to do anything about it, not until Ame is an enthusiastic partner in this dance.

"I'm comfortable now," she informs me. "Is this okay?"

My future mate wrapping herself around me as if I were a body pillow, using me for her comfort?

Fuck yeah, it is.

"Yes." I curve the arm she's resting her head on and clasp her back, holding her against me.

This is going to be a good trip.

20

JACK

FIVE DAYS OF INNOCENT TORTURE. During the day, I learn about my witch's life. During the night, I hold her in my arms.

Ame goes into detail about the traveling we did together, helping me rebuild the memories from the confusing twist mine exist in. Overall, our time on the road wasn't too exciting. At least, that's the sense I get from Ame. Morgana was probably having a grand time, spending most days in bookshops, sifting through texts to find a pearl in the sand. Ame spends more time describing the scenery. The campsites we stayed in and how the environments differed. She offers me her tablet to see the pictures she took and the notes she made about landmarks and the simple sketches of wildlife she attempted.

The way Ame speaks about that time reveals more of her than she might think.

But still, my witch holds herself separate from me with her distracted gazes, often lost in her own thoughts as I stare at her profile.

Even at night, with my arms twined around her, her body

draped over mine, there's a divide between us. Because the closeness means different things to us.

I'm cuddling with my mate.

She's … I don't know. Giving me what she knows I want?

I hate the idea. That she's only in my bed to soothe me. But I can't deny that it seems to be Ame's nature. Giving up her own comfort and wants to make someone else happy.

That's what she said on the dock after I confronted Morgana.

"I owe her."

Is that why she spent years seeking out dusty books that hold no interest for her?

I don't think Ame cared about the grimoires until she found me. Because she felt obligated to rescue me.

But I won't be a burden to the little witch anymore.

One more day, and I'll have access to my money and everything I need to be part of the world again. My documents—proof I'm not some strange being disconnected from the grid—are hidden away. My funds sit safely in my bank accounts, where I left them. All, except for the amount I gave to that traitorous pack.

Worst fucking mistake of my life.

Finnick had me convinced we were some kind of family. That we should share all things. That it would be best if I funneled my savings into the pack account when I officially joined.

Despite liking the picture he painted, I couldn't fully commit and only handed over a fraction of what I'd saved. But a single dollar was more than they deserved.

I gave that fucker the keys to my *car*.

My naivete makes me cringe now.

I plan to reclaim all I lost, and I'll take my payment one way. In blood.

When I approach the rental car Ame and I picked up this

morning—the RV is a pain to use for short distances—she's waiting at the driver's side with a questioning quirk to her brows.

"You're sure you can't get your things now? You could drive then. Even if your license is expired, you'd still have some ID."

I shake my head. "I need to go when it's dark." And I want to seek out the items on my own. Keep Ame away from the broken pieces of my past.

She relents, sliding behind the wheel and following my directions around the steep slopes of San Francisco streets. Everything looks like I remember, comforting in its familiarity. The buildings, all cut off at the same height; the ring and rumble of trolleys; the salty scent of the bay on the breeze.

I wondered if I would feel a sense of home once I was back here.

I don't. Not really. I guess I'm glad I made it back, that I'm able to see the city again. Once upon a time, I thought I'd never see anything other than the inside of a cage.

But there's no longing to stay. When I think of settling, I have a small town in northern Georgia that comes to mind.

Still, I have unfinished business here. Nothing I'll be taking care of on this trip though. The top priority in my life is Ame Shelly. Making sure she's safe and happy and cared for.

And making sure she's mine.

We spend the afternoon driving around, visiting restaurants and shops, new even for me. I avoid my favorite spots, worried I might run into familiar faces. I'm not ready for that kind of shitstorm.

The sun is almost done setting by the time we return to the campsite outside of the city. When I climb out of the car, the sky is dark and the woods around us shadowed. Time for my errand.

"Ame?"

When I say her name, she pauses in the process of

unlocking the RV and turns to face me, red brows raised in question. For a moment, I stare at her. In that oversize knit sweater, she looks young. College-aged. And it reminds me of a time of hopeful innocence, when I didn't know the horrors of the world. That's something that draws me to Ame every time. She has an air of goodness. Of taking the world at face value and ... not necessarily trusting everyone. But offering the truth whenever she can.

"Yeah?" she asks, prompting me to continue.

I clear my throat and recall my plan. "I'm going to head out now."

Her brows dip, eyes flicking to the car. "Do you need me to drive you?"

"No. I'm going to run."

I like the way her eyes trace over my body. She hasn't looked at me much today. As if the entire world interests her, but not me.

What do I need to do for you to crave me, little witch?

"Oh. Of course. Are you changing here?" She glances around the campsite. We're in a spot far enough away from others that things feel private, but I can still hear and smell campers nearby.

"I'm going to hike a ways." My chin tilts toward the trees. "Get plenty deep in the woods. Then change. After that it's a few miles, but I've run it before." More times than I can count.

Ame nods, still not meeting my eyes. Then, suddenly, she's in front of me, her slim arms wrapping tight around my waist, hugging me hard.

"Be safe, Jack," she whispers against my chest.

As much as I want to revel in this embrace, there's an odd note of finality to the exchange.

"I will." I stroke a palm over her loose braid, then grip her upper arms, holding Ame in front of me until she has to meet my stare. "I'll just be a few hours. Don't get into any trouble, okay?"

"Okay." Ame steps back, out of my hold, and retreats inside the camper, shutting the door behind her.

I stare at the door and try to shrug off the strange vibe. The one that says Ame doesn't expect to see me again.

"I'm coming right back," I mutter as if she could hear me.

The hike isn't long, only fifteen minutes and I'm good and alone. I raise my nose to the air, sucking in deep lungfuls of the surrounding scents to make sure. All I smell is nature with a hint of smoke. Northern California is plagued with forest fires again, but they're nowhere close enough to be worried about.

Coast clear, I strip my clothes, tuck them under the roots of a tree.

Then, I let my wolf out.

Darkness, thicker than the night sky, clings to me. A cool caress dripping over my body, almost tugging at my skin, as if eager to get to what's underneath. I chose my full wolf form to blend into nature in case I'm spotted running, though I don't plan to be.

This excursion has a purpose, and part of that requires being covert.

Finished with the transformation, I shake off the last tingles of the change and plunge into the woods. Spongy moss gives under my feet, and towering redwoods loom above me.

The forest slowly alters as I traverse mile after mile, the vegetation shifting from wild to cultivated, eventually giving way to residential streets. I stick to the shadows, thankful the house I'm looking for isn't in the middle of civilization.

When we found out what I was, my mother moved closer to the wilderness for me.

I come upon the house so suddenly I almost pass it by. I was moving fast, but I think a part of me expected the building to be gone.

Yet here it stands.

Does she still live here?

The lights are off, no golden glow from the windows. On the back porch is a familiar set of chairs, and the worn cushions bombard me with memories. Evenings when she would come home late and insist we sit outside together as I told her about my day.

Keeping low to the ground, I slink closer, searching for other signs of life. But there's no movement besides a red lantern swaying in the breeze.

My body locks up when I scent her. The smell of citrus and fresh printer paper is subtle, but strong enough for me to know she has been here in the past few days.

Wherever my mom is tonight, this is still her home.

Relief and longing and guilt and pain dig sharp claws into my chest, so it's all I can do not to whimper.

I'm so distracted by the roiling emotions that I don't notice anyone beside me until a fuzzy body presses against mine. The unexpected contact has me lunging to the side, a quiet snarl ripping from my throat.

Yellow eyes blink at me, unconcerned by the aggressive noise.

A cat. The thought creeps through my mind. *A gods-damn cat.*

The feline has a pitch-black coat—the same color that my prison body used to be. However, this feline is smaller than I was and smells female. Still, the similarity makes me uneasy.

The thing sits in the grass, staring at me in an almost-expectant manner. Then, the beast starts to purr.

I growl in response. *Fuck off*, I try to convey.

The purrs grow louder.

I snarl again and snap, my jaws clicking together an inch from the interloper's face.

The cat sprawls in the grass and starts licking her shoulder, unconcerned.

Fine. If she won't leave, then I will.

After a last glance at the empty house, I slink back into the woods behind my old home and soon find myself before a large boulder. My true destination. Bracing my hindlegs on the stone surface, I shove the rock over with a mighty heave only the strongest of humans would be able to manage, revealing a depression underneath. A waterproof lock box waits where I left it six years ago, at the time thinking I'd only be gone for a fraction of that.

Smoke swirls around my body as I resume my human shape, needing fingers to input the combination.

"Thank the gods," I mutter when the lid pops open to reveal a plastic bag containing my Social Security card, birth certificate, license—which *did* expire, but at least I have my passport too—credit and debit cards, and a roll of bills. My original intention was to leave this all with my mother, but she refused when she found out what my plan was. So I hid everything instead.

A meow from behind me has my hackles rising. I shift to wolf shape as fast as I can, snatch the bag up in my jaws, and dart away, aiming for a nearby pond. One more place to visit, and I'll return to my mate.

Then, she can stop talking like I'm leaving.

The shrinking moon reflects off the surface of the still water. There's only one house near the shores—a bungalow-type building. This one is lit up bright, pools of light spilling onto the ground and showing the interior.

Figures move behind the glass, and with even more care than before, I creep closer. The occupants of this house—if they're the same as I remember—don't have the acute senses of a werewolf, but they're close.

I crouch behind a bush, peering through the twigs and

leaves to spy on a large window that gives me a perfect view of the living space.

Familiar faces—one I expected to see here and one I didn't—steal my breath.

Niko Saito hasn't changed much in the past several years. He's lost some baby fat in his cheeks, but he still has a touch of roundness to his face that softens his sharp, dark gaze. The most prominent differences are the scruffy black facial hair and bags under his eyes. As the guy chats with the woman beside him, I get the sense he's perpetually tired.

Strange, when the man I used to know was so full of life that I sometimes had to hide from him just to get a breather.

The woman sitting beside him on a couch has undergone changes as well—her face maintaining the same shape, but now adorned with new wrinkles and a tight pinch between her brows. Her life has always been filled with stress, but she doesn't hide it as well now.

Maybe she's allowed herself to be a touch vulnerable because she's comfortable with Niko. He could always do that—ease everyone around him even if they started out as strangers.

The fact that these two still see each other, spend time with one another, even with me gone, comforts me.

They're better without me in their lives.

And I made sure that was how things would stay.

After a final painful glance, I slide out of my hiding spot and trot toward the woods, leaving behind a piece of my heart and a silent farewell.

Good-bye, Niko.

Good-bye, Mom.

21

AME

I DON'T EXPECT Jack to come back. When he said he was going on a run, I got the sense that he was leaving on a mission to seek out whatever that desire is that lingers on this coast.

Not ready for the final farewell, I leave my phone on the dashboard of the RV. I half-wish we hadn't picked him up that cheap cell phone on the drive out here because, now, I expect I'll receive a call or maybe just a text from him, saying he's decided not to return to Folk Haven. That I can head out and he'll slip into the conveniently waiting space of his old life. That the days of talking and nights of cuddling are over.

The nights—damn The Dark One's plans—those leave me aching and unsatisfied.

"I guess I could take care of that," I murmur to myself.

Every time Jack wraps me in his arms, my arousal builds, and there's been no opportunity to help it dissipate. No true alone time.

But now, that's all I have. Just me, this camper, and the wait until Jack's good-bye message.

Might as well fill the time by lying to myself for a short while.

I lock the camper doors before heading back to the bedroom. After stripping my clothes—because why not commit if I'm going to treat myself?—I crawl onto the mattress, sprawling out in the middle, starfish-like. Reclined naked on the bed, I draw a corner of the comforter to my nose and search for a familiar scent. There's a hint of pine needles crushed under heavy steps in the middle of the night, and I close my eyes, breathing Jack in.

On the back of my dark eyelids, I play out a fantasy.

Instead of the RV, I lie in my bed in the old Victorian house that feels like home. The room around me is dark, and I don't hear footsteps, but next thing I know, a heavy presence is above me.

Jack wrenches off the covers, exposing my body to the cool night air, and he crawls over me, surrounding me with his heavy heat.

Alone in the camper, I let out a gasp and slip my hand between my legs, cupping myself. Gods, I'm already wet. Feels like I have been since Jack asked me if I wanted to cuddle that first night.

The Jack in my fantasy asks dirtier questions.

"Do you want me to lick your pussy?"

"Do you want me to fuck your mouth, little witch?"

I press on my clit with two fingers and groan.

It's been years since I had sex. My libido is normally rather mild with the occasional spike if I meet someone who catches my eye. My last partner was a librarian in Des Moines, Iowa. Morgana was sure the library's special collections had two grimoires, if not more, and she asked me to distract the woman while she checked and then stole them.

We're witches. We're not perfect law-abiding citizens.

And anyway, magical texts are dangerous in human hands.

Not exactly sure how to be a good diversion, I asked to speak to the librarian in her office. Her desire for me was hard to ignore and ignited my own. I was baldly honest about how beautiful I thought she was. She was obviously shocked, her hazel eyes going wide and her dusky cheeks flushing with a blush. Somehow—because I made sure *not* to use my magic to influence her—my confession led to her fingering me until I came on her hand and me returning the favor by bending her over her desk and licking her clit until she came on my tongue.

Afterward, she kept repeating how she never did things like that, and I assured her I didn't either and that we never had to say a word.

Morgana got her books, and the librarian and I each got an orgasm. A good day for everyone, I'd say.

Now, I try to recall that memory. Use *her* to get me hot and bothered.

But Jack takes firm possession of my fantasies, selfishly ruling my subconscious with his growls and intense looks and strong body kneeling over me. Pleasure fogs my brain until all I can think of is thrusting and licking and panting.

"Jack." I groan his name as I massage hard circles against my sensitive bundle of nerves.

I come with a whimper, curling on my side with my hand between my legs and my face pressed into the bedcovers as the pleasure pulses through me. Over and over, I try to keep hold of the climax for as long as possible.

When he's officially gone, I get the sense that this—thinking of him—will hurt too much to do.

After the last vestiges of pleasure fade, I lie still in the bed, breathing slowly to calm my heart rate.

"I wish I could keep you," I whisper the selfish thought to the empty air, letting the confession go unheard by anyone.

After what that sorcerer did to him, Jack needs freedom

more than anyone I know. Which is why I refused to take advantage of his fleeting desire to try tying him to me.

Now, he's free to go.

I drag myself to the shower, hoping soap and water will wash away the sharp thorns stabbing into my heart whenever I envision driving home alone tomorrow.

When I'm clean—on the outside at least—I pile my damp hair in a bun on top of my head and decide to build myself a fire. Sitting alone in this RV isn't helping my melancholy.

But when I pop open the trailer door, I realize a blaze is already flickering in the firepit.

And a werewolf is sitting beside it.

Jack lounges in a camping chair, his legs stretched out, impossibly long, and his arms are draped over the back of the seat, making his T-shirt stretch across his chest. His face is drawn, eyes on the flames, but they flick up to meet mine when I stumble down the one step from the camper to the ground.

"You're back."

I wonder if maybe I dozed off after pleasuring myself and this is a happy dream. But then I step forward and smash my toe into a rock. I whimper as the pain spikes through my foot, and suddenly, Jack is at my side, hands cupping my elbows.

This isn't a dream.

"What happened? Did you hurt yourself?" His gaze tracks over my body, cataloging every inch.

"Stubbed toe."

He scowls at my foot, as if it's the enemy, and the sight has me wanting to smile. Him being here has temporary joy easing the thorns from my chest. But I can't let go of the ache completely.

Most likely, Jack came back to collect his things. Is an in-person good-bye better than a phone message? Maybe not. Not if I start crying anyway.

"How was your run?" I ask.

Jack turns his head away. "Fine. Got my documents. Saw what I needed to."

Did you find the thing you desire?

I don't ask because I don't want to know the answer. For now, his thrum of cravings still buzzes around me in an indistinguishable mass.

"That's good. Thanks for making a fire."

He shrugs. "The door was locked, and I heard the shower running. Figured you'd come out eventually."

When he lets me go, we do the same as the night before, only quieter. Make food, eat by the fire, stare up at the sky. All the while, I'm bracing for his announcement that he's staying. I don't know why he's dragging it out.

"Bedtime," he mutters after a while, shoveling dirt over the glowing embers.

Looks like I have to wait until tomorrow for the final farewell. I can't tell if I'm anxious or relieved by the fact. When I enter the RV, I head to the front, where I left my phone, and see I have a check-in text from Morgana. She wasn't a fan of this trip, still not trusting Jack, but I promised to send regular proof of life. I snap a quick selfie, hoping my strained smile doesn't reveal how sad I am.

Message sent, I turn and pause when I realize Jack isn't going about his nightly routine.

He stands in the doorway of the bedroom, frozen. I watch the muscles of his back tense and hear him suck in a deep breath.

"Little witch." He growls the words, sending goose bumps prickling up the back of my neck. "What did you do in here while I was gone?"

He can smell that?

Of course he can. He's a werewolf.

Thank the gods he can't sniff out what I was picturing while touching myself.

"I'm sorry." I cringe. "I didn't think." *Didn't think you were coming back.* "I shouldn't have done that. Not in the bed we're sharing anyway."

He's probably dealing with the same discomfort I feel when someone's sexual desires blare in my mind.

A small linen closet sits beside the bathroom, and I hurry to tug the door open. "We have clean sheets. I'll remake the bed."

Jack moves so fast that I don't register the motion. One moment, he was in the doorway, facing away from me, and the next, he has me caged against the wall, his arms bracketing me on either side, eyes almost pure black from dilated pupils locked on mine.

"Tell me who you imagined."

The demand has a note of menace, and I wonder if this is some great offense. I don't remember anything in my reading about werewolves having issues with self-pleasure, but books can miss things.

"I didn't mean to make you uncomfortable, I swear. It's just ... I didn't think you were coming back. If I'd known you were ..." *Would I have held off?* Probably not. I was—and still am —very horny. "I would have used the shower."

There's a popping noise, and my eyes flit up to see Jack now has claws, and they've punctured the vinyl siding of the camper.

Morgana will not be happy about that.

"I swear to all of your gods, if you keep saying I'm going to leave you, I will find the closest tattoo parlor and get your fucking name inked on every inch of my body because, damn it to hell, Amethyst Shelly, I am *yours*."

Mine?

"Tattoos don't work on werewolves," I murmur as my brain works through his proclamation.

In the brief moments where his desires have untangled

themselves enough for me to discern them, I've heard that he wants to make me his.

But ... he wants to be mine?

That can't be right. Not after years of imprisonment. Maybe Jack is still working through the aftereffects of the curse.

The shifter groans and drops to his knees in front of me, pressing his face against my belly, hands gripping my hips to keep me in place.

"What can I have of you, little witch? I have no pride at your feet. Give me anything. Any part of you that could be mine."

I see it then, the pulsing red glow that surrounds him. The desire so strong that it spills from the pores of his skin. My fingers take on a life of their own, stroking through his hair, and my eyelids flutter at the lovely, silky texture.

"I thought of you," I admit.

I don't know what else to say but the truth. I can't ask him for anything. He's already had so much taken from him.

But he wants a piece of me. Honesty—that's what I can give.

Jack growls, and his nose drags along the waistband of my sweatpants. "You want to touch me. To fuck me. Don't you? Tell me."

Be honest. Give him honesty.

"I want to put my mouth on you," I whisper.

If I thought he was tense before, it's nothing compared to the statue at my feet now.

I keep going. "The thing is, I enjoy oral sex. A lot. Getting it but also giving it. And you asked what I wanted." Could I touch him like I crave and make him feel good too? "Would you enjoy something like that?"

Jack stands suddenly, his hand coming to cup my chin as his eyes bore into mine. "You're *asking* to suck my dick?"

My tongue sneaks out to lick my lower lip. I can't help the reaction at the idea of him in my mouth. His eyes follow the movement, brows rising.

"It's what I thought about."

Slide into her mouth.

The nonverbal agreement makes me shiver, and my nipples peak against my T-shirt.

Yet, even as I hear the way he wants what I suggested, the wolf frowns. I brace for him to leave.

Jack stays where he is.

"You're supposed to ask for things for *you*. Like asking me to lick your *pussy*." He growls the last word, so like my imagination that I gasp.

My hand reaches out to palm him, finding the werewolf has grown hard.

"Please, let me," I beg, then chide myself, not wanting to coerce him. Still, my hand presses and massages while his lids drop to half-mast and short breaths spill from his throat. "I want to."

Let her.

Take her.

Make her mine.

He mutters a string of curses, head dropping back to stare at the ceiling.

Then, in a guttural voice, he responds, "If that's what you want."

22

———

JACK

AME SHELLY DOES NOT MAKE any sense.

But I find it hard to argue with her when she sinks to her knees in front of me, fingers on my fly, her green-eyed stare on the bulge in my pants.

This has to be some kind of fever-dream fantasy. Maybe I got hit by a truck during my run, and I'm in some afterlife pleasure dimension now. All the more reason to let what's about to happen move forward.

With a zip and a tug, the witch gets my pants and underwear far enough down my thighs to free a bobbing erection.

"Ame." I mutter her name, not sure what I want to say after that one word.

You don't have to.

Please suck me.

You've done too much for me already.

Gods, I'm obsessed with you.

Ame licks the tip of me, as if she likes the taste of my precum. I have to lock my knees and clench my thighs to keep from thrusting forward. As it is, my eyes are already trying to roll back in my head.

It's been years since I've been with anyone, and now, I have the perfect woman before me. Eager for me. Ame might be on her knees, but she takes control and shows me what she wants by gripping my cock and dragging her lips over the sensitive head.

I tug her hairband gently until the damp crimson mass spills around her shoulders. The wet strands amplify her earthy, minty scent and give me handholds to gently grasp as I work myself past her lips.

Over ... and over ... and over ...

The wicked witch swallows me deeper, and I almost spill in the tight cradle of her throat.

How is this happening? Why is she letting me do this to her? Doesn't she know I'm not worth it?

"Damn it, Ame." My voice has gone guttural. "This is too fucking good."

Good for me at least. But what is she getting out of this other than my cock in her mouth? I refuse to be selfish about my witch's pleasure. I need this to be mind-melting for her, so she's desperate to come back for more. So she's constantly battling the urge to touch herself to thoughts of me. Every day. Every night. Forever.

Keeping hold of her hair, I ignore the protest of my dick and ease myself free, loving the way her lips pop and flush red when I'm gone.

"Jack," she whimpers, straining forward.

"Little witch, listen to me."

Ame tilts her chin to stare up from her kneeling position, wide eyes meeting mine. "Yes?"

Fuck, she looks good at my feet. But my future mate is not here to serve me. We serve each other.

"I'm going to lie on the bed, and you can have my cock as

long as you give me your pretty pussy to taste too. Got it?"

She swallows hard and nods.

Thank fuck. I'm finally going to get to taste her.

Leaning over, I tug Ame up, and with an arm around her waist, I drag her to the bedroom. There, we fall back on the mattress with my aching cock pinned between us. I palm her ass, where the cheeks peek out of her sleep shorts.

"Get your clothes off and give me a taste," I growl.

Ame sits up, straddling me as she pulls the large T-shirt over her head. I groan at the sight of her creamy skin covered in freckles, a set of gorgeous tits begging for my hands. But she slides to the side before I can palm them.

Not that I'm complaining when she shimmies her shorts and underwear down her legs.

My witch is bare for me.

When I stepped into the doorway, I thought I would go rabid when I smelled her pleasure in this room. Knowing what she'd done in here while I was gone.

But this is the true trigger of my wild side. I grasp her bare thighs and drag her core to me, the folds glistening and smelling sweet, as if she dipped them in sugar water just for me.

"I'm going to eat you up, little witch," I snarl. Then, I plunge my tongue in deep.

Ame's hips buck, but I hold her in place with a steel arm across her lower back.

Mine. My fucking delicious pussy. Gonna feast all fucking night. The beast in me chants the vulgar thoughts, and I feel no shame.

As I lick her slickness, a firm pressure encircles the root of my dick, threatening to undo the small amount of control I still have.

She holds me upright, and I feel the hot puffs of her breath against my sensitive head as I earn gasps from her with each tease of my tongue. When her lips surround me, I let out a rumble of satisfaction against her core.

Ame begins to bob her head at the same pace of my licks, and we create our own pattern. Speeding up and slowing down to match the silent requests of each other.

Ecstasy builds at the base of my spine until I break away from her core and give her bare ass a gentle tap-out slap.

" 'Bout to come," I groan.

I expect her to take her mouth away, so I can finish on the sheets. But Ame responds to my confession by dragging me deep and cupping my balls while she's at it.

A string of curses spills from my throat just before I spill down *her* throat.

Too good. Too fucking good. Better than I deserve.

But that doesn't mean I'll give up any chance I have. Like the one right now, with her soaking pussy inches from my mouth, waiting for the same release I'm still shuddering over. I wrap both arms around Ame's middle and drag her flush against my mouth. With determination, I lick and suck and whisper dirty words against her intimate lips.

"Jack." She mewls my name before pressing her face against my bare thigh.

Power radiates through me, knowing that she's on the edge and *I* got her there. I'm not some wounded animal for her to save and send back out into the wild. I will destroy any thoughts of pity she has for me with orgasms. Time to finish her so well that she can't fathom a future without my mouth on her. Do it so well that I'm the only one she'll ever think about when her fingers caress her clit.

"I thought of you." My spent dick twitches at the memory of her words.

Dragging my hands along Ame's lower back, I grip her ass cheeks, spreading her wider as I press the flat of my tongue against her bundle of nerves.

The witch sobs and jerks, her body clenching with release. I feel her teeth bite into my thigh, and I groan, relishing the sting and the violently possessive note of the act.

Mark me, I want to tell her.

One day, I'll make sure she does.

Once her orgasm subsides, Ame stays sprawled on my chest, legs spread wide over my shoulders, vulva on full display.

I'm about to dive in for round two when a noise stops me.

Ame perks her head up, the witch having heard it too.

There's a scratching at the door.

23

———————

JACK

"You dropped other cats off at animal shelters. Why not *that* one?" I glare at the creature out of the side of my eye as I drive us down an empty highway in Nevada.

The fucker is rolling around in Ame's lap, swatting at a string the witch is dangling above her head.

When I left Ame in the bed last night to check who was outside the RV, a black blur streaked inside the moment I opened the door. Even with my fast reflexes, I couldn't catch the intruder.

"Fuck," I hissed, whirling around to search for the thing.

And that was when I saw the unwelcome visitor sitting beside Ame on the bed, butting her head against my witch's shoulder. An animal I would swear I'd seen before.

"Oh my goddess," Ame murmured, reaching out to stroke the no doubt flea-ridden pelt. "You're a sweet girl, aren't you?"

Disagree.

The thing gives me the creeps. That is, if I accept it's the same cat that I saw on my run. There is no way such a small

143

thing should have been able to travel the distance from the house to the camper. Not in a single night.

Which means it's magical in some way or I'm a black-cat magnet.

I don't like either answer.

"She's special." Ame smiles down at the black fuzzball, unconcerned by the potential threat in our midst.

"Like me? Found yourself another trapped mythic?" The words come out more accusatory than I meant them. But Ame finally let me touch and taste her last night. Now, her attention is taken up by this interloper.

I'm jealous of a gods-damn stray.

"No one is like you, Jack." She reaches over to pat my thigh, and if there wasn't so much space between the two front seats, I'd cover her hand and keep it where it is. "Although her emotional grid does seem slightly more complex than other cats." Ame gifts me with a beautiful grin that almost has me veering off the road to stare at her. "I think she's my familiar."

That has me clenching my jaw.

Great. There's no way I can get rid of the thing now.

"I don't trust it," I mutter.

Ame's happiness doesn't dim in the face of my surly tone, which a part of me is thankful for. I don't want to make her sad. But I also don't want her cuddling that arrogant feline.

"Why don't you trust her?" the witch asks.

To explain, I'd have to describe what I was doing on my run. It's not that I don't trust Ame with the facts of my past. I mean, she knows the worst of things. But it's best if I leave certain parts behind me.

"Black cats are unlucky."

Ame laughs. "*You* were a black cat. Were you unlucky?"

We come up on some traffic, slowing as we reach a stretch of construction. I glance over to my little witch, watching as she scratches her new companion under the chin.

When I came into her life, Ame was suddenly saddled with a werewolf. A werewolf mate once I convince her to be mine. And I *will*.

And like all werewolves, I'm a selfish brute.

"Yes," I grunt, "I'm the worst kind of luck." And she's stuck with me.

Ame snorts. "Think what you want." She scoops the cat under the thing's armpits, and it looks ridiculous, front legs sticking out straight. "Say hello to Lucky. Lucky Shelly. Newest member of the family."

I frown as it blinks big yellow eyes at me.

"Don't worry about Jack," Ame whispers to the cat, plenty loud enough for me to hear. "He'll come around. He's grumpy sometimes. But I love him anyway."

All of the air in the RV disappears. Ame resettles the cat in her lap, seemingly unaware of the magnificent bomb she just set off between us.

She loves me.

I hold myself still, worried if I change anything about my posture, she'll take the words back.

"Traffic is moving." Ame points out the windshield, and with the movement, I notice how much of the intense sun is touching her delicate, already-reddened skin.

Talk about love later. Need to take care of my witch now.

Before accelerating, I reach over to the glove compartment, pop it open, and pull out the new bottle of sunscreen I bought at the last rest stop.

"Put some of this on. You need to be careful in the sun."

Ame accepts the bottle and reads the label. "I didn't know they made SPF this high."

I shrug. "The higher, the better. You're already burned." I nod at the red flush twisting between her scattering of brown freckles.

I'm focused on navigating the massive RV on the one available lane, so it takes me a moment to realize Ame hasn't responded. When I glance over, she has her head turned toward the side window, hands fiddling with the sunscreen. But there's no scent of coconut, proving that she hasn't applied it.

Her shoulders are up by her ears again, like when she talked about her parents.

Something is wrong.

"Ame?"

She turns her head toward me but doesn't meet my eyes. "It's not sunburn."

My eyes track over the irritated portions of her skin again. "Sorry. My mistake. Is it another condition?"

An uncharacteristic grimace twists her lips. "It's a side effect. Of a spell."

"A spell?" I murmur, a careful prompting.

Ame sighs. "I told you about my parents. How they ... like to experiment."

Dread condenses, a heavy ice in my gut.

"Witches are kind of like shifters. We get our powers around puberty. But they wanted to see if they could bring mine out earlier."

The steering wheel creaks under my tightening grasp. "What did they do?" I manage to keep my voice level.

"The red powder—they mixed it in hot water. Then made me take baths in it. My mother would use a rough brush to scrub it into my skin." Her fingers trail over her arms. "The experiment worked, I guess. I made Anthony jump off that bridge without trying. And I started sensing the desires of those around me. Years before a normal witch gets their magic."

"That's fucking cruel," I growl.

Ame doesn't agree or disagree. "When Mor found out, she put a stop to it. Told my parents she'd toss all their ingredients into the ocean if they tried anything else on me. They had a lot of hard-to-find items, so the threat worked." Ame blinks her big green eyes at me, concern creasing her brow. "She was only fourteen, so it was the best she could do. When Mor turned sixteen, she got emancipated and moved out and took me with her."

Gods, after all that, Ame thinks I'll be pissed at her sister? Morgana was a kid too.

I reach out a hand, and Ame hesitates a second before taking it.

"So, the red is from the baths?"

She nods.

"You have the powder in your skin," I clarify.

Ame's lips purse. "I think so, but not much. Maybe it's worked its way out over the years. Now, I can't do what I did to Anthony without a dose of the powder on my palms. But it might be why I've always struggled to stifle my ability to sense desires."

She said that before, but her meaning is only beginning to dawn.

"When you say *sense*, you mean ..."

"What someone wants, what they crave, plays through my mind when I'm near them. Sometimes like a whisper, sometimes like a movie."

"All the time?" That has to be hell.

"Most of the time. I can't block it, but I've found if I concentrate really hard on something else, then I don't notice the desire. I know people think I'm kind of flighty. Airheaded."

"Who's said that?"

She waves a hand. "Doesn't matter. I'd rather have them thinking that than learn I know how they want to use honey as anal lube." She shoots me a look when I open my mouth. "Don't even ask. If it's not a desire to hurt someone, then it's their secret to keep."

Gods. She's so noble. Makes me want to pull this camper over and pleasure her until she moans my name.

Which has me realizing …

"My desires?"

Her eyes flick to me, then away. After a pause, she nods.

"So, you've always known …"

"That you're sexually attracted to me?" She chews her lip. "Yes. Since you returned to your man shape at least. And it's completely reasonable you would be, seeing as how I was the first woman you saw."

I rumble a growl and accelerate as traffic returns to two lanes. "That's not why I'm attracted to you."

Ame tilts her head, a small smile on her mouth. "Really? Well, that's the problem with this power. I know *what* people want, but never *why*. Can't read minds or anything. And most of the time, I wish I could shut it off."

That twists my guts. "Does being around me all the time make you uncomfortable?"

The cat hops off of Ame's lap and onto mine, and since I'm driving, I can't do much about it other than aim a quick snarl at the beast.

"It's strange. You seem to desire a lot, all at once. So much that they tend to blend together and make a pleasant buzz that fades into the background of my mind. You also drown out other people's desires, which is a nice relief." Ame grins my way.

I chew this over. "You're saying, I'm a desire white-noise machine?"

Ame chuckles, then laughs outright, and all the tension between us breaks.

"Exactly. You described it perfectly." She leans over to pet Lucky's head, and the cat purrs in my lap. "I'm glad you're coming back to Folk Haven for however long."

I decide not to correct her.

You love me, Ame Shelly. I won't let you forget it. I'm not going anywhere.

24

AME

"THIS PLACE SMELLS LIKE WOLF," Jack observes as we step through the front doors of the bank.

I raise my nose to the air, trying to pick out the subtle scents, like he does. But I can only discern the slight lemony smell of whatever floor polish the cleaning staff uses.

"That makes sense." I glance around the main room, searching for faces I recognize. "Wolf Trust Bank is owned and run by the local wolf pack."

"What?" Jack's question comes in a short, sharp tone.

The reaction has me realizing my blunder.

We arrived back in Folk Haven late last night, the return trip from California taking longer than the one out. Mainly because of the orgasms. The moment bedtime rolled around, Jack would lay claim to my vagina, using his mouth and fingers to destroy me with ecstasy. Not to be outdone, I would try my best to give him the same treatment.

Although I often got more than one out of him, based on the numbers, Jack is far in the lead on orgasm count. Not that

149

it's a competition, but I still feel greedy, knowing how much I'm getting without an equal return.

Inevitably, we'd pass out a few hours before dawn, and then Lucky would wake us up with a demanding yowl to be fed once she saw daylight. Jack claimed not to like her, but he would always jump out of bed to get the food, instructing me to sleep a few more hours.

Even with that and trading off driving, I'm still slightly sleep-deprived, and my thoughts are more unfocused than normal.

"I'm sorry. I should have told you. I forgot. I don't usually think of them as wolves. Just people who work at the bank."

But I should have realized. The last pack Jack interacted with betrayed him. Other werewolves are not at the top of his list for hang-out buddies.

"You said this is the only bank in town?" His jaw is hard, teeth gritting.

"It is. If we drive a half hour south, we'll run into another. Do you want to do that?"

He doesn't respond right away, and I'm already digging my car keys out of my pocket, ready to leave.

Jack shakes his head. "I won't let other wolves run me off," he growls.

Want to stand my ground.

I take in his tense form, feeling like this energy is too aggressive for a trip to the bank. "You sure you don't want to use the ATM outside? You won't have to talk to anyone."

Jack sets his hand on my lower back, drawing me forward. "I'm not here to take out some pocket change."

I realize I never questioned why Jack wanted to come to Wolf Trust. I figured it was to grab some cash, like he had in California. As much as I protested—never really expecting him to pay me back—Jack shoved big bills in the deep pockets of my overalls while listing off all the items I'd bought for him.

Now, we're even, giving Jack even less reason to stick around.

So, why would he need to meet with someone at Wolf Trust?

As we stand in line behind a human, Jack keeps me close to his side with a hand on my waist. I like the warm pressure of his fingers against my skin, and I press my body firmer into his hold. His fingers curl in the cotton of my shirt, and he shifts until our hips brush.

Like the length of Jack's time in Folk Haven, I'm under no illusion this affection will last forever—or even very long. I'm the steady presence as he regains his footing in a world that is six years ahead of what he last knew. Once Jack gets his bearings, his desire to clutch me close will fade.

I know what it's like to be useful to someone. And what it's like when your usefulness ends.

I'm going to enjoy him while I have him, but I won't hold on too tight. Or at all.

I wonder if my craving for him will go away after a time too. With the librarian, that one encounter was enough for me. Today, I think back on the hookup with fondness, but no longing.

I long for Jack even though he's standing right next to me. Crave him, even when he's gently thrusting in my mouth.

Maybe when he's finally ready to go home and I'm on my own again, I will recalibrate to the way I lived my life before.

Without the grumpy werewolf.

Please, Dark One, don't let me break apart too much when he leaves.

The human moves away from the counter, and Jack steps forward, once again drawing me with him by keeping that guiding hand on me.

The bank employee—Shanti, her name tag proclaims—is a

Black woman with short, curly hair that bounces as she gives us a welcoming customer-service nod and smile.

Then, her nostrils flare, and something flicks in her gaze. I notice the reaction but can't tell what it means other than she's probably just sniffed out that Jack is a werewolf, like her. I've seen her at Local Brew before, playing darts and drinking with other members of the pack. I like to go to the werewolf-owned bar on Monday nights because they have half-priced bacon cheese fries. Jack has probably seen Shanti too, as he was always in the corner booth with me on Mondays, growling at anyone who approached without food. His grumpy buffer was nice, so I could eat my food, drink a beer, and read my e-book without interruption.

"How can I help you, sir?" Shanti's voice sounds plenty pleasant, but the strange look in her eye lingers.

"I want to open an account."

She blinks once. Then twice. Then, she nods. "We can certainly do that for you. Are you a new resident of Folk Haven?"

I'm too confused to speak up and say that, no, Jack isn't living here. Just visiting. Just recovering really until he's ready to go back to his old life.

"Yes. I'm looking to transfer my savings to a local bank."

What in The Dark One's plans is he talking about?

Shanti nods, still smiling, though I'm not getting a friendly vibe from her. That is something my magic helps with. Vibes. Again, I'm not good at sifting out individual emotions other than desire. However, multiple emotions will often tangle together and push outside of a being to give off a general sensation.

Shanti's aura is sharp. That's the best way I can describe it.

"Our managers handle all new accounts. If you wouldn't mind waiting in our meeting area"—she waves toward a room with glass walls, a round table large enough to fit four people, and a potted plant with glossy green leaves and festive orange twinkle lights—"I'll go retrieve the manager on duty, and they'll be able to help you."

Jack gives Shanti a curt nod and follows the direction, still leading me along with him. Once we're seated side by side, I pluck a few pieces of Halloween candy from a bowl in the middle of the table and pick out the questions I want to ask.

"Why are you opening an account with Wolf Trust? This is their only branch. They're developing their online banking system, but I doubt they're convenient to bank with if you go anywhere else."

Jack stares at me, his dark eyes intense in a way I think only he can manage.

"You have an account here."

It wasn't a question, but I nod and pop a Reese's Cup in my mouth.

"You're staying here," he says, again no questioning tone.

After I swallow, I respond, "My sister is here. I like it here."

Probably not for the same reasons Morgana does, but Folk Haven appeals to me in a way none of the other towns and cities we drove through ever did. There's both a wildness and a safety to the town.

"If you're not leaving, then I'm not leaving." Jack says the words as if they make sense, but I'm still pondering them while anxiously eating candy when Baron, alpha of the Folk Haven Wolf pack, strides into the meeting space, shutting the glass door behind him.

I'm surprised to see the wolf. Not because he doesn't belong here. In fact, this is *his* bank. But that's just it. Wouldn't the owner of a bank have more important things to take care of than a new savings account?

"Hello. I'm Baron Moonson. And you are?"

In his human form, the pack leader is a towering white man with his brown hair carefully styled and strong jaw kept clean-shaven. Around town, I almost always see him in an expensive suit.

As the big man lowers himself into the seat across from us, his hard eyes stay locked on Jack's.

"Jack Lim." My friend's onyx stare is just as unforgiving.

"Mr. Lim." The pack leader speaks the name slowly as he relaxes back in his chair. But despite the casual posture, like Shanti, the shifter's vibe is sharp. "This visit is about more than a bank account, I'm sure."

Jack's body thrums with restrained energy.

I would need a magical blade to cut the tension in this tiny room.

A building full of werewolves.

How did I not realize this was a bad idea?

25

JACK

THERE'S something about the wolf that screams *powerful*.

I would hazard a bet that I'm sitting in a room with a pack leader.

Fuck.

When Ame told me werewolves worked at the bank, I still thought I could get through this interaction without too much trouble. All I want to do is open a fucking bank account.

This guy has other plans.

"No." I keep my sentences short. To the point. "It's not. I'm living here now, and I want a local bank. That's it."

The wolf's mouth curves into a smile while his eyes narrow and trace over me. There's a shadow of familiarity about him, and I wonder if this wolf knows Finnick. The two might be related for all I know. If they are, he probably won't take kindly to me offing the backstabber at the first chance I get.

"See," Baron rumbles, "now, that's where we run into a problem."

"If you need a character reference, I can provide one." Ame

leans forward, an open, honest expression on her face, her movement bringing me a hint of her mint scent, mixed with the chocolate she's stress-eating.

I want to throw her over my shoulder and sprint out of this room until I get her to safety. But this mythic might try chasing us down. I know how much wolves love the hunt.

When Baron flicks his attention to Ame, his smile takes on a genuine tilt. My hackles go up, and I barely suppress a snarl.

"Thank you, Ms. Shelly. But that's not the problem. The issue we have here"—he taps a thick finger on the meeting table—"is a lone wolf living in pack territory."

"I'm not in your territory." My voice hums with restrained hostility. "I'm living in the Shelly house. That belongs to *them*."

Instead of clearing things up, the wolf's brief pleasantness goes brittle. "That's Of the Wing territory. And they're witches."

"Better witches than wolves," I mutter.

Confusion twists Baron's brows before he clears the expression from his face. "You'll need to speak to Moira MacNamara, the owner of Folk Haven Realty. She can let you know about the property and land available in Of the Claw territory. Or, if you prefer, vacancies in town, which is a neutral living zone. But no matter where you live, all of Folk Haven and Lake Galen are the territory of the Folk Haven pack."

Baron reaches a hand into the lapel of his suit jacket and pulls out a business card. "Here's my contact information. Get in touch, and I'll send you instructions. You can stay in town as you petition to join. Decisions are made two nights before the next full moon. As long as there are no issues, you'll be a member of the pack in less than a month." The wolf offers me a confident half-smile, as if he's extending some kind of gift I should be grateful for.

Panic and rage claw at my insides.

"You'll be a member of the pack. One of us." Finnick's deep

voice creeps up from my past memories, and I don't know if I'm going to vomit or shift right here, in the middle of a bank.

I settle for another—less dramatic—option.

I pick up the business card, tear it in two, and toss the pieces into the bowl of candy.

"Fuck your pack." I say the words slowly, emphasizing each syllable. That way, he knows I mean each one.

The pack leader's face goes preternaturally still. "What did you say?"

When I stand, I do so with unhurried deliberation, almost mocking him with the casualness of my movement. "I would rather peel the skin from my bones than join your shitty power-play shifter club. Find another way to jerk yourself off. I'm not going to be one of your panting minions."

There are more insults I could fling, but I keep my mouth shut and reach for Ame's chair to help her stand. If she wasn't in the room, I'd go toe to toe with the guy, no problem. But I won't have my witch getting caught in the cross fire of a were-wolf brawl.

Baron Moonson lets out a low growl that fills the glass room as he also rises from his seat. "Listen here, you pup—"

"I don't think I will," I snarl over him, glaring at the glorified brute and fighting the urge to lunge for his throat just to show him who the fuck he's talking to.

As if the guy sees the caged beast in my eyes, he steps forward, fists clenching.

I'm half-ready to meet him head-on when I realize there's an obstruction in front of me. A tiny, witchy wall between the angry wolf and me.

"You won't touch him," she says.

Ame holds up her hands, but not in surrender. The normally pale palms are coated in red powder.

From the way the werewolf flinches back a step, he must

know what that means. What little Ame Shelly can do with a touch and some magic powder.

"Are you threatening me?" the pack leader asks, voice laced with warning.

"No." Her tone is steady, almost conversational. "I won't hurt you. But can you say the same? You're a respected leader in Folk Haven. Would you attack a mythic over nothing more than an insult?" Her hands begin to glow the faintest red. "Jack is my friend, even when he's being grumpy. I won't let *anyone* hurt him. Are you going to try?"

Baron's expression shutters. He crosses his arms over his chest, managing to maintain an air of intimidation in his surrender.

"This isn't over," he says, his attention returning to me. "You cannot come into this town and cause trouble."

I snort with pure derision. "Trouble for *you*, you mean?" With my hands on Ame's shoulders, I know I should shut up and leave, but his arrogance brings out every shred of hurt and rage that's been dug into my soul over the years. "I know *exactly* how much a pack is worth. Less than nothing. And you, the grand manipulator, enjoy every wolf fawning over you. But that's all they're allowed to do, isn't it? Cross you, and they're dead. Or worse than that. But not me. Never again. Every part of me is my own." Except for the large pieces that now belong to Ame. "I won't sell myself to you or any wolf just so you can turn around and hand me off to the highest bidder."

The guy's eyes go wide. "What—"

But I don't give a fuck what else he has to say. Denials. Placations. Threats. Doesn't matter.

Slinging my arm around Ame's shoulders, I walk us out of Wolf Trust Bank and into the bright fall day.

With fresh air clearing away the scent of wolf, I start breathing easier. We stride a handful of blocks before I'm calm enough to slow my steps. When I glance down, I realize Ame is cleaning the powder off her palms with a wet wipe.

Her hands are shaking.

Guilt tears through me, and I stop us in the middle of the sidewalk.

"Damn it, little witch. I'm sorry. I shouldn't have lost my temper."

Ame blinks up at me. "Oh, no. I don't blame you. Baron was kind of being an asshole. The way he didn't even *ask* if you'd like to join the pack ... I get why he set you off."

I take the wipe from her and finish the job of removing the magical powder, careful to clean between each finger, my eyes tracing the newly healed scar on her palm in the shape of an X.

"I didn't mean to scare you."

My little witch chuckles. "I wasn't scared of you. I never am. Not after that first night you changed back anyway. But that was really more surprise than anything."

"Then, why are you shaking?" I hold up her trembling hands as proof.

She studies them, as if surprised by her own reaction. She curls her fingers into fists. With my larger hands wrapped around her wrists, her hands look tiny and delicate.

"Must be adrenaline. I thought I was going to have to enchant the guy." Ame grimaces. "That would not go over well. Most people in town don't know what I can do. If they found out ..." My witch trails off, her face troubled.

Shame has me wanting to curl into myself.

I'm a selfish asshole.

Ame is trying to be a part of this town, and I'm stomping around, making trouble and forming grudges. If I keep going this way, I wouldn't be surprised if she opted to put distance between us.

"You won't have to enchant him," I promise her. "I can find a way to get along with the local pack."

"Really?"

One of her crimson brows creeps up her forehead, and I lean down to kiss the arch.

"Of course."

For Ame, I'll manage it.

26

JACK

AME TOOK Lucky to the vet. Without me. She said that I can go on cat errands when I stop glaring at the cat.

I don't like the rule, and having her out of my sight makes me anxious.

You can't have eyes on her at all times.

I know this is true, especially when I leave for my revenge mission. Who knows how long it'll take me to hunt down the three people who wronged me? My patchy cat memory means I don't know where to find the sorcerer. But he's not my first target. At least I can destroy Veronica and Finnick quickly.

Or slowly.

We'll see what mood I'm in when the traitorous wolves are under my claws.

Needing to alleviate some of my aggressive energy, I head to the guest room we pretend I sleep in and pull on a pair of athletic shorts and running shoes, planning on a long run. I leave my shirt off. Barely a week out from Halloween, but we're having a random hot day. Apparently, Georgia doesn't fully commit to the fall until November.

As I descend the stairs, attempting to move with stealth just to see if I can in this creaky house, I hear some angry muttering drifting from a back room.

Energy thrums in my body, begging for a good, long sprint. But if Ame were here, I know she'd want me to check on her sister. Time to offer a reluctant olive branch.

I find Morgana in the backmost room of the house, hunched over her laptop with her curly red hair in a messy bun on the top of her head. She must have been tugging at her hair because the bun looks ready to topple down around her scowling face.

"Damn The Dark One's plans. What the fuck is wrong with you?" she hisses at her computer.

"Hey."

Her head jerks up at my greeting, but her expression remains surly. "Hello, creep."

Remember that Ame loves her. Remember how she protected a young Ame when you couldn't.

I keep my body relaxed. "Creepy because I'm shirtless?"

One of her red brows ticks up. "How many times did you watch my sister change when you were a fuzzy little fake feline?"

I try to frown in response, but something has the corner of my mouth sneaking up. "Unlike you, Ame knew I was a man. She always locked me out of the bathroom when she took her clothes off."

Morgana lets out a huff, and I have no idea what it means.

"Good." The witch's eyes drop to her laptop screen, her frown turning more hopeless than angry. "Where is she anyway? I can't figure this out. Ame's the tech expert."

Morgana's comment surprises me. Not that I didn't think Ame was intelligent. She's the most intuitive, clever woman I

know. But most of my cat memories are of Ame handling physical books.

"Ame likes tech stuff?"

Morgana rolls her eyes. "She's always trying to pretend she
doesn't. Hiding her e-reader when I come around. Pretending
she's taking notes on paper instead of on that tablet. Claiming
she thought the HTML guidebook might be a grimoire in
disguise."

Is Ame a secret computer geek?

"It's like she thinks witches have to do everything the old-
fashioned way." Morgana waves toward the shelves stocked
with books. "But it's just that *I* like the old-fashioned way. She
can be a witch however she wants."

Morgana's description of her sister has me warming—
slightly—toward the curly-haired witch.

"What's going on? Computer troubles?" I ask.

Ame isn't the only techy person in this house now. I'm six
years behind, but I have the building blocks. No doubt I can
pick it up fast.

"Archival software problems," she mutters, half-paying
attention to me as she angrily clicks on her touchpad.

Software. Even better. I carefully remove a stack of books
from a chair, then bring the seat with me as I circle around the
desk.

"What are you doing?" Morgana is all suspicion.

"Seeing if I can help." I settle next to her and eye the screen.
"I went to college for computer science. Just started my career
as a programmer when the sorcerer shit went down. Tell me
what's going on." I gesture toward the screen.

But Morgana watches me. "How old are you?"

I sigh. "I was twenty-two when I got captured. Spent six
years as a cat. Did I age during that time?" I shrug, not sure how
curse magic works and not in the mood to see a doctor to get
poked and prodded to find out. "Twenty-eight maybe. Mind of a

twenty-two-year-old. Mind of a sixteen-year-old around your sister because she steals my ability to reason."

Morgana presses her lips tight together, and I think it's to stifle a smile. "I thought you were older."

"Anger ages you, I guess."

She makes a noise in her throat, then points to a window on her screen. "These files are supposed to be organized in a tier structure. At least, the software claimed I could create subcategories. But whenever I try to add one, I get an error message. It's fucking frustrating. Especially because this is just a cobbled-together organizational method anyway. There are better programs out there, but they're all web-based."

When she spots my confused look, she explains, "This is sensitive content. I don't want it stored in a cloud system that can be hacked. I want to organize everything in a closed system that lives here. You have to access it here. But the software available is limited. And fucking annoying."

"Do you mind?" My fingers hover over the keyboard.

She gives me a nod, and even though I don't need Morgana's approval to be with Ame, I find I like the idea of her being a Jack fan as opposed to us constantly dueling.

About five minutes later, I have the issue fixed, and subcategories are back.

"Fuck you," Morgana mutters, but there's no heat in the words, just a rueful smirk.

Considering the scale of my next offer, I figure, what's the harm? I plan on being around Folk Haven for as long as Ame is.

"I could build you a system. Ground up. That way, it would have all the capabilities you want. It would take time. And some more equipment."

Morgana stares at me, eyes wide. "You could do that? You *would* do that?"

I stand up, the restless energy back now that I don't have a puzzle to solve. "Ame loves you, and your happiness makes her happy. Besides, I miss working. Been a long time since I got to dig into some challenging technology."

Morgana looks confused, but not hostile. "I'll think about it. If you could do what you're saying ..." She trails off, no doubt imagining the perfect archival setup that doesn't currently exist with the level of safety she wants.

"Let me know." I turn to leave.

"Jack."

I pause at the door.

When our eyes meet, she seems reluctant. "Have you heard about Ramla?"

I shake my head. Ame has told me plenty about Folk Haven and the people living here, but no one named Ramla.

"Ramla University. Not too far south of town. I bet they have a tech support department for the students, and they might be hiring. Most everyone on staff is a mythic, and if you explain why you dropped off the face of the earth for six years, they're the kind who would understand that gap in your résumé. You know, if you're looking to get a job so you don't drain your savings, paying rent."

The tip has me smiling slow. *Could Morgana be warming up to me?*

Seeing the expression, she frowns again.

"Why should I trust you?" she asks, completely reversing tracks, as if rethinking her attempt at kindness.

Back and forth with this woman.

I stick to honesty. "You shouldn't."

You shouldn't trust anyone. Except for Ame because she is perfection.

Morgana's scowl tells me that was the wrong answer. Heaving a sigh, I leave the room, heading to the kitchen instead of the front door. I slip a boning knife from the wooden block on the counter and return to the study.

The witch's eyes widen at the sight of the blade, but before she can get any ideas, I score the sharp edge across my palm. As the warm red liquid wells, I stride across the room and grasp Morgana's wrist with my bloody palm, binding her to my oath.

"I swear on my blood, I will never physically hurt Ame"—thoughts of naughty acts in bed pop into my mind—"without her request. And I will try my hardest not to cause her mental or emotional distress. I'll give my life for hers and spend mine caring for her and making her happy as long as she wants me by her side. This I swear by my blood."

There's a zing of magic that goes through me and Morgana too, if I take her flinch as proof. I release her and fist my hand, knowing it'll take a few hours for my healing powers to seal up the cut.

Niko was the first to tell me about blood oaths. Warning I should only enter one if I was sure of the vow I was making. There's no taking it back.

From Morgana's shocked expression, she knows this too. Knows the weight of what I just claimed.

"You still shouldn't trust me," I say. "Ame is too precious for you to let your guard down. I know I won't."

27

AME

"YOU HAVE YOURSELF A PERFECTLY HEALTHY CAT." Dr. Zara Ironfeather offers me a kind smile over the examination table as she strokes a purring Lucky.

The black feline has been an agreeable patient throughout the whole process.

It's still odd sometimes—to hear purrs instead of growls.

"That's good to know. She was a stray, so I'm not sure what she got into."

Zara nods. "I'm glad you came in. I've seen you and this little one around town, and I've been wanting to introduce myself."

It takes me this long to notice how gorgeous Zara is. She has her thick black hair tamed into two French braids, displaying her brown eyes, the irises a shade darker than her dusky skin. The scrubs she wears can't hide the generous curves of her body.

If I didn't have a grumpy werewolf firmly lodged in my

heart, I might find myself infatuated with the veterinarian. But all I feel is the pleasant sensation of a fellow animal lover.

Then, her words register.

"Oh. No. Sorry. *That* cat was not *this* cat." I scratch Lucky behind the ears, and she butts her head against my hand. "That cat was Bee, who turned out to be Jack, a werewolf cursed to live as a cat by a sorcerer. Recently, we found a way to break the enchantment. Next time we're together and we see you, I'll introduce him."

"Bless The Winged One," Zara whispers, her eyes wide in shock. "He was cursed?"

The veterinarian is a mythic—a harpy—which is why I thought sharing the story was fine. But now. I consider how the magical creatures living in the safe barriers of Folk Haven might not have given much thought to the dangers that lurk in the larger world.

Not that my extensive travels ever brought me face-to-face with a sorcerer. But still, when I was constantly surrounded by humans, the risk never felt too far away.

"It happened years ago. And I found him in Maine. No reason to worry."

Zara swallows and nods, her smile returning. "I look forward to meeting him."

She walks with me to the front of her office, talking about flea and tick medications if Lucky is going to be an outside cat.

Folk Tails is a small operation, the only vet option in town. Zara shares the workload with a human named Keith, who seems nice enough, but I'm glad I got an appointment with her. She has a soft way about her.

Don't let any of them die today.

The desire is simple and pure and has the steady feel of a core longing. One that is always with her. All Zara wants is to help her patients and avoid as much death as possible. She's the type of mythic I wouldn't mind spending more time around.

Plus, she's filled the office with gorgeous animal-themed art. The sketches I sometimes make on my tablet of the wildlife I encounter are elementary compared to the colorful masterpieces.

"Who painted this piece?" I point to a beautiful image of an owl high in the branches of a tree. The wise bird watches me as I move.

"I did." A blush colors Zara's cheeks as she grins up at the painting. "I call it *Watchtower*."

Before I can compliment her, the door opens, and a familiar mythic walks in.

Delta—previous owner of the house that I now live in; mated to Calder, a selkie; and owner of Gigabyte, a nervous Chihuahua mut.

"Hi," Delta says, smile strained as she cradles a whimpering, quivering pup in her arms. "I have Gig here for her eleven thirty."

The dog lets out a tormented yowl.

"Is she injured?" I ask. That noise would indicate yes.

Lucky purrs in my arms, and I get the sense she's trying to soothe the scared dog.

Delta grimaces. "No. This is a normal checkup. She just hates the vet." The dragon shoots a sheepish look Zara's way. "No offense."

"None taken. Let me get Ame checked out, sanitize the examination room, and then I'll be ready for you."

The vet walks behind the front counter, which is decorated with black-cat cutouts and a large pumpkin with a paw print carved into the side. All of Folk Haven is getting into the spirit of the season.

Zara shakes the mouse of her computer to bring it to life. She starts typing on the keys, then mutters a curse and clicks on the mouse again. "Sorry. I'm still getting used to this new software. Keith insisted it was better, but I barely knew how to navigate the old one."

I have the urge to offer to take over the computer for her. I always do when Morgana is having issues with navigating things.

You don't work here. Don't be weird.

Gigabyte starts up a series of yelps, like a warning siren. Lucky leaps out of my arms—yes, I still need to buy a cat carrier because I never even considered putting her in one after living with Bee for years—and trots over to the bench, where Delta is trying to ease her dog.

Make her feel better.

Make her feel safe.

The desires are whimpers from Delta, the woman in quiet distress over her dog's anxiety.

I can help.

Normally, I don't use my powers in front of other mythics because I know the implications are frightening. However, I've never had any issues using my persuasive magic on or near animals. Sometimes, if I'm walking in the woods and I come across a skittish creature, I pacify them, so I can approach, just for a closer look.

And then I leave them with the desire to never linger on roads and to avoid people dressed in bright orange.

But what if I could do more? If I could do a small act of kindness for this dog who doesn't understand that she's somewhere good rather than a place to be feared?

As Zara mutters to herself while typing on the computer, I follow my cat over to the bench and sit beside Delta.

"Do you mind if I persuade Gigabyte to be calm? It won't hurt her. I won't be offended if you say no."

Delta tilts her chin, purple eyes widening behind her glasses. "If you think you can help, go for it."

Her trust warms me. With my mind, I reach toward the small dog. I've never needed the boost of red powder with animals. Maybe the amount lingering in my skin is enough to manipulate their simpler grid of emotions. The colors are slightly altered shades when compared to humans, but I find the dog's desire in a maroon-colored thread. With gentle, magical mental fingers, I hold on to a piece of Gigabyte.

Want to visit good place.

I don't know if my magic appears to others as words or urges, but I still keep my thoughts simpler when dealing with creatures.

Want to visit kind people.

Want to be good and get treats.

Want to relax.

At some point, I closed my eyes, focusing entirely on the emotions shared between the two of us. As I blink and take in the small waiting room, I find both mythics are staring at me in awe while my cat cleans herself and Gigabyte naps in Delta's lap.

"Goddess," the dragon whispers. "She's never this calm without medication."

"What magic did you work?" Zara asks, eyes popping between the dog and me.

"Just a bit of persuasion." I rub my tingling palms on my legs, then lean forward and scoop Lucky up. The cat immediately goes boneless, and the technique makes me smile as I think of Bee. "Is the computer working?"

Suddenly, I have an overwhelming urge to get home to Jack.

I'm not sure how much time I have left with him.

Zara nods and returns to the counter, although her focus stays on me. "Have you worked with animals before?"

The question brings up a mixture of pleasant and sad memories. "I used to work at an animal shelter in Maine. But they were absorbed into a larger organization, and my job disappeared with the merge." Around that time is when Morgana asked me to travel with her. There was nothing keeping me from saying yes.

Zara nods and accepts my credit card. "And what do you do now?"

"For work?"

She nods.

"I help my sister at the library." I'm proud of myself for not cringing as I said that.

The library is Morgana's dream. I'm simply there to help her achieve it—even if I'm bored every day. The truth is, I *like* books and reading, but I'd rather sink into a fiction story and use my sleek e-reader.

"Does that pay well?"

"It pays nothing. Nonprofit and all that."

Zara's brow furrows. "How do you survive without a paying job?"

"Oh." I clear my throat before answering, "I don't need to make money. I have enough. More than enough. When I get a job, it'll be because I enjoy the work."

"Well"—the vet offers me a hopeful smile as she slides a large piece of paper across the counter along with my receipt —"if you're ever looking for something, we've been considering putting up a Help Wanted sign. Would be nice to have a front desk worker."

The top of the paper reads *Job Application*.

"Oh. Okay. I'll think about it."

In a daze, I sign my receipt and carry Lucky out of the vet's office.

Could I work here?

Morgana needs me.

Would it be selfish to apply?

I don't need a paycheck.

What would people think if they saw the number in my bank account?

When the trust fund became available to me on my twentieth birthday, I wanted to give the money away. Even though all of my siblings got one too, mine felt too much like my parents saying *Here, take this money and forget what we did to you.* And that was what I started to do, mainly to animal charities around the country. Morgana convinced me to keep some of it. Enough to live off of at least. When she made her argument, I kept watching her eyes drop to the red flush on my arms. A silent message that I deserved the money.

So, why do I want to get rid of it all and start over?

28

———————

AME

THE NEXT DAY, Jack has an excited sparkle in his eye when he returns from his errand. He refused to tell me what the errand was, saying he wanted to make sure it was good news before he said anything.

"Will you tell me now?"

I would climb out of the window seat to pester him, but Lucky is curled up on my lap, and she seems disinclined to move.

The wolf's grin has a triumphant edge. "I got a job."

My brain works through the words, not comprehending them. We've only been back in Folk Haven for three days.

"A part-time job?"

Jack shakes his head and settles next to me, his cocky expression souring as his eyes land on Lucky. He growls a Bee growl that says, *Go the fuck away.*

Lucky snores louder.

"Then, what kind of job?" I press.

He returns his attention to me. "The tech department at

Ramla. I've got enough experience to at least help undergrads troubleshoot their laptops, and they're short-staffed. The head of the department is Felicity, a siren. She touched base with your sister about my troubles"—he grimaces—"these past six years."

"*Morgana* gave you a reference?"

He nods with a smirk. "We've graduated to her not completely hating me. Felicity is double-checking with her supervisors but said it's pretty much a sure thing. As long as everything checks out, I should be starting in a few weeks."

My mind requires a moment to reboot.

"You're working at Ramla?" I repeat. "Full-time?"

"That's right."

"Like, a career?"

"It's an entry-level position, but Felicity said I can sit in on evening courses if I want to update my skills."

My world reels. "But Ramla is in Georgia."

Jack's brows dip. "Yeah. So?"

"But you're leaving."

He sighs a grumble. "Not this again. I'm *not* going back to California," he insists.

Work here.

Live here.

Provide for her.

Make her mine.

The desires press on me, and I want to believe them so badly. But desires change, and his old life isn't the only thing that would draw him away from Folk Haven.

"Don't you plan to hunt down the sorcerer who cursed you?"

His face goes as blank as a new Word document. "What makes you think that?"

Seriously? I roll my eyes. "Because even if you were a cat most of the time, I *know* you, Jack. After what he put you through, you're not about to *not* retaliate. I figured once you recuperated here for a time, you'd leave on a hunt for him."

Jack's mouth twists, and he leans over me, bracing his arms on either side of my hips. Looming. "And do you have an issue with me going after him, little witch?"

"No."

He's so close. I can't help reaching up to stroke my finger over his brows, where they dip and wrinkle. My touch soothes them. Every night, he comes to my bed, tugs off my sleep clothes, delves his head between my legs, and ups his orgasm count. I'm just as desperate for the taste of him in my mouth, for the guttural noises he makes when he finishes. For the tight way he holds me close as we drift off to sleep.

Still, I want more.

If Jack could sense my desires, he'd know how I want him to stay. He'd know how I hope he'll continue to ignore the terrifying magnitude of my power. He'd hear how I pray to The Dark One that I can find ways to be useful in his life, so he'll push off his departure a little bit longer.

But he would also learn about the twisted parts of my mind.

How I long to see the sorcerer pay. How I imagine making him bleed.

Stealing his will.

Ending his life.

Maybe I'm not a strong, ferocious werewolf, but that doesn't mean I don't have a darkness in me, calling out for vengeance.

"I want to help," I whisper.

"Ame ..."

"I've already begun to plan."

I reach behind me and pull my tablet out.

Jack hasn't backed away, so I open the digital folder I've started filling with relevant information and sneak the screen up in front of my face, so he has to see the title of the collection.

"*Jack Lim's Revenge Plan,*" he reads. His fingers pluck the device from my hand as he sits back. "What is this?"

"I thought the title was self-explanatory." I sidle up next to him to read over his shoulder.

Jack taps to open the folder, displaying carefully organized and labeled documents. He taps on the first.

"*Targets,*" he reads, "*Sorcerer—name unknown. San Francisco alpha. San Francisco pack …*" He meets my eyes then. "What are you trying to do with this? Make it a game?"

"Oh gods. No. I'm sorry. Is that how it seems?" I chew my lip. "I'm trying to be proactive. And organized."

I reach out and tap the screen to navigate to another document. "Here are all the contacts Morgana and I have in Maine. I figure it's best we start there—ask around about a sorcerer. I wouldn't get your hopes up though, seeing as how sorcerers do their best to hide themselves from us, as we do the same with them." I scroll down. "This is a friend—a witch—who lives in North Carolina. Young in her magic but super powerful and with a *seeking* focus. She's located several missing persons for the police. Anonymously, of course, but she likes to help. She tried to seek the right transformation spell for you, but her magic usually requires a personal item. Not sure if she can help us, but she's an option."

I go to open another document, but his warm hand stops me.

"Ame." The shifter's voice is rumbly, and I realize his eyes have gone black.

My heart sinks. "You're mad. I'm sorry. I didn't mean to overstep. We can delete all this."

"No," he growls. "We're keeping your plans." He sets the tablet at my side. "We're getting rid of the cat."

"Huh?"

Jack unceremoniously scoops Lucky off the window seat and drops her on the floor.

"Jack!"

Lucky lets out a plaintive meow before strutting off.

He silences my protests by fusing his mouth to mine. The wolf kisses me deep and hard, stealing my breath and keeping me panting as he strokes his tongue into my mouth. His large body settles over mine, pressing me into the plush cushions of the window seat. Rain trickles down the windowpanes, and I grow as wet as the glass when he fits his hips between my thighs, rocking against my core with only our clothes between us.

When Jack breaks away to kiss down my neck, I gasp out a question. "You don't mind the Revenge Plan?"

"You're a good little witch," he murmurs against my collarbone, "helping me plot my revenge. Gonna make you come on my tongue."

"I'm only two documents in," I protest.

He groans and shoves his hand down the front of my yoga pants, fingers finding me slick. He teases my clit and licks the hammering pulse on the side of my throat.

"Tell me more," he whispers. "What's next?"

"Next?"

He dips one, then two fingers inside me, thoroughly distracting me.

"In the Revenge Plan." His teeth nip at my skin, setting my nerves tingling and my nipples tightening to almost-painful points.

"Oh. Yes. Um, I-I downloaded some maps."

"Mmm. Of what?"

He thumbs my clit and rocks his hips against my leg. I can feel his hard cock pressing against my thigh. My mouth waters, and I have to swallow before continuing.

"Maps of our driving route. I marked where we found each other."

"Fuck yes, we did."

Jack rears up, his fingers sliding out of me and finding the waistband of my pants. In a smooth move, they're off with my underwear, and I'm bare from the waist down.

His frantic energy pauses as he does, kneeling between my legs, simply staring at me.

"Jack?"

The wolf's attention traces up to mine. There's something wild in his gaze.

"I want to be inside you." Despite the intensity pulsing off him, Jack whispers the words. There's a vulnerability in his voice. As if he expects me to deny him.

I gaze at the man who has been my companion for years. He doesn't need me anymore, not with his body restored, his money in his pocket, and a new job.

But for now, he wants me.

And I want to experience everything I can with this wolf before he walks away from me.

"I have a birth control tattoo." Pressing to my side, I indicate a simple design in white ink on the back of my hip.

Jack's heavy hand lands just below the bit of magic. "What exactly does this do?"

"Prevents pregnancy. The only one who can break it is the witch who originally cast it, so it's a little bit risky to get. But liberating."

His thumb strokes over the long-ago-healed skin.

"So, we could *do it* without a condom," I explain.

The corners of his mouth curve upward. "*Do it*?" His hand leaves my thigh, only to land on the fly of his pants. Hot eyes stay on me as he slowly drags the zipper down. "What's *it*?"

Make her moan my name.

Make her scream my name.

Make her pray my name.

The desires spill out of him and into me, feeling like an erotic massage pressing deep into my muscles.

"Sex," I pant. "Penis," I say as his own pops free of his dress pants, already hard. "In me. In my vagina." *Goddess, what am I rambling?*

No matter how ridiculous my explanation is, Jack seems more than satisfied as he shoves his pants off, rips his shirt over his head, and hovers his hard body over mine with only enough space between us for him to reach down and finger my clit.

"Oh! Goddess." I writhe against him, clasping the smooth muscles of his shoulders as Jack strokes me the way he knows I like.

There's a pressure between my legs, the slick head of him pressing against my opening.

"Ame." When Jack speaks my name, the simple arrangement of letters becomes something special. Holy and rare, like a gods artifact.

He sinks in an inch, and I gasp, my body tensing around the erotic intrusion. Jack groans, his lids dropping to half-cover his black eyes.

"Tell me what else is in the file," he instructs as a flush rises up his neck. I want to lick the delicious color, but I do as I was told.

"A list," I stutter as he sinks deeper, "o-of towns"—more of him filling me—"near where we found each other."

Jack grunts, seating himself fully inside me, his balls cradled in the cleft of my ass. "I fucking love how you say that. *We found each other.*"

The wolf thrusts, long and slow, dragging a whimper out of me. My body is hot and full, and I want him to keep moving. As I spread my legs wider, my hands sneak around to his behind. I knead the taut globes and press him close.

"I'll always find you, Ame." He pants the claim as he thrusts, mirroring the firm presses of his finger against my clit. "You can't get away."

The sound of slapping flesh fills the room along with my mewling as he strokes me just right.

"I'm a selfish fuck." His eyes blaze as he stares down at me. "Come on my cock, little witch."

Make me yours.

"Jack." I sob his name as my body clenches with more ecstasy than I've ever experienced with a partner.

Maybe he has some kind of desire magic of his own, and I'm under his spell. I don't mind.

As the pleasure sweeps through me, red fills my gaze. The glow spills from his pores, pure desire seeping out of the wolf.

Any other time, I would try to avoid viewing the emotional vulnerability.

Now, I just cry out and bask in the glow.

JACK

My witch is beautiful beneath me, flushed and sparkling with sweat as she gasps through her orgasm.

Gods, I love her.

Ame is gentle and caring and—secretly—a little bit vicious. I never expected her to approve of my revenge, but she's already halfway into plotting the whole thing out. I'd better step up my game, or she'll have knifed the lot of them for me.

My balls are heavy as they slap against her slick skin each time I drive deep inside her.

"Jack," Ame whimpers, pliant and hazy-eyed beneath me as she comes down from her peak.

Treasuring the sound of my name in her sweet voice, I reward her by pushing up her shirt to suck a nipple into my mouth. My witch tastes salty and fucking delicious. I drag in lungfuls of her earthy, minty scent, intoxicated on the smell of the woman I plan to spend the rest of my life with.

"Oh goddess." Her reverent whisper comes before the tug of fingers in my hair. Ame holds my head against her body.

She wants me. I won't abide any more mentions of me leaving. Of going back to my old life.

Ridiculous. The only time I'll part from Ame is when I put her Revenge Plan into action, and that will be temporary. Probably shorter than I originally planned with all her prep work. The thought of that folder has my cock throbbing harder.

I raise my head, slip my greedy dick out from her tight heat, and flip my witch over, so she's on her hands and knees, staring down at her tablet.

"Read me more," I rasp as I sink into her from behind.

Let me see the darker corners of your mind, little witch. You're not all sunshine, are you? There's a taste of naughtiness, and I want to lap it up.

She gasps as I slowly press into her and pull out, over and over, loving the way her freckled ass—yes, the adorable brown dots are spread here too—pools against my hips when I'm buried deep.

"N-next is *spells*." She moans the last word when I drag my hand down her belly and under the hood of her, fingering that perfect bundle of nerves.

"Mmhmm. Tell me more."

"They're to ... to capture. To hold."

I give a rueful headshake and keep up my torturously slow movements. "I'm not going to be catching him, little witch." A punishing thrust has her groaning. "I'm going to kill him."

And I'll enjoy every bloody second of it.

She pants a few times, then tries for a response. "Killing lacks ..."

Morality?

"Creativity."

I sheathe my cock to the hilt as I register her meaning.

She wants him to suffer.

"Fuck," I mutter as my body shudders, curving over hers.

My fists plant on the cushion of the window seat, next to her pale hands. I bury my face in Ame's shoulder as I spill inside my little witch, hips pumping to get every drop into her sweet pussy.

Her fingers slide to the side, finding mine and holding on. Her need to grab, to clutch at me, sends my orgasm spinning higher until I might black out.

But I don't want to lose even a second of conscious time with this woman. I want her for my entire life.

Ame Shelly is everything to me.

29

JACK

THERE'S a wolf in the library.

Specifically, a wolf who is not me.

I scent the intruder only after the steam of my shower begins to dissipate. One moment, I was smelling Ame's mint soap that I rubbed all over myself, and the next, there's honeysuckle and fur.

A growl rips from my throat as I tear open the bathroom door and stalk downstairs.

"Ame?"

If anyone has hurt my witch, I'll burn this town to the ground.

"In the vine room," she calls out to me, referring to the room with vine-patterned wallpaper.

At a normal volume, she speaks to whoever I'm scenting. "This is our dragon section. Do you know Esme? She donated a whole bunch of books. Her mate is a dragon and has been checking them for accuracy. Morgana is hoping we can get more mythics to give their input, but we know a lot of our kind are private. Oh, Jack."

When I storm through the doorway, Ame is standing near a tall bookshelf with a vaguely familiar figure at her side. The woman turns, revealing a set of sharp, deep-set eyes, surrounded by almost-too-thick black lashes.

The werewolf from the wrestling match.

"Jack, this is Tanvi. She's a werewolf. Did you forget which dresser you put your clothes in?" My witch's eyes drop to my bare, still–wet chest.

At least there's a towel wrapped around my waist.

"Why are you here?" I didn't mean to growl the words. That's just how they came out.

Tanvi smirks. "What a warm welcome."

Ame glances between the two of us. "This is a public library," she reminds me. "Anyone in town can come."

Right. But why do I get a sense this wolf doesn't want books?

"Actually, I'm here to talk to you," Tanvi says, facing me.

Ah, that's why.

"I already told your alpha all I have to say."

Instead of getting defensive, the woman grins wide.

"I *know*. Gods, I wish I could've been there. He was so surly afterward." She chuckles, throwing me off.

"Baron Moonson is Tanvi's dad," Ame explains with a helpful smile.

Oh. Well ... that explains ... nothing really.

"Anyway"—Tanvi waves a hand, as if she can easily dismiss the alpha of her pack if she wants—"I'm here because I wanted to ask about you being a shifter. What's that like?"

Silence falls, and Ame and I share a confused glance.

I meet the stranger's eyes. "You're a werewolf. You know."

The woman's thick brows twist in confusion. "No, I'm talking about being a *shifter*."

I have no answer to that, which she must realize.

"Shit. Do you not know what you are?"

I scowl. "Of course I do. I turn into a fucking wolf every full moon. Hard to miss it."

But Tanvi is already shaking her head. "Gods, you seriously don't know." She struts to an overstuffed chair and plops herself down in it. "You, Jack, are a *shifter* werewolf."

As much as I hate to admit my lack of knowledge, I can't ignore the rabid curiosity inside me. This is what drew me to the San Francisco pack. I wanted all the secrets of my kind. The pieces of knowledge I should have gotten from my father if he'd bothered to stick around.

"And that is ..." I lean back against the wall and cross my arms over my chest.

"See, I'm a run-of-the-mill werewolf. I have to change into a wolf on the full moon, and I *can* change into a wolf outside of that, but it's a bitch to do. I can connect with a pack, utilize the power of that pack to be stronger, run faster, and heal rapidly. All that fun, normal werewolf stuff. But you"—she jabs a finger my way—"are a shifter werewolf. You're like me, but extra, you lucky bastard. I have two forms: this one"—she gestures to her current body—"and full wolf. You have three: two legs, wolf, and hybrid. I've heard of your kind, but never met one before. You're rare. Packs love having a shifter because you're supposed to be particularly powerful or something. And I've heard shifters are strong enough to turn back during a full moon. That you can walk around, looking like a human, even when she calls us. Can you do that?"

After hesitating, I nod, thinking of the night Ame changed me back.

Tanvi lets out an impressed whistle. "You really didn't know you were a shifter?"

Silently, I jerk my head, signaling no.

The onslaught of knowledge is almost too much to take, and I have no idea how to feel about it.

Then, a freckled set of arms sneaks around my waist and hugs me close.

I encircle Ame's shoulders with my arm and keep her tight at my side, soothed by her touch and support.

"I thought wolf shifters and werewolves were the same thing," my witch says to the quiet room. "I'm sorry. I was using the terms wrong this whole time."

Tanvi shrugs. "Other animal mythics in town refer to themselves as shifters, so I think we just kind of let the word apply to us too. Like I said, werewolf shifters are rare. I guess the pack didn't see it as an issue."

"But I'm here now," I point out.

The werewolf smirks my way. "Yep. Throwing everyone off. But I think the pack could do with a bit of a shake-up."

"I'm not joining the pack," I growl, and Ame rubs a comforting circle against my bare back.

Tanvi stands unhurriedly, appearing unconcerned with my grumpy ass. "Do whatever. Just know that the pack isn't going anywhere. If you plan to stay here, unattached, there might be issues. And not just for you." Her eyes drop, landing on my witch.

A snarl tears from my throat. "Are you *threatening* Ame?"

Tanvi holds her hands up. "No way. Seriously, I'm not." She sighs and shoves her hands in her pockets. "This is a small town. You can't escape the people you piss off. So, do you want to stockpile grudges, or do you want to make friends? It's up to you." The werewolf strolls toward the front door. "See ya, Ame!" she calls over her shoulder.

"Bye," my witch responds before the door shuts and we're left alone.

My thoughts are in a tangle with all the new information and subtle warnings.

"Let's get you dried off."

Ame slips her hand into mine and tugs me toward the stairs. I follow her without a word.

Despite the anger from Tanvi's implication that I should join the pack or suffer the small-town consequences, I feel a tinge of fullness, knowing more about myself.

I'm a shifter werewolf.

A part of me can't believe she gave me that whole explanation for free. The gesture was almost ... kind.

But that can't be right. Werewolves are assholes, the lot of us. We're selfish and violent, and we don't give a shit about anyone other than ourselves.

Only, that's not entirely true. Because I love Ame.

Other faces of people I care about flash in my mind.

Not that they would believe me anymore. Not after I abandoned them.

My mother and Niko didn't like Finnick from the start, but it got worse when he pushed for me to step away from my life to connect more fully with the pack. They didn't want me to go with him. I tried to explain to them how much I needed to be around wolves—to understand myself better, I claimed—but they didn't get it.

And Finnick? He was a persuasive, charming motherfucker. Gullible me fell for his descriptions of a supportive pack providing all the security and family I could ever hope for. What I thought I'd been missing my whole life. What I didn't realize I already had.

So, piece of shit I was, I burned my bridges. I told my best friend and my mother that I was choosing a group of magical strangers over them.

We yelled.

Screamed.

Said horrible things I don't know how to take back.

What I know now is that Dr. Anna Lim is better off without me. Finally, she'll be able to live her life for her instead of for me. I won't make any more demands of her. And as much as that hurts, I'm glad I'm capable of suppressing my selfishness here.

I should do the same with Ame. But giving her up is impossible.

All this goes through my head as Ame leads me upstairs and starts rifling through the dresser in the guest bedroom I don't even pretend to sleep in.

"How're you doing with the whole *shifter* thing?" Ame stares up at me as she passes over briefs, sweatpants, and a T-shirt.

"It's a lot." I grind my teeth. "The alpha in San Francisco knew I had a third form. He didn't say anything about it." With jerky movements, I tug on the clothes.

"Can I ... ask you about your parents?" Ame sets the question between us hesitantly.

She hasn't probed into my past up until this point, and that's what I thought I wanted.

But her asking now, wanting to know more about me, I like this better even though exploring the old wounds will hurt.

I suck in a bracing breath, then start. "My mom has always worked in academia. She has a doctorate in linguistics and teaches courses at a university in California, last I knew." A Google search still has her on the faculty roster. Same headshot and everything. "She's always been focused on work. Kind of a loner. And my grandparents passed away before I was born. When she was twenty-eight, she had a one-night stand with a guy. Guess her birth control didn't work because she ended up with me." I think, not for the first time, how hard that must have been. Having a kid with no support system.

Ame reaches out and presses a palm flat against my chest, holding it there, eyes on her fingers, where they rest against the cotton of my T-shirt. I don't know why this is the way she chose to caress me, but the heat from her palm quiets my pounding heart, and I lean further into her touch.

"Did you ever learn who your father was?" she asks quietly.

I shake my head. "She would always get flustered when I asked her about him. I think she felt guilty she never got his name. But it doesn't matter." I shrug. "He was probably a deadbeat anyway."

"But he was a werewolf?"

"Must have been." *Was he a shifter too? Is that how it works?*

I already have more questions and no one to answer them unless I seek out members of the Folk Haven pack.

Ame nods and kneads her fingers into me. "What happened to your mom?"

I tilt my head. "Uh, nothing. Far as I know, she's still in the same house we moved to when I was fifteen."

Ame's brows dip low between her eyes, almost but not quite a scowl. "But you ... have you gotten in touch with her since changing back?"

I shake my head, focusing entirely on the feel of her touching me.

"Why not?"

The final words I threw at her sear through my mind now.

"They understand me. They want me. You never did. Now, I don't want you."

I'm such a piece of shit. Mom was a single woman, trying to raise a werewolf. Yeah, she might have spent long hours working, and she might not have fully grasped what it was like to be a mythical creature.

But she tried.

And I treated her like crap for it.

"We had it out with each other. I said things I can't take back. She pretty much disowned me. And I did the same with her. Trust me when I tell you, she's better off with me gone from her life."

Ame continues to frown. "You don't think she'd want to hear from you?"

"No."

"Oh."

"Oh what?"

Ame flexes her fingers again, then pulls her palm away, leaving a cool spot where her heat just was.

"Just"—she glances up at me, spearing me with emerald, then glances away—"I was wishing I could meet her."

Words pause in my throat as an image comes to my mind. I see it so clearly—my mom making her morning tea, pouring an extra steaming cup, setting it in front of Ame, and the two women I love most in the world bending over the witch's tablet as the redhead explains the indecipherable nature of the witch language.

Mom would love the mystery.

But I destroyed any chance of that reality.

"I'm sorry," is all I can think to say. I am. I'm so fucking sorry.

"No, it's okay. I get it." Ame stares into space again, the way she does when her mind is tumbling down a pathway to try and block her off from the world.

"What are you thinking about?" Even if it's something silly, I want to know.

She jerks her head up, a flush spreading under her already-reddened cheeks, and the way she bites her lip looks almost shamed.

"Nothing important. Are you hungry? There are some burger patties in the freezer, I think. Or we could go out. Local Brew has great cheese fries. But the bar is a big werewolf hangout, so maybe not. What day is it? The marina has Margarita Mondays."

Well, now, I *need* to know. Slowly, like the predator I am, I stalk my little witch, backing her against the dresser and bracketing her with my arms.

"If it's nothing, then you can tell me. Right?"

Ame cringes and mumbles something so low that even my wolf ears can't pick it up.

"Louder, little witch," I coax her.

She sighs. "I was wondering if your mom would like me."

My body freezes, the vulnerability of her statement blasting through me in a frigid tempest.

"What?"

Ame finally meets my eyes, putting all her intoxicating focus on me. "She sounds smart and independent, and you obviously love her. But I usually make people uncomfortable. Sometimes, it's my magic. They're worried I'm going to use it on them. But I also don't make a lot of eye contact. And I lose track of conversations because I'm trying to block out all the weird desires projected at me. After a while, people avoid me. Not you yet, which is nice."

She must see horror on my face and misinterpret where it comes from because she places reassuring palms on my chest.

"It's okay. I don't mind, really. I like spending time alone. Or with animals."

As if to emphasize the witch's point, Lucky struts into the room and weaves around our legs.

Meanwhile, my heart is cracking apart for my little witch.

"Ame," I sputter. "My mother would *adore* you."

She takes her gaze away. "That's sweet of you to say."

She doesn't believe me. What the hell?

"I'm serious." I press in closer until we're chest to chest, her hands smashed between us. "She would probably like you more than me."

The infuriating witch offers a small, brave smile. "I doubt that's true, but thank you for being kind."

I'm not kind. I'm a selfish asshole.

I shove away from her, the dresser rattling with my aggressive movement, and pace around the bare bedroom, my thoughts tangling and tearing. Ame watches my movements with a concerned dip in her brows. As if she can't fathom *why* I'm agitated at her assumption that she's unlikable. She's the most fucking likable person in existence.

She thinks my mom wouldn't love her.

It's impossible. I cannot live in a world where Ame draws that conclusion.

"I'm going to call her."

30

AME

JACK HAS BEEN AGITATED the past half hour, ever since he made his declaration about his mother.

"You don't—" I begin.

He cuts me off with a wave of his hand. "I do. You were right. She should at least know where I am." He stalks to where I'm sitting on the bed, kneeling in front of me. "And she should meet you. I want her to meet you. If she's willing."

Jack settles on the floor of my—ours really, if I think about how he sleeps here every night—bedroom. He pulls out his phone and stares at the blank screen for a stretch.

I want to repeat that he doesn't have to do this, but I keep my mouth shut. He knows, and still, he's going to try.

What happened between the two of them that broke things this much? The few times he has talked about his mother, there was fondness in his voice. He loves his mother. And it sounds like she put her all into raising him. Would a parent do that for a child they didn't love?

My parents only paid attention to me when they wanted to

examine my powers for their experiments. When I had some usefulness in their eyes, I became worthy of affection.

The thought has me self-consciously rubbing the light-red stain on my skin.

Dr. Lim sounds like someone who *cares*. More like Morgana than my mother.

Jack reaches out, twining his fingers with mine before giving a gentle tug.

"I need you to sit on my lap." His voice is strained.

Without hesitation, I slide from my seat and straddle his waist, settling my butt on the cross section of his legs.

"Like this?"

His dark eyes gaze down at me. "Wrap your arms around me."

I do as he directed, embracing his torso and resting my head on his shoulder. Jack clamps an arm around my back, locking me against him, and then I hear the tapping of him dialing a number.

"Here we go," he mutters.

I squeeze him a touch tighter and feel the press of his lips on the top of my head. Though he holds the phone to his ear, the ringing is audible.

One ring.

Two rings.

Jack tenses more with each one.

After the third ring, the line connects.

"Hello?"

If I thought Jack was rigid before, it's nothing compared to this. He goes so stiff that I suspect his voice box has jammed up.

"Hello?" the feminine voice repeats with a touch of annoyance, no doubt believing a telemarketer dialed her number.

Jack clears his throat with a harsh cough. He lets out a choked breath, and I wonder if he'll be able to manage words.

Finally, he does.

"Hi, Mom."

The other end of the line is silent for a stretch, and I feel Jack's heart rate pick up where my cheek presses against his chest.

"Mom?" His voice is brittle, as if about to break.

I think the wolf in my arms is on the verge of shattering if something in this interaction goes wrong.

"Jack."

There's so much feeling in that single word that it seeps through the phone, and my magic soaks it in and deciphers it, even from a distance.

Find him.

Hold him close.

Dr. Lim did not give up on her son.

"Yeah. It's me. I know—"

"Where are you?" she cuts him off. "Right now. Tell me *right now*."

"Uh, in Georgia." Jack's answer is guttural, lower than normal, and he stutters, "A-a town called Folk Haven."

"Are you safe?" She says each word with precision, as if she thinks there's a limit to the amount she'll be allowed to speak.

"Yeah, Mom." His fingers clutch my back, then ease. "Very safe."

"Stay there. I will come on the next plane."

"I—"

"You do not leave. You *do not leave*."

There's a gasp, a choppy sob, then the sound of clattering on the other end of the line. I wonder what she's doing. Maybe searching for a pen? Or pulling out a laptop to book a plane ticket?

If this situation wasn't so heartbreaking, I might smile at the devotion she's displayed in a few short sentences.

Jack deserves that kind of love.

"Tell me your address. Jack. Jack. Oh God, *Jack*." There's

another sob as she repeats his name like a promise. Like a prayer.

But Jack doesn't respond.

I loosen my arms and lean back to find out why he's not talking to his crying mother. His face is blank.

The catatonic state worries me, and that's the only reason I tug on my power. I sift through his constant thrum of desire to pull out the individual pieces.

Does he want to hang up? Does he long for this conversation to end?

Or is it something else?

Pulling in a deep breath, I allow his desire to flow into me, acting as an empty vessel to hold it all for him, and I listen to everything he wants most.

Hug her.

Hug her.

Hug her.

Hug her.

Hug her.

The sentiment is simple but powerful. My chest aches like my ribs broke with his utter craving to travel across thousands of miles to hold his mom. To comfort her as she cries. Cries about him. About the pain of their separation.

When I drag my power back, I don't think Jack realizes I magically dissected him. He's still frozen by his inability to do the one thing he wants.

Time for me to step up and help the woman he loves most in the world. I slip the phone from his grasp and put it on speaker.

"Hello, Dr. Lim. My name is Amethyst Shelly. Jack has been staying in my house." I stroke my hand down his chest. "I'm his friend."

"Girlfriend," he mutters. The first coherent word he's managed in the last few minutes.

"Okay." I don't let the weight of that word derail me as I leave my hand just below his collarbone, rubbing soothing circles. "He was in a bad situation for a while, but he's out of it now. He's safe. And"—I reach up to give a gentle tug on the lobe of his ear—"he's doing much better. Barely growls at all anymore. He's quiet right now, but I know he wants to see you. If you text us your flight arrival times, we can come pick you up at the airport. I'd suggest flying into Atlanta, Georgia, or Greenville, South Carolina. Charlotte, North Carolina, would also work. Whichever is best for you. And you are welcome to stay in my home."

With Jack always sleeping in my bed, we have a guest room ready to go.

"Amethyst. Hello." Emotion is still thick in her voice, but she's pulled out that cold determination again. "Please tell me your phone number. And address." Despite the *please*, the words are a demand.

Somehow, Jack misinterpreted his relationship with his mother. This is not a woman who was glad to see the back of him.

I'm happy he was wrong.

I provide all the information she asks for, and I promise to keep my phone on and charged and tell her I will make sure Jack keeps his on and charged too. She asks if he's safe again, and he manages to assure her that he is.

"You'll tell me everything when I get there." That is not a request.

"I will," he promises.

She doesn't say good-bye. She only says, once again, "Do *not* leave."

The call ends.

Jack looks shell-shocked as he stares at the phone in my hand. I don't push him to speak, letting him come to terms with this reaction that was different than what he expected.

I try to imagine myself as Dr. Lim. What she might need in this situation. I'd want every bit of proof that Jack was okay.

I have an idea, but when I move to get up, Jack clutches me close.

"Don't go," he mutters.

In this moment, he sounds just like his mother. The similarity has me smiling.

"I'm coming right back. I promise."

Reluctantly, he loosens his hold, and I leverage myself out of his lap.

Lucky lies on the window seat and doesn't seem to mind when I scoop her up. I return to Jack's side and settle sideways in his lap.

"Take a picture of the three of us and send it to your mom. That way, she'll know you're okay. And what we look like. And that we have a cat."

"We have a cat?" he repeats slowly.

"She might be *my* familiar, but I think she likes you more. She's always following you around, meowing. It's not fair, but I'm dealing." I lean into his chest, making sure my face and Lucky's are close to his. "Go on," I urge him. "You don't have to smile. But also, please don't make it look like I'm holding you hostage."

Jack snorts, and the sound of his amusement eases a touch of my worry. He extends his long arm, and I stare at the camera and try for a smile that doesn't look forced. All I need to do is think of Jack to make my joy real.

My eyes flick up to him, finding his dark gaze on me, and I feel the muscles in my cheeks relax into a naturally pleased expression.

But when I glance back at the camera, he's already lowering his arm.

"Wait. I don't think I was looking."

But he swipes on the screen until he brings up the image,

tilting his phone so I can see. Neither of us is looking at the camera; we're staring at each other, smiling, as I hold up a floppy black cat. She yowls now, wanting to get down.

"I'll send this," Jack murmurs.

I watch him select his mother's contact, and he texts her the picture along with a simple message.

I'm safe. This is Amethyst. She makes me happy.

Warmth trickles through my body.

"You didn't mention Lucky," I point out.

Jack sighs, then leans down to press a kiss just below my ear. After that affectionate gesture, he sends his mom another text.

The cat is Lucky. She's our cat.

"Oh, good. Lucky will be glad you've finally accepted that." I set the cat on the ground, and she immediately uses Jack as a rubbing post.

He drops his phone and wraps his arms tight around me.

"My mom is coming to Folk Haven." He says this as if needing to convince himself of the fact.

"She's going to like it here."

"You think?"

"Of course. You're here. This will probably be her favorite place in the world."

That's becoming the reason that it's mine.

31

—————

JACK

LOOKING suspicious at an airport is never a good thing, but I can't stop pacing.

At least the drug-sniffing dogs know better than to approach me. They can scent the wolf on me, and they know I'm not a predator to be messed with.

"Do you want some beef jerky?" Ame lays her hand on the floppy cloth bag hanging off her shoulder, and despite the supposed vacuum seal on the bag, I can smell the dried meat.

But in a rare showing, the idea of any kind of food turns my stomach.

"No, thank you."

She's almost here. I have to keep reminding myself of that fact, worried it will change if I don't repeat it in my mind enough times while terrified of the truth at the same time.

Mom is coming to see me.

I never thought she'd want to see me again. Shame and guilt tear at my stomach when I think of how I chose strangers over her just because they could change into wolves, like me.

How, for even a second, did I let myself believe that made them more important in my life than my mother?

She shouldn't want to see me again. I don't deserve her love.

As I make an abrupt turn, my eyes catch on Ame. The witch stares up at the Arrivals board even though we saw the flight we're waiting for landed twenty minutes ago. The green glow of the letters reflects off her pale skin, and she pulls her cardigan tighter around her shoulders, as if catching a chill.

I don't deserve her love either. But the gods will have to pry her out of my cold, dead claws.

I stalk across the tiled floor until I loom behind her. Wrapping my arms around Ame's shoulders, I pull my little witch into my chest and offer her all the warmth of my body. Her hand clutches my forearm, and I realize she's nervous too. Just in her quiet Ame way.

"She's going to love you." I make the promise in between kisses to the shell of her ear.

Ame leans back against me. "I hope so."

With my better than average hearing, I pick up on a choked gasp in a pitch I recognize. Letting go of Ame, I turn and meet a set of familiar dark eyes across the baggage claim area. My mother stares at me like she's seeing a ghost.

I've never seen a ghost even though I'm a werewolf, but that's beside the point.

Next I know, Dr. Anna Lim is sprinting across the room, purse slapping against her side, sneakers squeaking on the floor.

Mom was never much for physical affection. She showed her love by doing things for me. Constantly making sacrifices and working hard so I could live a safe, happy life. She might have clasped my shoulder when she was proud or patted my hand when I did something to make her happy. I lived for those moments.

The last time she hugged me was at my college graduation. And that embrace was nothing like this.

Now, she slams into me, seizing me against her chest as her body heaves with sobs.

"My son. My Jack. I thought I'd lost you. Where did you go? I thought I'd never see you again. You're here, you're here, you're here—"

"Mom, please," I beg, clutching her tight, but restraining my strength so I don't crush her ribs. I'm at a loss for how to deal with this version of the iron-willed woman I grew up with. "Please calm down. You'll make yourself sick."

But she doesn't listen to me, only hugs me harder. So, I gather her close until she's on her tiptoes, and I breathe in the scent of citrus and paper and childhood.

"It's okay," I murmur over and over, hoping the sentiment will make it through and she'll believe me.

Around us, people mill about, more concerned with their own problems and apparently used to emotional reunions at airports.

Eventually, my mother calms enough to breathe at a normal rate and loosens her hold on me. She leans back, getting a good look at my face. Her fingers trace over my cheeks, her eyes flicking to every corner, as if needing to make sure I'm not some poorly made copy of her son.

"I thought you'd still be mad at me," I mumble.

She shakes her head. "What we said to each other—it doesn't matter. It's forgotten."

While I won't be forgetting the ungrateful words I yelled at my mother, no matter how much time passes, I still relax. Enough to remember who's at my side.

"Mom, this is Ame." Stretching out my arm, I clasp my witch's wrist and tug her toward us. "She's the one who saved me."

"Oh, no." Ame holds her hands up, eyes wide. "That's a misrepresentation. I didn't—"

"She spent years looking for a way to free me from a curse," I say over the humble evasion. "No one else believed her, but she kept going. I'd still be trapped if it wasn't for her. Actually"—I snake my hand into Ame's hair and cradle the back of her neck, guiding her eyes to mine—"if Ame hadn't found me and taken me in, I'd be dead."

My mother doesn't hug Ame the way she did me, but she scoops up the little witch's hand and cradles it between both of hers.

"Thank you." She presses Ame's knuckles to her forehead. "You brought my son back to me."

Ame's eyes go wide as she stares at the woman. "I, uh ... you're welcome."

Just when my chest feels too full to breathe, I glance over my mother's shoulder.

I recognize a face hovering in the crowd. My body jerks with the force of pain, love, and guilt.

"Niko?"

My childhood best friend approaches us at a reasonable pace, pulling two rolling suitcases. The normally jovial guy wears a harsh frown as his narrow gaze takes in every inch of me. When he reaches my side, he hits me with the hardest question possible.

"What took you so long to call? Gods-damn it, Jack. We thought you were *dead*."

Of course they did. I disappeared off the grid. But I've been back for a few weeks now and still never reached out.

"I ..." Shame lodges in my throat, and I have to clear it before I keep speaking. "I figured you all wouldn't want to hear from me."

My mom wasn't the only one I had it out with last time we talked. Niko tried to warn me about the pack. Said Finnick was demanding too much from me. More than any werewolf should. But I was desperate to belong. To be a part of a group of mythics like me. I was willing to sign on for anything.

Finnick knew that and used my desperate loneliness against me.

Niko was the only one who really had my back.

He was always more than a friend. He was like my brother. And I cast him aside like he was nothing.

"Asshole," he hisses.

Then, he lets go of the suitcases and wraps me in a crushing hug. The kappa might look skinny, but he's got a death grip on him. I return the embrace in equal measure.

"I am," I mutter into my friend's shoulder. "I'm an asshole."

"We have *one* fight, and you think I'm done with your furry ass?" His voice sounds thick, as if he's holding back tears.

For a moment, I'm content. My mate, my mother, and my best friend are all within arm's reach, all happy to be here. No one I love hates me and everything is right in the world.

But the happy reunion gets catapulted to the back of my mind when a memorable scent of peaches and wolf teases my nose. Jerking my head up, I stare across the room, meeting another gaze I know too well. Only this stare doesn't belong to someone I missed.

Veronica.

And the wolf isn't alone.

The San Francisco pack is here.

Looks like I'm about to commit mass murder.

32

JACK

"Some things changed while you were gone," Niko announces.

Our odd group—a witch, a kappa, and too many were-wolves—is gathered around a cluster of public picnic tables beside Lake Galen. The water seems too calm when compared to the roiling inside me. I didn't want the wolves here, in this town, where Ame lives. Where I live and plan to stay. The San Francisco pack has brought their taint to what is supposed to be a safe place.

But Niko asked me to trust him. Asked me to give Veronica a chance to speak in a safer place than a crowded airport.

I agreed because I owed Niko. And because Finnick wasn't with them.

When I asked Ame to drive my mom to the library, both women gave me an *are you serious* look. Now, Ame is sitting at my side on the sun-warmed bench, and my mother is waiting in the front seat of the car, reading a book and occasionally glancing up to make sure I haven't disappeared. Mom said she'd leave the mythical creature politics to us.

"Obviously." I glare at Veronica.

She's Finnick's girlfriend—though not his mate from last I knew them. The wolf has a blonde boho, white-girl vibe that makes you wonder if her job is selling handmade seashell necklaces out of her VW van parked beside a beach.

But I've seen her hunt, blood dripping from her mouth after taking down a deer.

If she's here to plead forgiveness for Finnick's actions, she's shit out of luck. The pack leader won't even earn forgiveness when his torn-out throat is in the palm of my hand.

And she doesn't get a pass either. Veronica was the one who brought me into the pack. She saw me on campus and sniffed out what I was right away. She was the first one who painted rosy dreams of a found family of mythics like me. She told me I could learn all about my kind. Be a part of something bigger than myself.

But I guess she was the honey in the trap.

I'm not about to fall for that a second time. I wrap a tight arm around Ame, keeping my witch close to my side. I'd rather not have her at this meeting at all, but she insisted, and I can't seem to say no to her. Not because of her magic.

Because I love her and I'm a wolf-shaped doormat.

Gods, I love the way her feet feel while trampling my back.

"Finnick is dead," Niko says, no more preamble.

I huff in shock, then snarl low in the back of my throat as fury slices through my body.

Because I wasn't the one who got to end his miserable existence.

"What happened?"

If they tell me that manipulative fucker had an easy death, I'm going to need a whole day's worth of running in the woods to get the anger out.

"I killed him." Veronica steps forward, wearing a hard expression that sits oddly on her pretty face.

"Lovers' spat?" I mock. *She stole my revenge from me.*

"No." Her pert nose wrinkles. "I found out what he did to you."

That's not what I was expecting. I grind my teeth together.

Trap. This is another fucking trap.

"We didn't know his plans," she says. "All of us thought you were going to join."

She tilts her head toward another table, farther away but still within earshot, where the rest of the San Francisco pack lingers. The group is quiet, even as they watch us, expressions varying from curiosity to hope to wariness. Eight members now that their alpha is gone.

"Then, Finnick showed up after a full moon run and claimed you decided to skip town. That there was another pack you wanted to join. That you said fuck us and good riddance."

"That piece of shit sold me to a sorcerer," I snarl, furious that he thought he could so easily blot me off the face of the earth.

He almost did.

Veronica nods. "We found that out eventually. Took some doing, but I got him drunk enough one night that he let it slip."

"And you what?" I sneer. "Broke his neck and sent him on a quick and peaceful trip to the afterlife?"

She slams her fists, knuckles first, on the tabletop and glares straight into my eyes. "I locked him in a magicked cage, like he did you. I filled his food with wolfsbane. I made him suffer until I got every last detail out of him. Then, I stabbed him in the gut until his pathetic heart stopped beating." Her eyes sparkle, cheeks flushed, as rage radiates off her like the rays of the sun.

But not only rage. There's also a compelling sort of power. Finnick had it. So does Baron.

Guess I know who the new San Francisco alpha is.

"My parents were killed by a sorcerer. At least, I *hope* they're dead," Veronica hisses. "I only got away because they hid me. I never saw them again. Anyone who deals with those twisted fucking magic leeches deserves what's coming to them." She straightens and wipes her palms on her jeans like they're dirty. "We've been working with Niko and your mother these past six years to find you. But Finnick didn't have much to give us. And the sorcerer disappeared."

I look to my best friend, and he gives a nod, even as his eyes stay locked on Veronica.

There's something in his stare I don't want to think about right now.

I clear my throat. "Well, here I am. You found me. Now, you can go home."

Veronica scoffs. "Not likely. There's still that evil fuck to find." She crosses her arms over her chest. "I know you're going after him. Consider us your backup."

"Like I'd ever trust your pack at my back."

Her face turns to granite, but she gives a short nod. "I understand why you feel that way. However, it doesn't change things. No matter that Finnick agreed to the deal, that sorcerer stole one of *my* pack members. This fight is mine too."

The wolf straightens her shoulders, and only now do I realize the sheer amount of power she emanates. Even more than Finnick did. On par with the Folk Haven pack leader. I wonder how Finnick ever claimed the leading role in the first place.

Maybe he dealt with the sorcerer in other ways too.

"I and my wolves are willing to undergo measures to prove our trustworthiness to you," Veronica announces like she's giving me an official gift.

I snort. "My measures are, leave me the fuck alone."

Ame shifts beside me, and I adjust my arms so she's more comfortable. My witch lays her tablet on the table, and I wonder if she's getting bored with this conversation. I know I'm ready to be done with it.

I promised Niko I would hear them out.

Veronica holds my eyes across the table. "If I'd known what he'd planned, I never would have let him go through with it. I would have thrown down on the spot. You belonged with our pack. I *liked* you, Jack."

Veronica puts extra emphasis on *liked*, as if she's trying to convince me with the force of that word. From the corner of my eye, I swear I see Niko flinch.

Ame stiffens at my side, and the tensing of her body translates into mine, although I don't know what's suddenly stressed her out.

My witch leans over the table, waving a quick hand in front of Veronica's face. "Please stop thinking those thoughts that you're thinking right now."

Veronica jerks her head back and blinks at my witch. "What?"

I also stare at Ame, noticing the grimace twisting her mouth.

"I can hear strong desire. You're being very specific with *how* you like Jack. I never thought I was a jealous person, but I'm having to reevaluate. Please try to rein in your attraction to Jack. Maybe save it for a later time when you're alone with your thoughts." Ame delivers this shocking revelation with an almost-apologetic voice.

Barely acknowledging that Veronica might have or had a crush on me, I home in on the witch at my side. She seems intent on scrolling through documents on her device rather than continuing with this direction this conversation has taken.

"You're jealous?" I purr the question, loving the possessive implication of her feelings.

Ame's green eyes meet my probing ones. "Sorry."

"Don't be sorry."

She worries her lip. "I don't want to be possessive of you. You're a free man."

"No"—I lean in closer, letting my voice drop deeper—"I'm not. I'm yours. You own me."

That kicks her eyebrows up. "I don't *own* you. You don't have to stay with me."

You're not getting rid of me, little witch.

"Do you want me to leave?" I ask anyway.

"Well, no. But I won't keep you if you want to go."

"Well, I never want to go. So, it looks like we're good."

"Great. Really sweet. Can we get back to the matter at hand?" Veronica snaps the question, a scowl on her face as she observes us.

Looks like Ame isn't the only one experiencing jealousy. But my witch is the only one with claim to me. Veronica has no right.

"The matter at hand is the same," I say. "I don't want—or need—your help. Unless you know where the sorcerer is?"

"I don't," Veronica admits. "But a pack hunting for one man has a greater chance of finding him than a lone wolf."

"And a witch," Ame adds, raising her hand briefly. "What are your pack members' names?" she asks, and I let her curiosity interrupt the back-and-forth, so I can take a moment to solidify my cool disdain.

Veronica flicks her eyes between us, then surprises me by immediately listing off each of the wolves. "Jill, Roberto, Hazel, Kelly, Liam, Monroe, Zora, Reese."

I recognize every name, except for the last two, who I assume are new members since I last ran with the pack. But even though I can match the other six names to their faces, it doesn't mean I *know* them, much less trust them. Finnick kept me separate, claiming we'd interact all the time when I was part of the pack.

Which, of course, never happened.

Ame's freckled fingers guide a stylus over her screen. I realize the folder she has open is her Revenge Plan, and she's started a new document. At the top, she's written *Potential Allies/Helpers*. Beneath the title, she's listed out all of the werewolves Veronica just named.

"Ame." I try to gentle my voice, even as I speak through gritted teeth.

"Yes?" she asks so innocently that my fucking heart melts and I want everyone to disappear so I can curl around her and kiss the hell out of her.

"We're not doing this." I tap the title of her page.

"But look, I wrote *potential*. We don't know what we're getting into. This might be an *Ocean's Eleven* situation."

"What do you mean?"

She meets my eyes in the way she rarely does with others. The undivided attention always has me feeling special. "Sorcerers want power. I don't think he's going to be living in some secluded shack with no defenses. He's going to use his power to get more, and he'll guard what he has. We might need more than you and me."

"And me," Niko says.

"And Niko," Ame repeats. She opens another document, titled *Allies/Helpers*, and adds *Niko Saito* under a short list of other mythics.

Gods-damn it. I'm about to get hard in the middle of this meeting from her Revenge Plan.

"You mentioned undergoing measures to prove you all are trustworthy," Ame continues in the voice of someone conducting an interview. "Did you have anything in particular in mind?"

Veronica pinches her lips together, probably at having to negotiate through Ame instead of working this out with me. I enjoy the idea of this pissing the wolf off. I cross my arms over my chest, and allow Ame to take the lead. I'll step in before she makes any binding promises.

"Blood oaths. All of the members are willing to undergo them, swearing to tell you the truth about Finnick. Which none of us knew."

Ame gives a small nod and makes a note but doesn't say anything encouraging. Still, even I have to admit that's a big deal. If they went against the oath, they'd experience excruciating pain. Possibly death. Blood oaths are no joke.

"Would you swear never to betray Jack?" Ame asks.

Veronica doesn't hesitate. She shakes her head. "I won't ask my wolves to bind themselves that way to anyone. Not even me. Jack might be a decent guy now, but if he decides to go on a mass murder spree one day, no way will I bind myself to that."

The response earns her a touch of grudging respect from me.

"Understandable," Ame murmurs, writing down more notes. "We will consider your offer of help. Is there anything else you'd like to add?" She hovers her electronic pen over the screen.

Veronica sucks in a deep breath and shoves up from the table, circling around to a stop at my side. Before anyone can make a move, she digs her blunt fingernail into the flesh of her forearm, dragging downward with enough force to leave a ragged gash, weeping blood. She presses her palm into the crimson liquid and grasps my wrist.

"I swear on my blood to always tell you the truth." Power zings from her to me. "I did not know what Finnick was planning. I would have killed him before he could sell you. I killed Finnick *because* he had sold you. The pack failed you. I failed you. We only want a chance to right some of the past wrongs, though we know there is no way to undo what happened. There will never be a day in my life I do not feel guilty over what was done to you."

Every word is the truth—I can't deny that.

The wound on her arm has already started to heal as she steps back from me—faster than my injuries seal up, and I wonder about that. *Do shifters heal slower? Does being a part of the pack help?*

Gods, I hate that I still want something from other wolves. That they know more than me.

Veronica turns her attention to Ame. "We'll stay in town at least until this is done. Let me know if you get a lead on the sorcerer, and we'll be at your back."

Then, the wolf strides away from us, done arguing her case. She waves at her pack, and the group gets up to follow her to their rented van. A few throw looks my way.

All of them are tinged in guilt.

My thoughts sit in a muddle. If I believe what she just said —which it's kind of impossible not to after that blood-vow display—then the betrayal really only was Finnick. The San Francisco pack didn't sell me out.

What does that mean, going forward?

I guess there's a smaller handful of people I have reason to be pissed at.

Still, the resentment remains.

Looking for any kind of distraction from my thoughts, I glance down at Ame's hand as she writes a note next to Veronica's name.

Willing to get bloody.

Fuck. I love this witch.

33

JACK

"You trust this witch?"

This isn't the first time I've asked Ame the question, but I want her to really think about her response. Ame is too free with her trust.

Take me, for example. I'm a selfish piece of shit, like all werewolves, who refuses to leave her life even though she'd probably be safer without me.

She needs to be more discerning about who she spends time with.

"I used to babysit Calli. She's, like, one of my only friends," Ame says by way of response.

And now, I feel like an even bigger asshole for trying to make Ame doubt one of the few people she's close with.

I blame the San Francisco pack. After our tense chat two days ago, they booked up an entire B & B, and now, Folk Haven feels entirely too full.

Yesterday, we ran into Veronica at Coffee & Claws, where the wolf was buying ten pumpkin spice lattes. Apparently, the pack loves the stuff. And my best friend, Niko, does, too, because he was there with the blonde. He also opted to stay in the B & B instead of the library.

It's pretty obvious the kappa has a crush, and I don't know how to feel about it. I don't know how to feel about *any* of this shit.

Now, Ame and I sit next to each other at a picnic table near a peach orchard in South Carolina. Calliopia Starfell grew up in Maine with Ame, but she attends college in North Carolina. Ame worked out the logistics of the meeting while I went on a brooding run through the woods after getting my mom settled in the library with a stack of books in a language she'd never seen before—aka her favorite kind.

"There she is." Ame stands and raises her hand as a beat-up station wagon pulls into the dirt parking lot, kicking up dust with its back wheels. As we wait for the witch to climb out of her car, Ame settles back beside me and takes my hand in hers. "She might not be able to help."

"I know."

I think this whole meetup is a waste of time, but Ame put it in her Revenge Plan, so how could I deny her?

She tilts her chin my way. "Kiss?"

She's started doing this lately. Randomly asking for a kiss, no matter that I've told her repeatedly that she can grab my face and lay one on me at any time of day in any situation and I will immediately be on board.

But she insists on asking, and the one-worded question has started making me hard because, fuck, if I don't love how she cares about me.

With one hand cradling the back of her head, the loose weave of her braid pressing into my palm, I lean in and give my little witch a chaste kiss. Well, chaste for me because I only use a hint of tongue instead of sucking on hers until she's moaning and writhing.

When I lift my head, I spot movement from the corner of my eye.

The witch approaches, wearing an orange shirt that reads *Spooky Bitch.* She's taller than Ame, though not as tall as Morgana, with pale skin and purple-painted nails. Brown hair with natural golden highlights falls in a wavy mass around her face, brushing the top of her shoulders, which lead to strong arms. The witch has a few curves but walks with more strength than sensuality.

Powerful. The word blares in my mind.

But I also get the sense she's not trying to exude that power. She merely exists that way.

And when Calli grins at my witch, I detect nothing but genuine joy.

"Ame! I can't believe we waited *years* to meet up! What took us so long?" Calli comes around to give Ame a hearty hug before settling across from us at the table.

My witch smiles and shrugs. "Life. I didn't realize that much time had passed."

Calli nods. "You were in town for my eighteenth, right? Now, I don't have to sneak into bars anymore." She winks, then turns her curious attention my way, expression unguarded.

This witch hasn't experienced much pain in her life. She'd be more cautious if she had.

"Sorry. Hi!" She gives me a wave. "I'm Calliopia. Friends call me Calli."

"Jack." My short answer seems aggressive in the face of her enthusiasm. I add, "Nice to meet you."

Her nose wrinkles with a smile. She's a cute girl. Round cheeks and long lashes. Still doesn't do anything for me.

"Happy to meet you, Jack. Ame said you were hoping to find someone? I'm your gal. At least, I'll try to be. My aunt says I'm plenty powerful, but I still need certain assists to make a spell work. Why don't you give me the rundown?"

The rundown. How do I tell a stranger about the horror of my life the past few years without this turning into a *poor Jack* sob story?

When I hesitate, Ame sets her hand on my knee, drawing my attention to her.

"Would you like me to explain?" She rifles in the bag beside her, coming up with her tablet. "I made a list of the relevant details."

Mouth shut tight, I nod. Ame slides her finger across the glass screen, and I spy the title at the top of a document.

What Happened to Jack.

The straight-to-the-point words have me fighting a smile.

In a no-nonsense tone, Ame tells Cali about the pack that betrayed me—although maybe they didn't, and it was just that Finnick fucker—the transformation to feline, the years of captivity, the escape. Ame finishes the story with how she found me—aka one of the best days of my life—and the eventual discovery of the spell to change me back.

"Oh goddess! *You* were the one she wanted that transformation spell for? Hell, I'm sorry I couldn't help there. Finding things like that—a general item or piece of information you're interested in—I can't do it. Not yet anyway. My aunt says with years of study and practice, I could get better. But, fuck, I'm sorry you had to go through all that." Her mouth twists with anger, and she pounds her fist on the old wood of the table. "Sorcerers are the ultimate douche bags of the universe." Her anger morphs to a grimace. "But ... crap ... I don't know if I can help you find the guy. Unless"—Calli's expression turns hopeful—"do you have something of his? Even if it's small. That's what you want, right? For me to help you find that twatwaffle?"

"Yeah," I mutter. Any other time, I'd chuckle at her colorful insults. But she pointed out why I didn't get my hopes up about this plan. I'd barely gotten away from him with my skin intact.

Hadn't paused to grab souvenirs on my way out. "I don't have anything."

Calli's face falls, and she spreads her palms flat on the table, staring at the backs of her hands, going quiet in thought.

"I have an idea." Ame claims our attention with those words, and I find her green eyes on me, her stare unwavering, even as her teeth worry her lip. "You can say no to this. You can say no to anything."

My heart clenches at the sentiment lingering under her words. The reminder of my freedom. That I'm in control of my life now.

"I know," I murmur. "What's your idea?"

She faces Calliopia. "The sorcerer thought of Jack as his. As a pet and also as a tool. Wrong though it was, he owned Jack."

My body vibrates with rage at the description, but I'm not mad at Ame. Just at the truth in her words.

Calli's eyebrows pop up. "You're suggesting ..."

Ame nods. "Use Jack to find the sorcerer. Is that possible?"

Fuck. The genius of the idea rocks me.

When I glance at Calli, I spy a thoughtful expression on her face that slowly transforms into hope. I'm hit with a twisted sense of triumph.

That asshole's arrogance is going to ruin him.

I'm coming for you, dead man.

34

AME

"Fits perfectly. Just like I said it would." Esme, a harpy seamstress and our former landlady, grins as I descend the stairs.

"I didn't realize you were making me a *gown*." I run my hands over the silky green material that drapes to the floor. A lacy ivy pattern covers the tight-fitting bodice and snakes over my shoulders, only to plunge low in the back.

Much sexier than anything I normally wear, but perfect for a ball we're attending tonight.

Folk Haven's annual Halloween ball.

"You'll fit right in. I'm booked months in advance for this thing. You're lucky Morgana planned ahead."

Honestly, I forgot about the Halloween Ball. We hadn't gone last year, what with us being in the middle of moving into this house. And since it's a mythics-only event, there were no helpful fliers posted around town to remind me. Everything passes by word of mouth, I guess, and despite being holed up in this library most of the time, Morgana tries to keep her fingers on the Folk Haven pulse.

In her mind, us going to this ball will build bridges. Get more patrons. Keep her dream of running a library alive.

No way I could back out after hearing that. If my sister needs me to pretty up and make friends, I'll do my best. Preferably, with Jack at my side, his white noise of desire will help me keep track of conversations and meet eyes rather than hear about the odd cravings townsfolk have.

I've already picked up how Esme wants her dragon mate to burn off her dress later.

To keep from hearing more, I focus on how Lucky bats around a fake mouse Jack's mom brought her.

Sadly, the *no humans unless they're mates* rule means Dr. Lim is not allowed to attend the event. Not that the woman seems too broken up about it. She leans against the doorway, holding a stack of grimoires she can't possibly read, but still seems fascinated by.

"Are you sure you're okay here on your own?" I ask her.

She nods, attention already tracking back to the shelves. "I want to read some more before I have to pack."

Want to read them all.

The stray desire has me smiling and reminds me of Morgana. My sister is able to shield her desires from me, but I bet if she couldn't, hers would be similar to Dr. Lim's.

Now that the woman knows Jack is safe, she's booked a flight back to San Francisco, still in the middle of a teaching semester. But with the way she was asking questions about the linguistics program at Ramla University, I get the feeling Folk Haven will soon have a new resident.

"I'm not sure anyone in town has seen me without a layer of dust this past year," Morgana says as she appears at the top of the stairs.

She looks dangerously curvy in her black gown. The lace

sleeves have an intricate spiderweb design—perfect for the holiday.

She's a Samhain goddess, ready to curry favor among the locals. I think she's still worried The Council will take the deed to the house back from her.

I'd never let that happen.

And with a werewolf on my side, I might be able to manage an element of protection.

Said werewolf is missing. He drove to the nearest men's apparel store to find something suitable for the evening.

I'd told him he didn't have to go, getting the sense Jack would rather not be in crowded spaces. But he'd said if I was going, then so was he.

"You look gorgeous," Esme announces, scooping up her sparkly gold skirts as she heads toward the door. "And y'all were my last stop. Time to collect my man and head over. I'm gonna get drunk on pumpkin punch and town drama." The harpy throws a wicked grin over her shoulder. "See you there!"

I'm not sure I want to do either of those things, but I am hoping this event will distract me from what else is occurring tonight.

Calli is casting her seeking spell.

The power of Samhain—similar to yet more potent than the full moon—buzzes in the air like static electricity, waiting for a chance to shock. The young witch plans to use the boost to supercharge her spell and hopefully get us something we can use. Even narrowing down the search area would be helpful.

But there's nothing to do now but wait for her to call, so why not go to the Halloween Ball?

After feeding Lucky—and giving her more treats than Zara would probably recommend—I end up driving Morgana's car as she reads off the handwritten directions Esme gave her along with the gowns. Even if we had an address, electronic navigation never works well in town limits.

I texted a picture of the directions to Jack, and he told me he'd meet us there.

When I make the last turn onto a dirt road, tree stumps with thick, waxy candles sit along the edges, spaced evenly and guiding new arrivals to the final destination. Trees crowd in on either side, so close that I wonder if their leaves are at risk of catching on fire. I expect the event coordinators have some Of the Flame mythics on hand just in case, although I've heard their kind are rare in Folk Haven. But there should be a phoenix or two. Maybe a salamander, which Morgana claims is *not* merely a tiny lizard that eats fire. They're a mythics we— and I quote—*should not fuck with*, if her books are to be believed.

Still, I'd like to meet one if I get the chance.

We come to a crowd of cars, and I park us in the first free spot.

"Good thing I didn't wear heels," I say, stepping onto the soft grass.

"Speak for yourself," Morgana mutters, wobbling in her stilettos.

When she dresses up, she dresses *up*. My sister enjoys reading epic fantasy novels, and I think the grand balls were some of her favorite scenes. She has a longing in her for elegance. No doubt that was part of the appeal of the old yet beautiful Victorian house that's now our library.

After spending most days in sweats, she deserves a chance to feel gorgeous and sophisticated.

Luckily, there's a stone path just past the parking area that leads to a lakeside pavilion. This last day in October means the water is cold, but the night is pleasantly mild. Still, I bet this area could easily be spelled for temperature control the way it seems to be magicked to repel bugs.

Or maybe the Halloween decorations are drawing a larger than usual number of bats who have decimated the insect population. The venue is strategically lit with torches and candelabras, the corners draped with black gauze. An eerie mist swirls about the feet of the mythics dancing to a live band playing a hauntingly lovely tune. Drinks of different odd colors wait on floating trays around the edges of the space.

Spooky and playful and enchanting.

Normally, I'm not one for social outings—lots of desires trying to creep into my mind all at once—but I'm suddenly regretting missing last year's ball.

Did it look the same as this, or do they change the decorations every year?

The moment we step into the pavilion, multiple sets of eyes turn our way. I glance down at my dress to make sure I didn't tear Esme's hard work at some point, revealing my hot-pink boy shorts. They're my least favorite pair of underwear, but tomorrow is laundry day, so I had few other options.

"Guess we're the newbies on display," Morgana mutters under her breath.

The eyes on me send desires brushing against my magical senses.

Find a hottie to go home with.

Trip the hateful shrew who has the same dress.

Make him notice me.

Show her I don't care.

Convince them to leave town.

That last one seems to be directed at us, but I'm not sure whose desire it is. Maybe there's more than one mythic who doesn't like the witches living in Of the Wing territory.

"Look." Morgana tilts her chin. "There's Selena and some of the coven. Let's go make friends."

Ah, yes. The Folk Haven coven. The group of witches we've yet to receive an invite to join, even after living here for a year.

"We're both bad at making friends," I point out.

Morgana gets frustrated with people easily, and I go too quiet as I try not to listen to how they want to be spanked with a frozen pizza.

Don't ask.

"We'll get it right one of these days as long as we keep trying."

She guides me toward the beautifully adorned group of women. Each gown I spy is more impressive than the last.

I wonder, *Is this night a competition?*

Intimidate them.

Look the best.

The most beautiful ...

Leave them awed.

Sounds like it might be.

"Selena," Morgana greets the witch council member first.

The woman nods her head in acknowledgment, the candle-light flickering off her dark skin, steel-colored hair, and gold jewelry.

Selena introduces us to the witches gathered around her. I remember none of the names as I count the number of drinks on the floating trays to keep my mind away from my magical observations. Jack has been in my life for less than a month, but in that short time, I've gotten used to being around him and how his desire for me drowns out all others'.

I want him here, so I can breathe.

"And when is this funny little library going to be open to the public?"

I catch the question as a witch with hair the same shade as mine and skin just as pale smirks. The woman doesn't have my reddened skin though.

"The library is open," Morgana says, keeping her smile mild. "Has been for five months now. You're free to visit whenever you'd like. And if you call ahead about your topic of study, I'll pull relevant texts for you."

As my sister deals with the politics of witches and this strange double-talk, where she pretends they aren't actively avoiding the library, I decide I'm free to wander away. I'd probably ruin the charade of pleasantries by saying the wrong thing.

Like asking why the red-haired witch wishes she could shove Selena into Lake Galen.

Skirting the edge of the dance floor, I circle the space and admire the different gowns and costumes, all sparkling under the glow of candles.

Eventually, I reach the food table, which is loaded with Halloween delights. Pastries full of autumn spices. Maple-glazed bacon bites. Roasted pumpkin seeds. Cauldrons filled with steaming stews. And a whole tower of candied apples.

I pick up what looks like a bone but smells like chocolate. When I bite it, I find the center is made of a pretzel and peanut butter.

Creepy and delicious.

The moment I finish one, I'm already reaching for another. But a body steps between me and the snack table.

The scent of seaweed teases my nose, and I swallow hard, losing my appetite.

Bend her over the table ... call me daddy ...

"Hello, Hamish." When I raise my eyes to the selkie's chin, I see him give me a toothy grin.

"Amethyst Shelly. You look divine this evening. That dress appears to have been made for you."

"It was." At least, that's what Esme claimed, and I have no reason to think she'd lie.

He chuckles, as if I told a joke. "Aren't you going to compliment my outfit?"

He waves a broad set of hands down his body, and I follow the movement.

The man is dressed in a crimson suit. The outfit is bold and fits him well.

"That's a handsome suit," I say.

Please go away. You smell so *bad.*

He steps forward, into my space. "Red and green. Together, we look like we're celebrating Yule rather than Samhain. But we're still quite a match."

The way he says *together* makes me twitch.

Moan my name ...

There's only one name I'll say the way he wants me to. The selkie is wasting his time.

"Let's dance." Hamish's hand comes to my lower back, and he draws me toward him.

I lock my knees. "No, thank you." I can't take much more seaweed scent, paired with dirty thoughts.

"Come. This song is perfect for you and me."

Hamish pulls me into his arms, sweeping me into the throng of dancers and pressing me close. My chest against his. No space between us.

Every breath I take reeks of salty water plants.

No. Don't like this.

"Let me go. I didn't agree to dance. I don't *want* to dance." *Not with you anyway. I want my wolf.*

Instead of listening to the very clear words I spoke, Hamish chuckles again and gives me a charming grin and tries to meet my eyes. The disregard makes me so uncomfortable that I lose control of my limbs other than staying on my feet.

Why can't I fight back? Why can't I be tough, like a wolf?

Would Veronica let a man treat her this way?

No.

"Let go of me, Hamish." I try to put a growl in my voice. A Veronica growl. A Bee growl.

But I sound like a child playing pretend at tough.

His grin grows wider. "Mmm, I like how that sounds. Say my name again."

I want this to stop. I really want this to stop.

Why do I have to be the desire witch? Why can't anyone else in the room feel how much I want to be free of this?

And suddenly, I'm furious with myself. For needing saving. For expecting someone else to take care of my problems for me.

Stop looking for a caretaker. Make him leave.

I could do it. I could make him want to stay far away from me.

Everyone will see. They'll think I'm dangerous. They'll make me leave Folk Haven.

But I don't know how else to end the uncomfortable embrace. Would using my magic on a mythic without The Council's approval earn me the label of a trouble starter? Would I horrify everyone in attendance? Would I ruin Morgana's dream of owning a library?

I can't see my sister in the crowd. I can't see faces at all as Hamish twirls me.

"Stop," I say, my voice steadier than my nerves. "I want you to stop."

Stop before I make you. Stop before you make me ruin everything.

But he doesn't. The selkie leans closer, a red glow pulsing out from his skin, and I catch on his eyes. His wanting hurts my head.

Gods, I want to tear this tight dress off her. Tie her wrists with the fabric till she whimpers. Palm her pale ass as she leads me upstairs and shows me all the library's secrets—

Then, he's gone, and I can breathe.

There's a grunt and a wheeze and a whimper. In front of me, Hamish curls in on himself, clutching his stomach, where Jack just rammed his fist.

35

AME

"Do you know what *stop* means?" Jack snarls, and the seething tone reminds me of how Bee reacted whenever Hamish talked to me in the past. "Why don't you say it now?" The werewolf grasps the selkie's hair and wrenches him upright. "I'll listen as well as you just did."

"Y-you can't—"

"Can't what? Defend my mate from some fucking fishy asshole who likes to grope unwilling women?"

Jack's eyes are full black as he stares around the gathering. I see now that the room has come to a standstill as the drama unfolds. The music still plays in a creepy ballad, the enchanted instruments unaware.

Morgana shoves her way out of the crowd, her stare circling between the gasping man and me and Jack's fist in the selkie's hair. There's a dangerous edge in her expression when she next glances my way.

Some of The Council members step forward as well. Selena

is expressionless, but I get a sense of sharp intent as she stares at the wheezing Hamish. Moira, a selkie herself, glares at Hamish, and I recall gossip that they used to be a couple.

Seems things didn't end well.

Baron is here too, looking more thoughtful than anything.

"Jack."

When I speak his name, he immediately gives me all his focus, though he doesn't let go of Hamish's hair.

Bless The Dark One, he looks devastatingly handsome in his all-black suit. Whatever store he found must have had the exact right size because the thing looks like it had been stitched for him. He's even slicked back his hair, the product turning his normal brown strands onyx.

Dig my claws into his gut and tear.

Take her far away.

End him.

Keep her safe.

Make her happy again.

The last has my heart clenching with love despite his murderous rage.

"Yes, little witch?" The way Jack asks that is too suggestive for an audience. And still, I find myself smiling.

"Thank you for making him stop. But there're usually a few more steps to take before violence."

He smirks. "Not for me."

"You will release my son this *instant*." A man storms forward, looking like an older version of Hamish and speaking with a Scottish accent so thick that I almost don't understand him.

Jack doesn't bother to glance at the older selkie. He keeps his gaze on me, and I find meeting his eyes surprisingly easy. I extend my arms, fingers splayed.

"If he touches me without my permission again, I promise I will spell him to be afraid of his own penis."

The entire ball is silent at this point, which means my declaration rang through the space.

The threat was surprisingly easy to make.

I don't want their fear. But I would rather them be scared of me than have Jack in jail for eviscerating Hamish.

My shifter grins wide and wolfish as he releases Hamish and strides into my arms. "I knew you had some wicked in you, little witch." He kisses me deep.

A collection of gasps sounds from the crowd. A werewolf and a witch making out in public is not a normal thing. Monster bias still exists in this town. But when we break apart, there are no raised pitchforks, so that's a plus at least.

"What are you going to do about this?" Hamish's father hisses, his scowl on the Council members.

Selena turns her attention to the man. "What am I going to do about your son assaulting a witch?"

The man sputters, and Hamish, still looking queasy after getting his guts pounded, attempts to defend himself. "We were *dancing.*"

"She refused you multiple times," Jack says in a calm voice as he stares into my eyes and strokes his thumbs over my cheeks. "Plenty of shifters heard." Black seeps over his gaze again, his voice going as calm as death. "And they all *ignored* her."

Over his shoulder, I spy multiple heads dip, as if ashamed.

He's not wrong. Plenty of mythics have better than average hearing. More than one would have heard my protests. But Jack was the only one who did something.

I wrap my hands around his wrists to keep him by me. I don't want him to murder anyone on my behalf. Not tonight anyway.

"Hamish." The strong feminine voice draws my focus, and I see Moira MacNamara step forward. "As the Of the Fin council representative, I demand you admit fault and apologize to

Amethyst Shelly as well as agree to stay at least fifty feet away from her at all times." She turns to me. "If you would like to demand greater actions be taken, please approach me at your convenience."

Hamish's face has gone from green to red, matching his suit. "I didn't—"

"If"—Moira speaks over him, her voice carrying greater power—"you refuse to adhere to this extremely reasonable request, your suit will be brought before The Council, and further action against you will be voted on."

Everyone who knows anything about The Council knows that won't go well for him. Obviously, Selena will vote against him in this case, and it's clear Moira is not on his side. Levi Abadi, the monster council member, is Moira's mate, so automatically, he's not a Hamish fan. The Of the Wing council member is a wild card, and I don't have a clear read on the Of the Claw member, the pack's beta. But that's still three to two.

I can't help thinking how the Folk Haven mythic justice system, at least in this case, is working far better than the human one. In the latter, I would never be able to demand retribution for a man getting handsy on a dance floor.

But here, the insult creates waves.

"Thank you," I say. As long as Hamish keeps his distance— and out of the library, thank the goddess—I have no further problems with him.

Levi Abadi materializes from the crowd, the monster seeming to relish his job of escorting the sputtering selkie father and son from the gathering. Moira and Selena follow, and I wonder if more punishments will be doled out where others can't see.

Baron nods to his beta, who also joins the departing party. Then, the alpha comes our way, and Jack tenses.

"No one is going to give you grief about that punch," he says by way of greeting.

"Good to know."

Baron tilts his head, studying Jack. "I'm only surprised you didn't do more, given what you are."

36

JACK

THE PACK LEADER is just trying to rile me. Make it seem like he knows more about me than I do. That worked well for Finnick, but he wasn't lying. Finnick *did* know more than I did because, back then, I knew next to nothing about werewolves.

Does this guy know his daughter took a trip to the library to give me some lessons?

"I know enough about myself to not want any input from you."

Unlike in the bank, Baron doesn't let my dismissive words piss him off. He stares at me with intense eyes.

"You're a *guardian*." He says the word in a careful tone, as if expecting some reaction from me. He doesn't get one because I have no idea what he's talking about.

"If you're saying I guard what's mine, that's true. And it would benefit everyone in this town to remember it." My arm circles tighter around Ame's waist, my thumb stroking over the vine designs of her dress.

What would that selkie have done if I'd decided not to

234

come tonight? What would all of these mythics have let him do?

Ame has magic. She can protect herself.

Another voice whispers, *Magic she doesn't want to use because she hates how people look at her when she does.*

"Yes, that's part of it. But there's more. Can we talk elsewhere?" His eyes track around the space, where there are plenty of mythics listening.

"I don't trust you enough to speak to you alone," I say. "Also, I don't want to. Now, my witch and I have a ball to get back to."

Ame has been quiet through the exchange, and I wonder about the thoughts swirling behind those pensive eyes. When I hold her in my arms and lead her into the middle of a throng of dancers, she stares at my collar instead of meeting my stare, her lips twisted.

"How are you?" I press my mouth against her hair and speak the words quietly.

"That's what I want to know too." And of course, Morgana is suddenly beside us. "What happened?"

"It's over, Mor," Ame says. "Let's just move on."

The older witch's frown says, *No way in hell.*

Ame sighs. "Fine. Let's go outside. By the lake."

She leads the way, clutching my hand in hers, and Morgana follows behind, her heels clicking on the hardwood.

In the blaze of the lamps set up lakeside, their red hair glows, and their faces seem luminescent. Morgana faces her sister, arms crossed, waiting.

Slowly, as if recounting the events causes her pain, Ame admits to dealing with months of the selkie's detailed sexual thoughts, his overly friendly hands, and his inability tonight to listen to her *no*.

If he were still here, I'd rip his testicles off and skip them across the glass surface of Lake Galen.

"Goddess, Ame. I'm not trying to sound like an accusatory

bitch, but why didn't you *make* him leave you alone?" Mor asks the same question I decided not to voice.

Why not magic the guy? I'm glad I kept my mouth shut because Ame's face goes pale and pinched in the waning moonlight.

"Because Hamish wasn't *really* dangerous."

Disagree.

"That's bullshit," Mor snaps.

And something in my little witch breaks free. Her eyes burn, and her lips twist. "It's not bullshit, Mor! I don't want to use my powers. I don't *like* them. They make me feel gross. They make people uncomfortable and afraid and want to stay away from me!" Her voice cracks, and a tear traces down her cheek.

That small bit of water breaks my heart.

"Mom and Dad shoved this power into my skin"—she rubs at her perfect, red-tinged arms—"and when they realized what they'd made, they wanted me as far away as possible. It's always like that. When people find out what I can do, they avoid me. Why do you think the only friends I have live states away from me? Because no one else can stand to be around me! Not even our brother—" She stops herself on a choked gasp, slapping a hand over her mouth as tears trail down her cheeks.

"No, little witch." I gather her in my arms, pressing her face into my chest, wanting her sobs and sadness to sink into me so she never has to feel the pain again. "People love you," I murmur against her earthy and minty-scented hair. "I love you."

I wish the first time I'd told her wasn't in the middle of her crying, but I don't regret telling her.

Morgana takes a tentative step forward, gently laying a hand on Ame's shoulder. "I'm sorry," she whispers. "I didn't realize. I should have."

Ame's shuddering continues, but her sobs quiet. I only worry she's trying to silence herself for our benefit.

"Little witch," I murmur, "do you want to walk for a bit?"

After a pause, Ame sucks in a wet breath and straightens. I let my arms fall, but my hands land on her waist, unable to fully let her go. She wipes brisk hands under her eyes, smearing some of her black makeup.

Even with puffy eyes and a red nose, she's gorgeous.

"A walk sounds good."

Morgana hovers, her face uncertain. "Ame, what Anthony does—"

My witch shakes her head. "I shouldn't have said that. And I just … I just want to go on a walk. With Jack."

The older witch looks almost vulnerable in the moment as she stares at her sister. And I remember how Ame said Morgana was the one who raised her.

"Okay. Do you want Jack to drive you home too?"

Ame nods, staring out over the dark lake.

Morgana shifts, as if to walk away, but pauses, a determined tilt to her brow. "I hope you know, the only time you scare me is when you choose to hurt in order to keep others from feeling uncomfortable. I will always choose *you* over everyone else. Over everything else. I want you to choose yourself too. And if this town can't handle how amazing and powerful you are, then I'll close the library without a second thought."

As the witch strolls away, stabbing her pointy heels into the soggy grass, I smile at her departing form.

Morgana Shelly is okay in my book.

When I return my attention to Ame, I see her green eyes have gone wide. She's thoroughly shell-shocked. With a gentle hand, I guide her into a meandering walk along the grassy shore. Some parts of the lakeshore slope dramatically to the waterline, but this is a gradual dip. Almost flat and easy enough to stroll along.

As we wander, my thoughts cycle through her words. How much they clarify things.

Ame's tendency to keep to herself. The way she jumps to help whenever she can, as if to prove she's a nice, useful, nonthreatening person.

The fact that she's positive I'll eventually leave her.

My witch thinks that if the world gets to know her, they'll be scared of her.

The belief isn't entirely unfounded. Her power could be used for dark purposes.

But once you know Ame, it's clear she's the last person to manipulate someone on a whim. There's no need to fear her unless you're a dangerous asshole.

Which I guess is a category I fall into.

But I'm *her* dangerous asshole.

The music fades as we get farther from the ball, letting the natural sounds of the night seep in. Water slapping the shore, bugs chittering, and the squeak of bats overhead blend together and fill the silence between us. Ame is the first to break it.

"You called me your mate. When you were confronting Hamish," she says, as if I might have forgotten. "Why?"

I tilt my head to stare down at her. "Because you are."

The witch chews her lip. "How do you know?"

"Because I want you to be."

Niko was the one who told me that when mythics find the person they love and want to spend the rest of their life with, they refer to that person as their mate. Now, they tend to get married too. But that's not required.

"That's not normally how mates work." Ame strokes her thumb over the back of my hand, as if knowing her pushback will upset me.

It does, but I'm glad she's not being agreeable for agreeability's sake.

I frown down at her. "What do you mean?"

"There's different lore for different mythic groups. But there's usually an element of fate to it." My witch closes her eyes, as if the next part pains her. "You probably have a fated werewolf mate."

Every part of my body rebels at the idea of someone else in the world trying to take me from Ame.

"I don't."

"You might," she insists, her words soft but still gutting me.

I'm about to drag her to the ground and take her here and now just to prove that she is the only one I'll ever want.

But we're not alone.

"It's the scent." Baron's deep voice sounds behind us, and I turn with a snarl.

The alpha is quiet when he moves. I didn't hear his approach.

"What do I have to do to get you off my back?"

Baron meets and holds my eyes, unrelenting. "I'm trying to answer your question about werewolf mates," he says.

That's probably the only thing he could have said to keep my attention.

"Fine," I mutter, sounding like a sulky teenager. "How do werewolves identify their mates?"

The pack leader's eyes flick between Ame and me, and he sighs. "We don't believe in one true mate. We believe in mating *potential*."

"Explain."

He pauses, probably considering if my asshole personality is worth dealing with. It's not. He should leave me alone.

"Your nose will tell you. You'll meet someone, and they'll smell like"—his eyes go hazy—"ambrosia."

I jerk, the statement speaking to a deep part of me.

"We see that as a hint from The Clawed One. Saying, *This one would be good for you. Pay attention.* Then, it's up to you to do something about it. But you could meet more than one person with mating potential. Some wolves have encountered a handful, some tenfold. Some none at all. In the end, you choose your mate, and they choose you. The pack has a ceremony. A werewolf wedding, so to speak."

Mating potential. Interesting.

"What about you?"

"What about me?"

"How many potential mates have you met?"

His expression turns bleak, and I'm not sure if he'll answer.

"Just one. And I lost her years ago." He shakes his head. "But the scent isn't necessary either. I didn't have it with my ex-wife, but we still married and had a daughter. Although we're divorced now, so ..." He shrugs.

But that example doesn't apply here. Because when I finally came to as a man again and saw my little witch sitting in her spell circle, power radiating around her, one thought blared bright in my mind.

She smells so fucking good.

I grin down at her now, cradling her face in my hands. "You're my mate."

And the pack leader has to go and interrupt the special moment.

"Mates, no matter if they're wolf or not, are considered part of the pack."

"*I'm* not in a pack. Not yours. Not the San Francisco pack. None of them."

When I glare at him, the alpha looks thoughtful rather than offended. Finnick used to get into brawls at the slightest provocation.

Maybe the urge for violence isn't what makes a good leader.

"Tanvi told me she met with you. Explained about shifters. But she left out that because of a shifter's third form, they are outside of the pack structure. Above it in many ways. A shifter's only duty, responsibility within the pack, would be protection. That's why I called you a guardian."

"You expect me to believe you're eager to have someone *above* you in the pack?"

The man offers a rueful smile. "I'm an arrogant son of a bitch. I know that. And if I thought you were here to challenge my authority as pack leader, we'd be having a different conversation. But I want my wolves safe. And if our lore tells true, guardians are the best defense our kind have."

I want to point out that I couldn't even protect myself from a human wielding evil magic. How could he expect me to guard an entire pack?

The feeling of fingers winding through mine draws my attention downward, and I find Ame has caught hold of my hand.

"I don't think Baron is demanding any kind of decision in this moment, right?" She looks to the wolf, and he offers a curt nod. The witch stares up at me. "You can think on it. We can talk about it."

"Fine," I mutter. "I'll think on it." And look how easily swayed I am by my mate's sweet voice.

More likely I want to get her home. Comfort her. Give her pleasure. Chase away all the bad memories this night brought up for her.

And convince her to call me her mate in turn.

37

———

AME

THE MORNING after the Halloween Ball, I wake up to a long text message from Calli.

"She found him."

Jack drags me into his side and burrows his face against my neck. "I found you," he murmurs in a low, sleepy voice.

"Yes, good job. But I'm talking about Calli." I turn in his arms, trying to meet his unfocused gaze. "She thinks she found the sorcerer."

That wakes him up. Jack's body goes rigid, and then he sits up fast, drawing me with him.

"Where?" He growls the single word.

"Can I read the message? There are links and things. And she's not one hundred percent sure it's him."

He gives a stiff nod. I lean into his chest, trying to offer him comfort as I scroll to the top of the message.

Hey, Ame—and Jack, who I'm sure is reading this over your shoulder.

I cast the spell last night around two a.m. Figured that would put the guy in bed in most time zones in the US. Wanted to catch him in his house.

The blood-and-hair combo worked great. One of the smoothest spells I've cast—only set a couple of things on fire. Bless you Samhain! Anyway, you were close with Maine, but the magic pointed just over the border to Vermont. LUCKILY, I stocked up on local maps in those areas—I'll send you the bill. Was able to narrow it down to a street. And guess what. There's only one house on it!!! This might be where the good news ends. The house belongs to this guy.

She included a hyperlink in the text.

I'm half-hoping he's your man. Half-hoping he's not. You'll see why.

With a light press of my thumb, I open the link Cali sent. A news website pops up, and an article loads. When the article's picture appears, Jack flinches hard.

"That's him," he snarls.

The bold headline underneath explains Cali's cautioning words.

NEW MAYOR ELECTED IN LANDSLIDE VOTE

38

––––––––

JACK

AME TALKS me out of immediately hunting down Lucian Smite
—small-town mayor and sorcerer—and tearing him to pieces.

First, because I have to drive my mother to the airport,
which I do without letting her know shit is about to go down. I
don't want her worrying about me anymore.

But after I escort her to the security line, Ame still insists I
hold off. My intelligent witch points out that running in
without a plan is a good way to get captured again.

"He kept you captive for years. And he probably found
another mythic to siphon power from. He'll have normal security that political figures get, plus all sorts of magical ones he's
cooked up."

I could argue on the first point, seeing as how the town he's
mayor of isn't a large metropolitan city. For now, he's satisfied
himself with a smaller fish.

No doubt this is just a stepping stone to a bigger power
grab.

And it looks like Mayor Smite is originally from the

Vermont area. Wonder how he ended up all the way over in California.

But Ame is right about the magical protections. Likely a part of him expected me to come back for revenge once I escaped. My bet is, if he hasn't grown lazy over the past three years, he has a few werewolf-specific traps set up.

Maybe he even hoped I would return, so he could get his little pet power source under his control again.

And a pet was exactly what I let him think he'd made me into. Even with my limited mental faculties as a cat, I eventually realized I couldn't fight my way out of his clutches. Once I accepted that, I had two options. Option one: give up. Option two: give up, and when the sorcerer was sure he had me tamed, find an opening to escape.

I let him stroke me. I never growled. I kept my claws sheathed at all times.

There were times I even rubbed against his shin. As if I liked him.

He fell for it. Maybe not entirely, but enough to let his guard down.

And to leave a door open.

I escaped, and I'm free, but he still breathes air, which means I can't move on.

As much as my rage demands I wait for nothing, I shove the urge into an iron box in my mind. This isn't supposed to be a suicide mission. This is a *murder this evil son of a bitch* mission, so I can spend the rest of my life on the *loving and fucking my little witch* mission.

And of course, that little witch has to come up with even more ideas that make sense but also set me on edge.

"We need help."

Reluctantly, I agree. We call in Niko, although I'm not clear on how a kappa is going to be a good battle buddy. I mean, I trust the guy to the ends of the earth, but he's basically a big frog. Although he does have a wicked set of sharp talons.

The San Francisco pack is a harder sell.

"They have something to prove," she explains. "They are strong, they have the numbers, and they owe you."

And so I relent there too.

But as we approach our first strategy session, it seems like the group is growing without my input.

"What the hell is he doing here?" I growl the words when I see a familiar yet unwelcome face strolling toward the front door of the Victorian house.

"I invited him."

When I whirl around, I find myself alone in the front hall with Morgana.

"Why?" The question grinds through my teeth.

We were just beginning to get along, and now, this?

"Because you're going to take down a sorcerer with a motley crew of mythics, which includes my sister." Morgana steps close, her eyes burning. "You plan to make her stay behind, but you won't be able to. Get over that notion now. Put your energy into figuring out how she can be as safe as possible during this confrontation."

"You think calling in an arrogant alpha will protect her?"

"He's arrogant for a reason. He's not some baking bear shifter. You go against Baron in a fight? My money is on *him*. And he's not the only one I called."

Driving her point home, there's the sound of other car doors slamming shut.

"Who?" I snarl.

"Levi Abadi—aka a leviathan and the town's monster council member. Aka the mythic with whom you do not fuck. Selena, the witch council member. We get stronger with age. Her spell work is likely unmatched by anyone in this town."

Sure, they sound impressive, but that doesn't mean they're ready to leave their cushy lives for a murderous ambush.

"I'm a fucking outsider. They're not going to help me."

Something in Morgana's face softens. "You're used to that. I am too. And believe me, there are plenty of mythics in Folk Haven who couldn't give a shit about you. But there are also people here who will help you just because it's the right thing to do." She smirks in response to my scoff. "If you don't believe that, at least acknowledge that sorcerers are a threat to everyone. They'll clear him out for that reason alone."

Our group ends up in the vine-wallpapered room because it's the largest—best able to handle a pack of werewolves, two alphas, a shifter werewolf, three witches, a kappa, and a monster. Morgana set up a long table with reading lights evenly stationed on the dark wood surface. Good for studying and plotting revenge.

In front of the full bookshelves, our assortment of mythics fills the room.

Once everyone settles down, Ame steps forward and spreads a map on the table, showing the town of Pentonville, Vermont.

"Thank you for coming, everyone. We're gathered here today to plot the destruction of the sorcerer named Lucian Smite."

We never expressly agreed that Ame would be the one to speak. But there was a brushing of hands and a meeting of eyes that seemed to say, *You're better at speaking without growling at people*, and her response was, *Sure, I'll handle it.*

And she does so brilliantly. Without getting too flowery about the past, Ame lays out the events that led up to my capture, the years of enslavement I underwent, my escape, her discovery of me, and now, our location of the evil being who held me against my will.

I feel a heavy pressure on me and glance around to see multiple stares directed my way. The most intense is Baron.

I glare back, not wanting his pity.

"If you are in this room, I assume you have an interest in aiding this effort. Am I correct?" Ame sweeps her gaze around the room, not directly meeting anyone's eyes, but collecting all of their silent nods.

No one objects. No one says that hunting a man is an immoral thing to do. We are a room of mythical creatures, and we all know the dangers of a sorcerer. We all know there is no human law to apply to this case.

Tell the authorities Mayor Smite's cat was a man the whole time and the politician was using twisted magic?

Yeah, that won't get us far.

Sometimes, this world is brutal. We just have to be more savage than the other guy.

"Good. Time to introduce ourselves. Please state your name and mythical type, plus any special skills you believe will help with this mission."

Gods, she's sexy when she goes all commander.

"I am Amethyst Shelly. Witch. Desire specialty. If I can get skin-to-skin contact with him, I should be able to control his choices."

The San Fran wolves stare at my mate with wide eyes.

Yeah, she's fucking impressive. I'm proud of her for putting herself out there like that when I know she'd rather tuck her magic away and never use it again. If anyone hints at being afraid of Ame, I'll give them a reason to fear *me* instead.

Also, she's not going to be within touching distance of Lucian if I have anything to say about it.

"Morgana Shelly. Witch. This is my library, and I've begun gathering spells that should help us with this confrontation."

"Selena Evermore. Witch. I'll give those spells all the juice they need." She nods at Morgana, who returns the gesture.

"Levi Abadi. Monster. I'm here for muscle and to represent The Council along with Selena."

"Niko Saito." My friend waves at the group, offering his affable smile. "Kappa. Guess I'm muscle too."

The San Francisco pack introduces themselves, and I watch as Baron eyes each one, as if taking mental notes.

"Veronica Hunter. Alpha of the San Francisco pack. Muscle."

"Baron Moonson. Werewolf. Alpha of the Folk Haven pack. Muscle."

Ame nods at the group. "Thank you—"

A tapping interrupts her, and every head turns to stare out the large glass window. The portal normally shows a beautiful view of the forest with a hint of Lake Galen in the corner.

Now, the clear panes reveal a smiling, *handsome enough to burn out your retinas* stranger.

Open the window, he mouths, pointing to the latch.

Morgana circles the table, unlocks the window, and cranks a small lever that pushes the whole thing outward. There's no screen, which seems like an oversight on a lakeside house in Georgia. The mythic could easily climb in through the ground-floor opening.

Even simpler, he could have used the front door.

But he doesn't make a move to enter, and still, the room fills with the staggering weight of his power.

"Am I late?"

Who in the fucking hell is this? I try to ask the question with a glare at Morgana, but the witch lifts a single shoulder as her brows dip in suspicion.

The stranger doesn't seem to notice how his presence has ratcheted up the tension in the room. He just tosses a luxurious fall of golden waves over his shoulder and grins at the group. Carefree. Shirtless.

With sharp eyes that say, *Try me and find out.*

"Why are you lingering outside?" The question comes from Levi, and the monster council member wears an expression that combines wariness and exasperation.

"Such a lovely day, isn't it? Seems a waste to spend it inside." His voice has a slight accent. But not the Southern lilt a lot of Folk Haven residents speak with. He sounds European, but I can't place the country. My mom probably could.

Levi sighs, as if he's used to this mythic's strange behavior.

"Sev here. Monster. Baddest of the bunch." The way he introduces himself, in the same format as everyone else, makes it clear he was listening in on our meeting. His eyes rest on Ame, and he does a slow perusal of her that has me growling low in my throat. Sev doesn't bother to look my way. "And you can use me however you'd like, my crimson-haired temptress."

A hand on my arm holds me back. I realize Morgana crossed the room and is gripping me.

She flits her eyes from me to Ame in a clear sign of, *Let her handle it.*

I'm about to shrug off the bossy witch when my mate speaks up.

"Don't flirt with me." Ame holds the monster's eyes with an unwavering stare. "I know what you want. I'm not it. If you're going to cause trouble, you're not coming."

The room falls silent, and the monster's eyebrows rise slowly at the blunt rebuff. Levi's lips press tight together, as if he's struggling against a laugh. I stay tense, ready to defend my little witch if the powerful being takes offense.

But Sev loses a touch of the predatory gleam in his gaze and leans against the windowsill in a casual slouch. "Whatever you say, commander."

"Good." Ame steps up to the table again and brings her tablet to life.

She opens the Revenge Plan folder.

"We aim to go after the sorcerer on the night before the next full moon, when the wolves are at their strongest. We have less than a week to form a plan of attack."

39

AME

Lucian Smite has vastly different life goals from me.

From the forest shadows, I gaze out at the sorcerer's mansion. The thing is huge, gaudy, and cold. It looks more like a resort than a home. The man wants to make himself a modern-day monarch. I guess that is the type of personality that would have a human searching out dark means of generating power.

He doesn't want to earn his wealth and acclaim through the normal channels.

He wants a sure thing even if it comes with blood and pain.

Despite my natural magical ability to manipulate those around me, I've never had the urge to dominate or subjugate.

And maybe that's why I've yet to have a pack of bloodthirsty mythics storm my home.

Jack shifts beside me, eager energy radiating off him. We've spent the last week plotting out as much of this confrontation as we could. The assault would likely be safer if we waited longer, planned more, but I'm not sure how long Jack would have been willing to push off his revenge. I didn't want him charging in without backup.

And what if another mythic is locked up in this overcompensation of a house right now?

How long have they suffered? Waiting even another day might have been too late to save them.

"You two ready?" Niko crouches on Jack's other side, dressed in workout clothes, symbols of the witch language painted on his skin.

Everyone has some of Selena's markings, helping with stealth and protection. They aren't impenetrable armor, but cuts won't go as deep, and enchantments meant to manipulate minds will have trouble grabbing hold. She warned us that the magic drains her, so she will cut connection to the markings after a certain point. Then our safety is up to our own strengths and abilities.

Hopefully, the sorcerer will be destroyed—his toxic spells along with him—before she wears out.

"I am," I whisper back to him even though I think we're too far from the house to be heard.

"Ame." There's a guttural note in Jack's voice as he says my name. "Please—"

"I'm not staying behind." I lay my hand on his shoulder to soften the harsh edge in my words.

We've had this argument multiple times a day, leading up to this.

He scowls at the ground, and then with jerky movements, he starts stripping his clothes. Once he's bared to the night, standing tall above me, the already-dark shadows grow opaquer as they cling to his skin.

When the creeping tendrils disperse, a massive wolf man on hind legs towers over us. Jack is going in as his hybrid form. Perfect for wreaking the most havoc.

"Stay close," he snarls in his beastly voice, crouching to stare into my eyes, his burning black.

I push myself up enough to kiss his snout. "I'll stay close."

Niko, the communication member of our little group, reads a message from his phone. "Morgana says she only feels one human emotional grid inside."

We all arrange ourselves around the perimeter of the house, the plan to come in at multiple angles and confuse any defense spells he might have in place.

One human. Most likely, it's him. And it's possible that he has more people, only shielded from us somehow. Sorcerer magic is a mystery to us. What they can and can't do with their toxic, twisted magic. No doubt, even if we end his life tonight, this place is already painted with his evil.

"The rest are ready," Niko tells us.

Jack nods his great, shaggy head. "Go."

We decided to opt for speed over stealth. At the very least, he'll have some kind of alarms or cameras. We just need to make sure they go off too late to help him.

A seven-foot-high brick wall surrounds the property with only one iron-barred gate. Jack scoops me into his arms and leaps clear over the barrier, and I realize in that moment how much my mortal speed is holding him back. He sets me down gently on my feet as floodlights flare to life, illuminating the property leading up to the mansion.

"Go ahead without me. I'm following," I tell him as Niko scrambles over the wall himself, as easily as climbing a ladder.

"Together," Jack growls, and he lopes toward the house but at a pace I can maintain.

Breathing hard, I keep up, only stumbling when I hear a night-rending howl, followed by a chorus of snarls.

To the right, I spy one of the wolves, a brown-coated creature, struggling under a glowing net.

"Trap," Jack growls. "Not hurt." He barrels toward a sliding glass door.

His message is clear. We guessed there would be spells meant to catch Jack if he ever came back. And since a sorcerer needs a live mythic to sap power from, it wouldn't make sense for those traps to be lethal.

The reminder gives me a new thrust of furious energy.

How dare he! No one will take Jack's freedom from him again.

I'll make sure of it.

The brown wolf might be out of the fight, but we'll get them loose before we're done tonight.

Killing the sorcerer is the priority.

Even I, a relatively passive person, know he can't live. We don't have mythic jails.

Jack pauses long enough to wave for Niko and me to stop moving. I slow, using the time to suck in some gasping breaths. Maybe I need to add jogging into my *weightlifting boxes of books* workout regimen.

The shifter turns his body into a battering ram and crashes through the glass door.

"He didn't even want to check if it was unlocked?" Niko mutters, and I snort.

We both step carefully through the doorframe, our sneakers crunching on glass shards.

We're in some kind of formal dining room; a long table, set with gold plates and cutlery, takes up only a portion of the grand room.

Does he host evil dinner parties here?

Hopefully not. The idea of a whole collection of sorcerers makes me shudder.

What kind of damage could they do?

Jack stands tall on his furry, muscular hind legs, lifting his nose to the air. I see his muzzle wrinkle.

"Up," he growls.

There's the sound of smashing from other parts of the house, and I pray to The Dark One that the rest of our group is making aggressive entrances rather than finding themselves in traps.

Jack digs his claws into the hardwood and propels himself deeper into the house as Niko and I jog to keep up. Eventually, we find a staircase, and like Jack's nose told him, we go up. Paintings hang from the walls, each one displaying some old, constipated-looking guy.

Suddenly, a ghostly white hand reaches out from the nearest one and grabs for my throat. I only have time to gasp before there's the sound of tearing canvas. Niko produced a set of claws and shredded the picture, the one that had come alive and tried to grab me.

"An illusion?" I whisper.

The hand looked real, but I didn't feel anything on my skin.

Either way, wolfy Jack tears the frame from the wall and chucks it down the stairs, where it bounces a few times before smashing into a tattered heap at the bottom. He then follows Niko's example, dragging his claws through all the rest as we ascend the steps.

A long hall stretches out, closed doorways lining either side. On the opposite end, two wolves in animal form appear along with Levi. The monster nods to us, then kicks in the closest door, disappearing into the room.

Jack uses a different method, once again scenting the air. He alone knows what the sorcerer smells like. He passes the first few doorways before shoving one open on his right. The thing swings open so violently that it lets out a bang as it slams into the wall.

Did Jack find him?

As a precaution, I reach into my pockets, coating them with the powder I both hate and need. Without it, what use am I?

Jack's nose led him to what looks like an office. A plush rug lies across the hardwood floor. A massive oak desk commands the room, a sleek monitor sitting on the surface, but no scatterings of papers. The shelves along the walls are also neatly organized. Everything precise. Like this is a show room. Not something that a human actually functions in.

This can't be the right place.

But Jack stays in the middle, sniffing and turning and searching and sniffing again.

"Do you smell him here?" Niko asks.

"Yes," Jack huffs.

"Could it be a trick?" I ask as I approach a bookshelf full of legal-looking texts. Does the sorcerer bring people here to show them how boring and human he is? "Maybe he spelled his scent to confuse you?"

Jack gives a whole body shake, and I'm not sure what that means. I abandon the bookshelf when a strange glitter in the wallpaper catches my eye.

Is it gold paint?

The pattern is a simple twining of lines, and I touch my powder-coated finger to the glittering one. Heat flares along my skin, hot and agonizing.

Find a way out.

I'm too stunned by the random desire to shout a warning.

And this time, when a hand reaches from the wall to grab me, the limb is all too real.

40

AME

I'm pulled *through* the glimmering wall before I can think to scream.

The sensation of passing through what was supposed to be solid turns my stomach. The too perfect office disappears, and I find myself in a hidden room. The space is dim, lit by a bulb hanging overhead. The arm around my throat is strong, and while it doesn't cut off my airflow, the threat of that lingers in the press of fabric against the skin of my neck.

"Who the fuck are you, and why the hell are you in my house?" Despite the cursing and anger, the voice speaking is deep and pleasant. A voice you want to listen to. A soothing voice that might be easy to trust.

A politician's voice.

Is there a point in lying? He already knows we're not friendly. The whole *storming his house* situation makes it pretty impossible to sell the idea that we stumbled into his mansion.

"Assuming you're Lucian Smite, I'm a friend of a person you hurt. We're here for revenge."

"Who is your *friend*?" My captor spits the question.

"Have you hurt more than one person?" Why give him a name if he doesn't already know? "Do you have a long list of enemies?"

With a snarl, he shoves me away hard enough that I slam into a table full of menacing tools across the small space. A rustling sounds in the stale air. There isn't much in this room, not even dust. But the place feels dirty.

When I turn, I face a different version of the man pictured in the article Calli sent. Lucian Smite is not polished now. His monogrammed pajamas are wrinkled, and his carefully styled hair is in disarray.

Still, he's handsome in that way some men are when they reach their fifties and time decides to add a distinguished air rather than dragging their cheeks into jowls.

Why does evil get to wear a nice face?

Mayor Smite stares at me, angry disdain in his eyes. "I've never seen you in my life."

I straighten, ignoring the ache in my hip as I attempt to pick up one of the wicked-looking knives from the table. The weapon doesn't budge. None of them do. It's as if he superglued them all to the scarred wooden surface.

Brain working hard to come up with a plan, I keep my eyes off the crate in the corner and focus only on him. "Like I said, I'm here for my friend. You don't know me."

His blue eyes drag over my body, and his desires pulse against my mind.

Find out who they are.

Keep any mythics.

Take their power.

Become stronger.

Be the greatest man this world has ever known.

"You really are an evil villain," I mutter, wanting to press away the selfish desires before they overwhelm me. But there's nothing to distract me.

In this secret space, all noise of the ambush is gone. My werewolf has to be only a wall away, but I don't hear a trace of him. My hands clench reflexively, and I feel the rasp of red powder.

"Why didn't you make *him leave you alone?"* My sister's words tease through my brain.

Make him.

Make him.

I don't want the people I love to fear me.

But I can see Jack's face, hot eyes and eager grin as I read off my Revenge Plan.

I can hear my sister growl, *"That's bullshit."*

They *want* me to be frightening. Because the people I love want me to be safe.

There's more rustling from the crate in the corner, and I don't have to look to know what's in it. I can sense the emotional grid from here.

More complex than any animal's should be.

"How many—" The sorcerer's question cuts off with a gasp when I lunge for him. He throws his arms up, defending from an attack.

But all I need is a grip on his bare wrist. My fingers wrap around his vulnerable flesh.

Find the red thread.

I spear into his mind so fast that he groans. But I find the string of desire and wrap my mental grip around it.

Lucian Smite is strong. I can feel him fighting me, and an ominous gray presence creeps toward me. There's an itch on my arms, and I realize Selena's spells have begun to work for me. Whatever defenses Smite has, they need to battle a seasoned witch before they get to me.

Priorities.

I don't know how much I can make the sorcerer do before

Selena's magic taps out and he breaks free of my hold. There's a pressure in his mind, something pushing Selena out but also dragging me closer. Twisted spells I don't understand.

I'm not sure I'll even get one command through, but I need to try.

When there's a puff of panicked, pained breath from the crate in the corner, I know what I have to do.

"You want to let the rabbit go." Magic weaves around and into my words, reaching through the space between us and wrapping around the mind of the man.

Lucian stills, blinking at me. Then, he turns to stare at the cage in the corner.

There, behind steel mesh, is a small brown rabbit, shuddering in fear.

I've found Jack's replacement.

"I ..." The sorcerer slowly shakes his head.

I tighten my hold on his wrist, pushing with my power and moving with him as he steps toward the cage.

"You want to free the rabbit," I coax. "You don't want it anymore."

"I don't want her," he mutters.

The sorcerer crouches beside the cage, me shadowing his moves. His fingers hesitate on a combination lock.

The grip I have on his mind—his will—weakens as the gray sludge slinks up the red strand of desire toward me.

Get him to let you *go*, I can imagine Jack telling me.

"Let her go. She's not useful. You want her far away from you. Out of this room. Out of this house." My voice is light with persuasion as I ignore my flagging energy.

The magic pulls on my muscles. I quiver but hold.

Finally, he enters the combination, opens the little door, and scoops the rabbit out. From the way she shakes in his clutch, I can only imagine what his visits normally involve. Rage pulses hot and low in my gut.

Whoever that is, he's hurt her.

He hurt Jack.

"You want to free her. *Now*."

I ignore the menacing gray presence brushing against my magic, which is no longer leading his desire, instead shoving it with the force of my fury. He stumbles to the wall and thrusts the rabbit through, as if the surface were a mirage.

His hand comes back empty just as Selena's presence flickers out of the symbols on my skin.

I'm alone.

I release Smite and dive toward the same spot the rabbit went through. My shoulder slams into solid concrete, and I yelp in pain.

"Your power ..." The murmur has an edge of excited menace.

I turn to find the sorcerer staring at me with wild eyes, a creepy grin spreading across his face.

"I felt it. My God, it's more than I've ever imagined."

He's no longer under my spell. I'm out of his mind.

And yet I feel like I've sunk neck deep into gray quicksand. Clinging to me, suffocating me.

He sucks in a shuddering breath, eyes fluttering closed in ecstasy. "I could decimate armies with you, my beautiful little well of power."

Understanding is quick and dreadful. When I went into his mind, I must have opened a door to whatever incantation sorcerers use to sap the powers of mythics.

That's where this weakness is from. He's draining my magic.

Jack will find a way through the wall. He'll come for me.

And then the sorcerer will use my power to capture Jack, enslaving him again.

And it'll all be my fault.

Tears stream down my face at the thought.

I should have stayed behind.

Lucian is directly in front of me now, staring at me like I'm the perfect little gift. Like he's thinking of what animal he'll turn me into to keep me passive.

When that happens, I'll have no chance. He's lost two. He'll never let another get away.

"Don't fight, little witch. That's what you are, correct? I can feel it now. My little witch."

Something breaks in me then. Hearing Jack's loving nickname for me, used by this piece of human garbage.

A rabid, terrorizing desire rises in me then.

I want to claw the smug satisfaction from this man's eyes until my nails are bloody. But my arms are heavy at my sides.

And still, the need grows. To see all his hope leave, not in a slow drain, like he drags at my magic. Like a swift, sharp stab to the heart. No doubt, no hesitation.

I want this man to *fear me*.

"So beautiful," he whispers, leaning closer, like a lover before a kiss.

You hurt the one I love. Never again.

With a scream of hatred, I lunge forward.

41

———

JACK

THE WALL STOLE MY MATE.

I throw myself against the barrier.

Tearing.

Ripping.

Rending.

Doing absolutely nothing.

There's not even a nick in the wallpaper.

I let out a howl of rage and resume my attack.

I can't hear her. I can't scent her.

I can't feel her.

There's no internal clock in my animal mind that lets me know how much time has passed. How long it takes for a voice to pierce my furious haze.

"Jack! JACK! Look at me! Let me help! I can get her! I can get you to Ame!"

That last sentence is the only one that could ever get me to pause. Panting so hard that my chest heaves, drool and blood—I tried to bite my way through the wall—drip-

264

ping from my snout, I turn to meet a set of liquid black eyes.

Niko.

"Please, Benji, *trust* me. I can get us through the wall."

"Ame," I rasp in a desperate whine.

"I know." He puts a hand on my massive shoulder and presses me back from the wall.

He's the only one I'd allow to do so, and even with him, the man like my brother, I have to suppress the urge to bat him aside and keep up my useless demolition.

"It's a spell. A magical barrier," Niko explains as he tugs his shirt off and shoves his pants down his legs.

The guy is commando underneath, standing butt-ass naked in the middle of the sorcerer's office.

"I can drain the magic, but you need to stay back." He glances over his shoulder, and I realize more of our raid party has entered the room. "All of you. If you don't, I can't promise I won't hurt you accidentally."

"Get on with it already." This is from Veronica, the pack leader looking flushed as she scowls at the ceiling above Niko, as if his nudity offends her.

Wouldn't think it would matter to a werewolf.

Niko sucks in a deep breath, then shudders as his body expands. Shivers race over his skin, leaving an aqua color in their wake. His mouth and eyes widen, his nose flattens, and when he straightens, he stands over seven feet tall, looking more like the Creature from the Black Lagoon than a human.

And like all kappas, he has a bowl-shaped dip in his skull, full of silvery water.

I asked him once what it was about, and he simply said, "It's power. Best it stays full at all times."

"Back," he rasps now.

Though it feels like tearing the flesh from my own bones, I stumble back another step.

I won't be able to keep my distance for long.

Oddly, that's the moment a rabbit pops out of the wall. The little creature sits in a quivering mess at Niko's blue feet, then makes a break for the exit. Only there're too many mythics in its way to get free.

Morgana shoves to the front of the group, crouches to the floor, and scoops up the terrified animal, murmuring soothing nothings to the creature.

Disregarding the strange occurrence, Niko faces the wall again and spreads two sets of webbed fingers, each ending in a wicked sharp claw.

Then, he tilts his head forward, deliberately spilling his skull water onto the ground.

The moment the liquid loses contact with him, the mysterious sparkle disappears, leaving a puddle of ordinary water at his feet. But the shocking bit comes when his bowl is empty.

Niko becomes a magnet for my soul. He's a black hole, sucking me forward, and I realize all the other mythics in the room are leaning toward him too. Morgana, with her armful of rabbit, stumbles forward a step. Veronica, bleeding from a mystery wound, clasps the doorframe, even as her torso bends like a flower toward the sun. Two wolves crawl on their bellies across the floor until Baron steps through the door, crouches, and grabs them by the scruff of their necks.

This is more than a physical draw. It's as if my friend were leeching the soul from my body. I clamp my mouth shut, terrified I'm about to puke the essence of my existence onto him.

The kappa rasps a wheezing noise, sounding like a gilled creature trying to breathe air.

Then, he plunges his talons into the wall. They sink deep, the barrier as soft as melted butter for him. Niko's mouth falls wide, and he lets out an eerie wail that's both terrible and beautiful.

The building trembles, and I remember the handful of

earthquakes we experienced in California. But this isn't the ground shaking the house. It's my quiet, kind friend.

The fake wall flickers, and the magnetism eases. I realize there's an inch of water in the kappa's skull bowl.

He's refilling his power. Using the sorcerer's magic for fuel.

As the magic drains from the barrier and into the mythic, I catch a flash of a bare lightbulb hanging from a ceiling. A hint of red.

Is that—

A scream fills the office, and I don't hesitate, diving over my friend through the failing barrier. Shards of a half-formed spell cut into me, but not enough to make me stop.

What I find is not what I expected.

The sorcerer, the man of my nightmares, is on his knees before my witch, clutching his face as crimson liquid seeps from between his fingers. The same dark color stains my mate's face.

Ame's wild green eyes meet mine as she spits out blood and what looks like a gob of flesh. The minute her mouth is clear, she starts screaming again. But this time, she uses words.

"Kill him! Kill him! KILL HIM!"

Third time's the charm.

In a single step, I'm behind him, my massive not-quite-hands, not-quite-paws on either side of his face. With a twist and a tear, his head separates from his neck, and I heave the useless object over my shoulder. The sorcerer's skull hits the offices floor with a wet thunk.

"Gross," someone mutters.

"I preferred the rabbit," another adds.

One more stride, and I have my precious witch in my front limbs, careful as I gather her close.

"Hurt?" I ask. "Where your wound?" I have trouble with proper grammar in this form, but Ame understands.

"It's his blood. All his." She hugs my neck hard, gasping in deep breaths, as if she just sprinted to me. "He was draining my magic. I saw what he wanted to do with it. He was going to try to take you all."

"Did good," I growl to her.

"You bit his nose off?" Veronica asks, and while I keep a hold on my witch, I glance behind me to see the alpha at Niko's side, a hand on the kappa's shoulder. She gives my witch a toothy grin. "Badass."

"Uh … thanks," Ame mutters, and I spy the twitch at the corner of her gore-coated mouth.

Fuck yeah, she's a badass. One more reason to love her.

My mate is willing to get bloody.

42

―――――

LEVI

AT SOME POINT during the storming of the mansion, I realize Sev broke off from the group.

The monster is—and always has been—a wild card. When he volunteered for this mission, I knew he had to have a reason other than eradicating a twisted magic user. Giving Sev free rein of a sorcerer's house is not a good idea.

I suck in a deep breath of air, trying to scent him.

Nothing.

My nose isn't superior like werewolves, just better than the average human's. Instead, I reach out with my mind, flexing that sixth sense that allows some mythics to get a general idea of the power levels of the others around us.

A pulse of great magic reveals itself downstairs. I jog through the house, finding the basement entrance. The sorcerer has been located and terminated upstairs, so why would Sev be down here?

Up to no good, I'm sure.

The basement level isn't some dank, dark space, left only

for laundry and a water heater. The large room is as finished as the upper floor, a leather- and wood-filled den. There's even a fireplace, which my quarry lingers in front of.

"You should go back with the others, my friend. Save some more poor bunny mythics from the big, bad human." His tone is light, but there's an edge to the words.

"You think we should have left the sorcerer alone?" I throw out the guess, not sure what has his false charm dropping away.

"No. Of course not." Sev offers a sharp grin over his shoulder. "Don't mind me. Just reflecting on how nice it is to have someone care about ridding the world of evil. Must be lovely to be saved."

I know next to nothing about Sev's past before he found his way to Folk Haven. But I can guess it wasn't exactly pleasant.

With his body angled toward mine, I realize the monster wasn't staring at an empty fireplace. Instead, he seems to have found a compartment behind the mantel.

"What do you have there?" I take a step closer.

Sev's eyes flash. "I have why I came."

He reaches into the opening and pulls out a small gold and glass object. Balancing the knickknack in his palm, he holds it up high enough for me to see. It's an old-fashioned sand timer. Before I can lean in for a closer look, Sev slips his treasure into a wooden box, which promptly disappears into an unknown pocket.

"What was that?" I dare to ask.

He smiles wide, showing all his teeth. "The newest piece of my collection."

Chills creep in a warning down my spine.

I've never seen the extent of Sev's collection, but he has revealed one other item of it in front of me. A small bird statue that held amazing power. I watched it turn what seemed to be a living creature into a pile of fish bones.

A gods-made artifact.

"How did you know that was here?"

Those objects aren't supposed to be traceable.

Sev shrugs and strolls away from the compartment, which I now see is filled with lots of odd items.

"Lucian Smite is—was, pardon me—a sorcerer with an insatiable appetite. I figured it was likely he would have something. And now, *I* have something."

"What does it do?"

The monster offers a smirk as an answer, which could mean *I don't know* or *I'm not telling.*

"What about the rest?" I gesture to the fireplace hidey hole.

Sev waves a dismissive hand. "Trinkets. Dangerous trinkets, but nothing like my beauty. Squirt a little of your cleansing magic on them, and they'll be as harmless as kittens."

The image of me *squirting* magic makes me feel like a cheap water gun. Or a teenager getting too excited with his first dry-hump.

Heaving a sigh, I let Sev pass me by without further comment and head to do as he suggested. This isn't a battle worth fighting.

I might be the monster council member, but Sev is the most powerful of my kind I've ever encountered. That's saying something when my father is the leviathan of legend.

But for this task, I pull on my mother's legacy. As a cleansing witch, she passed on her ability to purify to me. Nowhere near the same scale as she can manage, but I'm strong enough to scrub a cabinet of twisted magic.

I crouch before the collection and grimace at the slithery, slimy tug of them. Inside my mind, I find the calming pool of magic that is part of my being.

Then, I pour the power out.

No squirting necessary.

43

JACK

KILLING a sorcerer and burning down his house is a big deal, as it turns out.

At least big enough to require a post-decapitation/arson Folk Haven Mythic Council meeting.

Luckily, Levi and Selena were there and vouch for the legitimacy of Lucian Smite's sorcery. Plus, Selena was the one to pick up the mayor's head and set it back on the guy's shoulders, claiming it would be better if all his bones were discovered together.

Then, she set the fire with Morgana's help. The two of them had found a spell to bottle dragon fire, kindly provided by Xavier, a dragon and local fireman.

A lot of mythics helped. I only now realize, as I stand in the middle of the council meeting, I would not have won against the man alone. I *needed* these people.

I don't know how to feel about that.

After hours of bureaucratic nonsense, we finally escape

Town Hall into a sunny fall day, and I'm glad to be done with the politics.

"Two wolf packs. That'll be interesting." Ame grins up at me, shielding her eyes with the hand that's not clasped in mine.

I smirk. "Just don't get in the middle of them."

That's another reason the meeting ran so long. Veronica showed up and declared she wanted her pack to live in Folk Haven. They would be separate from the already-established pack, and she'd maintain her role as alpha.

Baron, who was also in attendance to relate his version of events, did not seem pleased by the idea.

The Council decided to give them a six-month trial period. So, I guess they're waiting to see if any werewolves start brawling in the streets.

Luckily, I'm not in charge, and Baron will be so busy with Veronica and her pack that I should be able to live, undisturbed, with my witch in her library.

"Mom said she'll meet us here. Let's wait on the bench." I nudge Ame toward the seat.

My mom was only back in San Francisco for a short stay before she was booking another plane ticket out here. Only, this time, she called Folk Haven Realty and set up a time for Moira MacNamara, local selkie, to show her the available houses. Anna Lim is pulling the same move as Veronica.

I wonder how the townsfolk will feel about the sudden influx of outsiders.

Ame plays with my fingers as we wait, seeming lost in thought. Since no one else is nearby, she must truly be thinking about something rather than trying to distract herself from hearing someone else's desires.

Leaning in, I run the point of my nose along the curve of her ear. "What's up?"

"Kiss?" she asks.

I chuckle and give her a quick peck before pressing my forehead to hers and staring into her eyes. "What's up?" I repeat.

"I don't regret what I did," she says eventually. "Attacking him. Demanding that you kill him. Leaving everything as ashes behind us."

"I don't regret it either." I relish it, but I keep that to myself.

Ame's brow crinkles. "I think our world is more violent than I gave it credit for. I see violent desires all the time. But I think I convinced myself that people desire things they can't have. But that's not true. Lucian was going to make all the sick things he wanted into a reality if we hadn't stopped him."

Keeping my mouth shut, I let her work through this.

"A little healthy fear is a good thing. And I think ... no." She firms her jaw, glaring into my eyes. "I *know* now that I'm okay with being a person that some people fear. Especially if it keeps the ones I love safe."

"Am I one of the ones?" My voice is low and husky, as I'm entirely too turned on by my witch right now.

A smile spreads slowly, unfurling like a stretch of relief across her mouth. "Yes. I love you."

"And do you trust that I'll stay?"

Wetness glitters in the corners of her eyes. "Yes."

"That's a good mate." And this time, I kiss her deep.

That is, until a horn beeping interrupts us.

"My mom is such a cockblock," I groan, recognizing a familiar face behind the wheel of the offending vehicle.

"I love your mom," Ame says, grinning wide as she jumps up from the seat and waves. "Let her know. In case she ever needs me to bite off a guy's nose for her."

I chuckle as I follow after her, loving these glimpses of her bloodthirsty side.

Ame could be right in more ways than she knows. The world of mythics exists within the human world, but also separate. We try to be civilized, but sometimes, the darker parts of ourselves keep us safe. Keep the ones we care about safe.

Maybe werewolves are selfish assholes, including me. And maybe that's okay.

I shake my head with a huff, pushing off the thoughts to consider another day. Today, I'm going to hang out in a library full of magical books and enjoy listening to my academic mother bombard Ame and her sister with questions about the witch language.

As we approach, Mom climbs out of the driver's side and responds to Ame's wave with her own, just as enthusiastic. It still throws me off-balance to see the eager gestures of affection that she's added to her repertoire. I knew Dr. Anna Lim always cared about me, growing up, showing it in her contained sort of way. Now though, Mom is taking every chance she can to remind me that she does and always has loved me.

As if she's scared I'll disappear again if she doesn't remind me.

But I'm not going anywhere.

"How did your meeting go?" my mom asks.

Niko climbs out of the passenger's side, wearing a sheepish smile. There's a large duffel bag in the backseat.

Could Folk Haven be in for another resident?

"Meetings." I shrug, then scoop my mom in for a hug. She likes these now too. "Don't know that anything got done."

"Jack is being cynical," Ame says before hugging my mom too. "The Council made headway on multiple issues. I think change is coming. Good change hopefully."

"That's not all that's coming!" Niko says too loudly, then blushes redder than Ame's hair. "Sorry. That sounded wrong. I just meant, I'm gonna look for a room to rent in town. Folk Haven seems like a cool place."

Joy makes my throat tight, and I dive forward to embrace my best friend. My brother.

"It'll be good to have you here. Got a lot to catch up on." My voice is thick.

"Don't you cry," he mutters. " 'Cause then I'll cry and it'll be a whole mess."

Laughing, I let him go with a hearty—very manly and not emotional—slap on the shoulder.

"I don't know if *I'm* good," Mom says. "But I am also one of the changes that's coming to this town. I've already—" My mother breaks off in the middle of her sentence. Her entire body freezes, and her eyes widen in something like horror.

She's not staring at me. She's not staring at Ame. Her gaze is fixated over my shoulder.

Scooping up Ame's hand, I turn around to see what has my mother acting weird. Other people who attended The Council meeting are exiting the building. Veronica catches my eye and nods before flicking her gaze to Ame, then Niko, then strolling off down Main Street. The one walking down the steps in our general direction is Baron, the wolf entirely focused on talking to the man at his side, Juan Greymark, beta of the Folk Haven pack and Of the Claw council member.

Baron squints his eyes in the noonday sun, as if just realizing he's outside, and scans the street as his beta talks. When the alpha spots me, he gives a slight smile, and I grimace in return. Then, his eyes move on, landing on my mother.

He goes as still as she did.

Before I can comprehend what their odd reactions could mean, my mother shoves me aside and strides up the stairs of Town Hall, straight to Baron.

Not sure what has my mom on a warpath, I follow her in time to hear her say, "If you have werewolf sperm, then you need to learn how to properly put on a condom." To emphasize this revealing statement, she whacks the werewolf pack leader in the arm with a purse that I know could double as a weapon.

Baron, for his part, stares at my mother, as if she were the northern lights—a sight he never expected to see, but is awed by.

Multiple pieces of information collide together in my mind.

My mother had a one-night stand with a werewolf.

She did not know he was a werewolf during that one-night stand.

She didn't stick around long enough to get contact information from him and was never able to find the man again.

Baron has scented one woman who could potentially be his mate.

He lost this woman years ago.

I assumed that *lost* meant dead. But maybe that was a miscalculation on my part. If this familiar way that my mom is scolding Baron means what I think it means, then the only conclusion is …

"Is Baron your father?" Ame gazes up at me with her beautiful green eyes, full of wonder and wariness. She doesn't know how I'm gonna react to this.

I don't know how I'm gonna react to this.

My mother is still berating Baron with her words and beating him with her purse. The alpha werewolf seems perfectly content with the minor assault, and the beta watches with a bemused expression.

"Dude, your mom is going to get arrested," Niko mutters.

Town Hall doubles as the police station. Won't be long till a cop sees a small woman bludgeoning a town leader.

"If she does," Ame whispers back, "I'll get her out. They owe me."

Niko doesn't have a response, and I don't know whether to laugh or run away.

"What is your name?" Baron growls.

"You don't remember my *name*?" my mother shouts, pausing her purse attack.

"You never told me, you wild woman!" Baron encircles my

mother's upper arms with his large hands, but the gesture doesn't seem aggressive. More possessive.

I don't know how to feel about that. I don't know how to *feel* anymore. I am an empty cup, and I think it's a defense mechanism because I *cannot* handle what is happening in this moment.

"That can't be right," Mom pants, worn out from her violent exercise. "I'm sure I told you my name."

"Do you know *my* name?"

There's a long hesitation that is answer enough.

"My name is Baron Moonson, and I have been searching for you for *twenty-nine years*. Where have you been, wild woman?"

"I've been raising my son," Mom hisses at the alpha. Then, she does a grand wave toward me, where I stand, unable to peel my feet from the pavement.

Baron's eyes land on me, their weight heavier than if the entire Town Hall had collapsed on me.

"Son? How old is your son?"

"*Our* son," she snaps, "is twenty-eight years old."

"You have a sister." Ame clutches my hand against her chest, smiling up at me. "Tanvi is Baron's daughter. She works at the bank and bartends at Local Brew sometimes and likes arcade games and ... you have a *sister*." She grimaces. "Sorry. I'm just pointing this out because I don't know if you like your father. You two seem to fight a lot. But Tanvi is fantastic." Her callous hand rubs over my arm. "I'm sorry. I'm piling even more on top of you. I'll stop talking. I'm here when you need me."

Despite Ame doing exactly what she said, giving me even more information to process, I find my witch rattling off facts soothing in a way.

I have a sister. I met her.

The sharp-eyed werewolf who gave me information about myself without asking for anything in return.

I have a father. He's standing in front of me.

Baron didn't know I existed. I always had this idea that he *was* aware and chose not to be my father. But that was never true. He didn't abandon my mother and me. He never even had the *option* to reject me in the past. Of course, he has that opportunity now.

My body tenses, ready for a blow, as I'm worried he'll turn away—

Baron lets go of my fuming mother, strides up to me, and lifts me off the ground in a rib-collapsing bear hug. Or more accurately, a wolf hug.

"Hate me all you want," the alpha mutters. "You're my son."

Fuck.

Now, he's never going to leave me alone.

44

AME

One Month Later

"WHEN ARE you going to be done in here? I want to take a shower," I ask the man lingering at my bathroom sink. *Our* bathroom sink.

Jack is here to stay. In Folk Haven. In this house. In my bed.

And in my bathroom. He's been brushing his teeth far longer than the dentist-recommended two minutes. He's risking wearing away his tooth enamel.

Jack eyes me in the mirror before bending over to spit the foam from his mouth. Even as I wait impatiently, I can't help but admire the way the muscles of his back flex and ripple. I want to stroke them, but if I do, he'll pounce, and I'll never get to shower.

"Go ahead." He waves a hand toward the tub while toweling off his mouth. "I'm not stopping you."

"I can't shower while you're in here."

He faces me, leaning back against the sink. Getting comfortable. "Why not?"

"Jack." I try to mimic one of his many growls as I say his name, but the word comes out breathy instead.

That won't do.

The shifter smirks, holding my eyes as he reaches for his shaving cream. "I'm not done in here. And I've seen everything you've got, little witch. In every possible angle you could imagine."

I chew on the inside of my lip before answering, "Not suspended."

Jack pauses with the bottle poised over his hand. "Excuse me?"

"That's an angle you haven't seen me in. You standing. Me suspended. From my ankles specifically." I sidle past him, toward the shower, and turn on the hot water. "I'm not saying it's the most flattering angle. But it would be new."

There's a rumbling over my shoulder, and I glance back to see his hot eyes tracing over my body. Maybe I shouldn't have corrected the wolf if I wanted him to give me some space.

"We can have sex later," I scold him. "I need to shower now."

Jack faces the sink and squirts shaving cream in his hand, pointedly *not* agreeing with my statement.

With a sigh, I strip quickly and pull open the glass shower door. The warm water feels heavenly. These early December days are chilly, and even though it has nothing on the cold season in Maine, I'm constantly hunting for the coziest, largest sweater to keep warm. Jack has made it his mission to get more bulk on my bones. Whenever I forget to take my lunch with me to my new job as a receptionist at the vet's office, he stops by on his commute to Ramla, stomps in all grumpy, carrying a turkey and mustard sandwich, scolding me like I'm an errant toddler.

I kind of like it.

But right now, *I'm* being the responsible one, trying to get through my shower in time for our guests to arrive, even with the heavy weight of his eyes on me.

"Stop it."

"Stop what?"

"Stop staring at me. You're giving me goose bumps. And when I have goose bumps, I can't shave my legs properly."

"Sorry." He doesn't sound sorry, and I know he's not when he steps closer to the shower. "Use the soap again. You missed some spots."

"I did not."

"I can get them for you."

"I did not miss *any* spots."

"You're rushing. Normally, you take your time."

I pause, a tiny tower of shaving cream in my hand, as his words roll over me.

Jack, the man, hasn't seen me shower alone before. Not when I'm just trying to clean myself.

But Bee snuck in a time or two when I forgot to close the door.

"I *knew* it." I pull open the shower door and slap my cream-covered hand against his bare chest, leaving a white smear. "I knew you were just trying to spy on me while I was naked!"

His brows dip. "Of course I was." Jack shoves his pants down, his cock bobbing up to slap his stomach as he steps into the shower beside me. "I was a cat for years, and I wanted to see some boobs. *These* boobs." He palms them, rubbing his thumbs over my nipples until both peaks harden. "Gods, I fucking love your boobs."

So much for shaving my legs. But Jack doesn't seem to mind the prickliness when he wraps my thighs around his waist and drives into me, leaving possessive hickeys on the boobs he loves so much.

Good thing I was already in the shower because he gets me messy.

When we're both panting on the bottom of the tub, Jack kneads his fingers into my butt. I think he finds the gesture soothing, so I let him play.

"You're sure you don't mind me going?"

Tonight, the night of the full moon, Jack is meeting with the Folk Haven pack for a run.

He hasn't decided if he wants to join—still dealing with the trauma of his last pack experience—but Tanvi has been by, trying to get to know him. The siblings are wary around each other, and her *full-moon run* invitation is a clear olive branch.

"I don't mind as long as you don't. I have no problems with wolves." I press a kiss to the center of his chest before sitting up. "In fact, I am very fond of them. But keep your furry butts away from my spell circle."

My mate smirks and helps me balance as I rise to my feet. Then, he assists me in actually finishing my shower, only claiming one more orgasm from me by massaging my clit as I condition my hair.

He's the most delightful devil.

Dressed in a robe, I hurry around my bedroom, not wanting to be naked when our guests arrive. Lucky and Bunny—as we've taken to calling the mythic we rescued from Smite— watch me as they cuddle together on the window seat. My familiar has taken charge of the not-really-a-rabbit, and Bunny is slightly less panicky when the cat is around.

And this time, no one has questioned my one hundred percent surety that Bunny is in fact definitely a mythic, trapped in a bunny body.

While Jack is running with the pack, I'll be performing another enchantment-breaking spell to free the mystery woman. But I won't be alone. Morgana is coming to lend her power to the spell, and maybe one other will be at my side.

Hoping for a third would be silly.

"They're here." Jack has his head tilted, as if he's listening to something. "At least, I figure that's their car in the driveway."

I squeak and hurriedly dance into my loose jeans and tug on my favorite green sweater, then sprint for the stairs, dodging Niko on my way.

"Sorry!" I call out to him.

He laughs. "Got somewhere to be?"

"They're here," Jack explains, following me at a slower pace.

"Cool. Be down in a second to meet them." Niko has been staying in the spare bedroom Jack never bothered with, renting from us as he looks for a more permanent place. He's especially nice to have around because he cooks more delicious food than the other three of us could ever hope to manage.

Also, Jack loves him like a brother.

Speaking of brothers ...

I burst through the front door in time to see Broderick and Anthony climbing from their rental car. The former shouts a hello and opens his arms wide for a hug. I plow into my brother's chest, holding him tight.

"It's been too long," I say.

"Damn right it has. We should've been here a month ago." Broderick sets strong hands on my shoulders to hold me far enough away for a proper brotherly glare. "What's this I heard about you going up against a sorcerer? *Without* me?"

"I ..." My cheeks flush, and I flick my eyes over the car hood toward Anthony, who's staring up at the house instead of looking at me. "I didn't think to call you."

Broderick wears a scowl that looks out of place on his normally jovial face. "You should always call us. We're your brothers."

I sigh and smile and silently disagree with him. "You're right. I'm sorry."

Broderick might have come for a magic fight, but Anthony wouldn't have, and it's hard to separate these two.

"She handled her own." The deep voice I love so much sounds from behind me.

Jack appears at my side, and then introductions commence. I give Anthony a more sedate hug and try not to notice how stiff he is in my arms. Both my brothers eye my werewolf, as if they think I'm Little Red Riding Hood and Jack just ate my grandmother.

But if he can win Morgana over, I expect it's a matter of time before they warm up to him.

When our group enters the house, Lucky and Bunny are sitting at the top of the stairs, waiting to check out the new arrivals.

"Oh my gods, is that a rabbit?!" Broderick leaps toward the stairs, hands already outstretched.

"Hold up." Jack easily catches the back of my brother's shirt, holding the grown man like an errant toddler.

"Bunny isn't a bunny," I explain.

Broderick frowns in confusion, then tries to glare at my wolf, who is still holding his shirt. While he's contained, I give a general overview of what the sorcerer did to Jack and what that means for Bunny.

"So, no manhandling her," Jack warns, finally letting my brother go.

He huffs, smoothing a hand over his shirt as skin paler than mine flushes. "She's so freaking *cute* though."

So was Bee. I smile at the memory of my grumpy cat and gaze up at Jack.

He blinks under the sudden attention, then slips his arm around my waist.

Later, when it's almost time for Jack to head out, I find him in our bedroom, pulling Lucky away from a section of wall the cat insists on scratching every so often. The woodwork is covered in her little claw marks. Good thing we never plan on selling the house.

Jack settles on the window seat, holding a purring Lucky. I plop down next to him.

"Have a good night, casting spells," he murmurs, leaning in to press a kiss against my neck.

"Have a good night, werewolfing." I kiss the corner of his jaw, breathing in the scent of his shaving cream. I might not have an urge to sniff out his mating scent like he does with me, but I still find his smell plenty tempting.

Jack lets out a little growl, and the sound makes me smile.

It's his *let's skip out on responsibilities and have a bunch of sex* growl. He's expanded his growl vocabulary.

As he sets Lucky on the ground, I rise again before he can tackle me.

"Not now. You need to get going. In the morning," I promise.

"Now," he demands.

I smile wider. "*Later*," I insist. "My whole family is downstairs."

"Little witch," he coaxes, knowing what that nickname does to me.

"Bee," I say, and his eyes flash. I lean down to kiss him. "You're an animal."

"*Your* animal."

I nod, our noses brushing. "Since that night on the road, you've always been mine, and I've always been yours. And I'm not going anywhere. Except for downstairs. Right now."

"I'll kiss you into submission," he warns, gaze darkening.

I slap a hand over my mouth and sprint from the room, a wolf hot on my heels.

EPILOGUE

ANTHONY

I wander around the house, running my eyes over the shelves but keeping my distance.

It feels like the books are reaching for me.

My siblings aren't uneasy around grimoires. They see history and possibility and inanimate tools.

Me? I see ... a pulse.

The heavy, steady beating of the magic gives me the creeps. Especially the way I sense the same power lying in a restless sleep under my skin.

Magic is a dangerous tool, and all I have to do is choose not to use it.

It's the same thing I've told myself my whole life.

And yet I'm always the one who feels like a tool to be manipulated by the force.

Why couldn't Morgana and Ame have moved to the suburbs? Gotten a normal house with no spells lingering in the walls and collected snow globes from roadside attractions?

But, no, the rest of my family is fine with magic. They embrace it.

They don't have a reason to fear it, like I do.

Just as my feet point toward the front door—my mind made up to leave—a swish of dark hair in the next room distracts me. When I lean to the side to get a clear view, I'm stalled by the sight of a stranger.

A woman.

A beautiful woman.

She slides a book off the shelf, flips through a few pages, then tucks it under her arm and heads farther into the house.

I follow.

She must be a library patron.

A set of comfy chairs is arranged next to a window with a view of the forest, and she settles in one of the seats. Black hair hangs loose around her shoulders, and she tucks a section behind one ear, showing off a profile with a sharp nose and chin, paired with soft lips.

I meander closer, pretending to study the books instead of her.

She doesn't notice me, and I take advantage of her inattention. There's a beauty mark—a small dot, like Marilyn Monroe had—sitting sweetly on the dusky skin just above her plump lips. Her complexion pairs perfectly with long onyx lashes and dark eyes, which are completely uninterested in me.

Look at me, I have the sudden urge to beg.

But that's not the way to approach the image of scholarly perfection. She tucks one leg—encased in loose, worn denim— under her knee and leans closer to an ornate lamp giving off a warm pool of light.

Only when my foot lands on a squeaky wooden floorboard, the old wood giving a groan louder than a doorbell, does she glance up.

The library patron offers me a smile that shows off a lovely set of teeth with the barest hint of a gap between the front two. I find the little space endearing and fantasize tracing my tongue along it.

"Hi there." She might look like she stepped out of a Bollywood movie, but her accent is all Georgia. The sweetest drawl my Yankee ears have ever heard.

"How's it going?" The question is too casual for my curiosity. What I want to say is, *Tell me every detail about your life.*

"That all depends on your perspective," she says, laying her book flat in her lap and smoothing a long-fingered hand with blunt nails over her page.

Her odd answer only intrigues me more, and I shuffle a step closer. "My perspective on what?"

Her smile is teasing, but not coy. "On what you mean by *it*, obviously."

I lean a shoulder against the nearest shelf—these aren't grimoires, so I don't feel like they're grabbing at me—and enjoy the weight of her eyes on me. "I'm interested in multiple *it*s."

"Well"—her husky voice draws the word out—"why don't you list them then?"

"Okay. How's your *day* going?"

She fiddles with the edge of a page. "No dogs died today. So, better than yesterday."

At my widening eyes, she offers me a smile that's more acknowledgment of my surprise than actual happiness. "I'm a veterinarian at the clinic in town. A day without the death of a pet is better than I can hope most times."

"Oh." Fuck. A vet. Which means she's *way* smarter than me. My personality—and social media influencing job—consist of dead-eyed stares and sarcastic comments. "If I saw a dog die, I would cry." That's not sarcastic. That's the whole damn truth.

She nods. "Sometimes, I do. But in my office, so I don't upset the owner."

"That's rough." I don't know what else to say.

"It is," she agrees. Her eyes drop to her book, then find their way back to mine. "You said *multiple its*."

"I did say that."

Only I thought she'd give me a light surface answer. Something insubstantial enough for me to tease her about. But this woman just revealed way more than normal in an introductory conversation.

"If I made you uncomfortable, you're free to say you forgot the rest and retreat." She waves toward the rest of the creepy house that's far less interesting than this woman. "I'm not very good at small talk. The animals don't usually require it."

Retreat? I only want to get closer. I settle in the cushioned chair beside her.

"Can't do it. Got more *its* to cover. How's your reading going?" I nod toward the book in her lap.

"Just started, so I'm not sure yet." She closes the volume and shows me the worn cover.

MONSTERS OF THE FAR EAST

"What made you pick that up?" I figure that's a better question than, *Are you a monster?*

"I'm not a monster," she says, as if reading my mind.

"Okay."

"But I might make one."

My eyes go wide, my muscles tensing.

Making mythics is not natural. Mythics are meant to be born.

"Sorry. That sounded Dr. Frankenstein-ish, didn't it?" Her beautiful smile isn't sad this time. More rueful. "I swear I don't have a bunch of random body parts I'm stitching together to form the perfect monster man. Your limbs are safe."

At ease again, I mock frown. "What, none of my pieces are good enough for this dream monster man?"

Her dark eyes drag over me, and I enjoy the shiver that follows in their wake. "Maybe I spoke too soon. What would you suggest? Pitch your pieces to me."

Smothering a grin, I try for an academic expression. "Well, there's no ignoring my face."

"No, there's not," she murmurs.

A thrill tingles along my nerves, but I don't let it throw off my flirting.

"My chest could fetch a good price at auction."

Her cheeks plump as she attempts to suppress a smile.

"But what you really want are my ... toes."

"Your toes?" She chokes on the question, delight sparkling in her eyes.

I nod sagely. "They're wily toes. I can pick stuff up with them. Could probably type a dissertation with the things."

"Fingerlike monkey toes. Got it."

The beautiful stranger grins at me, and I lose my breath, unable to keep teasing as I struggle to drag air back into my lungs.

"But," she continues, "as I said, I'm not building a monster." She resettles the book in her lap and opens the worn cover.

"Enlighten me. How do you plan to make a monster then?"

Her attention stays on the reading material as she rattles off her answer in a distracted way. "I plan to date a mythic. Then fall in love with that mythic. Then mate and/or marry them. Then have one baby with them."

"That's a very specific to-do list," I manage. I'm not sure how I feel about her clearly planned future when all I had plotted out were a few flirtatious lines that might convince her I was someone she'd like to make out with.

She nods. "I know what I want."

"And you don't want another witch?" *What if it's a witch who does his best to pretend he's not one?*

One of her brows lifts, and then she chuckles. "Oh. No, I'm

not a witch. I'm a harpy." She gives a slight flap of her arms, miming the wings she would sprout in her secondary form. "Males of our kind are rare. The only one I know is gay, so he's not in my dating pool. And humans ..."

A shadow moves across her eyes, and I feel a stirring in my gut.

Something like ... anger.

What did humans do to her?

"Humans are not an option. So, it's another mythic. And if we have a child, like I want, it'll be a monster." Her finger taps the book cover. "Best to know what I might be getting into."

She's smart, funny, and on the husband hunt.

This woman is not for me.

Despite how much I suddenly want her to be.

"I'll leave you to your reading." I forcefully peel myself from the chair, wondering if someone left a sticking hex on the cushion because it's a struggle.

She nods, eyes already refocused on the pages. "Nice to exchange odd conversation with you, man who still hasn't properly introduced himself."

I bite my bottom lip to keep from smiling. "You haven't told me your name yet either."

The corner of her mouth twitches. "I'll introduce myself the next time I see you."

"I'm not staying in town long." My plan is a week at most and only to make sure my sisters are happy and whole.

One of her shoulders lifts. "Then, I guess you don't need my name."

I'm tempted to stay. To keep bantering with her.

But she's right. I'm leaving soon, and there's no point in me making connections with anyone in Folk Haven.

I don't need her name.

But, damn all the gods, I *want* it.

The End

~

Thank you so much for reading SHELTER FOR A SHIFTER. I hope you enjoyed Ame and Jack's love story and that you leave a review! Do you want to spend more time in the mythic-filled Folk Haven? Check out the following books for more small town, sexy, fated mates romances.

SEDUCED BY A SELKIE
Folk Haven Book 1

Delta Novac hates Folk Haven, and as soon as she's done cleaning out her father's mess of a house, she's giving the town her taillights. But after she dives into the lake to save a drowning man that's not actually in danger, she finds herself with a sweet and sexy selkie shadow ready to do anything to get her to stay.

SUCKER FOR A SIREN
Folk Haven Book 2

Seamus MacNamara refuses to believe in the selkie mating myth: that his one true partner will rescue him from great danger. So, when the adorably beautiful barista he has a secret crush saves his life, Seamus ends up insulting her instead offering heartfelt thanks. Now he just wants a chance to redeem himself...and he's willing to go down on his knees to earn her forgiveness.

SWEARING AT A SEA MONSTER
Folk Haven Book 3

Moira MacNamara takes shit from no one, and that includes Levi Abadi, the enticing, infuriating monster who thinks he can dictate what she does with her own property. She makes a deal with him, sealed in blood. But now she can't help noticing how her veins thrum with heat every time he comes near...

If you enjoyed SHELTER FOR A SHIFTER, please consider rating and reviewing the book. Reviews help other readers discover my books, which helps me make a living and funds my ability to write more mythical romances for you!

Keep reading for a sneak peek of *Fire Magic & Ice Cream*, the story of Quinn, a fire elemental whose powers are directly connected to her lust, and August, the owner of an ice cream shop she can't help crushing on...

FIRE MAGIC & ICE CREAM

QUINN

"This is a horrible idea."

I shouldn't have gotten out of the car, but I realized where we were too late. Harley already pressed the button to lock the doors.

"It's my idea, which means it's genius. This is exactly what you need, fireball." Harley saunters across the steaming parking lot.

With another mighty tug, I try heaving open the car door. My effort is futile.

Cat hovers, dancing from foot to foot. "You told me you wanted to try this place."

Sometimes, I wish my little sister had more evil in her, like Harley. Then, I could give her a proper glare for outing my secret longing.

"I said I *wanted* to try it, but that I *can't*. It's too much of a risk."

"Stop being so dramatic. It's not like you're walking into an ammo store, about to set off all the gunpowder," Harley growls

297

at me, already at the front door. "It's an ice cream shop, for goddess's sake."

I know exactly what it is. Land of Ice Cream and Snow. The newest addition to the strip mall where I get my biweekly pedicures. Every time I hobble out of Tulips Nails with my fresh coat of polish, the acid smell of acrylics clears from my nose, and I get hit with the most delicious scent imaginable.

Waffle cones.

Even though it's torture, I tend to take a roundabout route to my car, just so I can glance in the windows. Not that I ever see much. The interior is dimmer than the blazing Arizona sun.

The easy solution would be to walk into the shop, but I've never done it. Not once.

"I can't go in there!" I lean back on the car, arms crossed.

"Why not?" Harley glares, fists on her hips.

"You know why! The second I step through that door, I'll melt their entire stock. I'm a menace!"

"Oh, Quinn. You're not a menace." The distress in Cat's voice almost makes me take the description back. Just to keep from upsetting her.

Harley stalks across the parking lot, coming to stand in front of me. "Listen here, little miss firecracker. You might not be able to control your powers yet, but I can. You start to spark, I'll shut you down. Now, get your apple bottom in gear because I'm practically orgasming from the smell of that place, and I'm not about to rush through eating because you're pouting in the car."

We meet scowl for scowl, but I give up first. Probably because this ice cream shop has been taunting me for months.

"You really think you can keep my heat in check?"

My big sister loses her annoyance at my hesitant question, replacing her glower with a saucy grin. "Hell yeah, I can. Could help you out other times, too, if you weren't such a prude."

"Gross! I don't care how kinky your job is. We are *not* that kind of family."

She rolls her eyes. "I'm not asking to be in the room with you like some poorly written porno. I could sit outside your door, read a magazine or something, and make sure you don't burn the house down." Harley tilts her head as she looks me over. "Are you super loud or something?"

"Gah!" I cover my ears and sprint for the front of the shop. "Stay the hell away from me and my sexy times!"

Through the earmuffs I've created with my hands, I pick up my sisters' laughter. Ignoring them, I take the step I've been holding back from ever since Land of Ice Cream and Snow flipped on their Open sign.

I grab the handle and slide in through the front door.

What greets me steals all words from my throat. My nose was already full of sweet scents when I stepped inside, but before my eyes can scan the room, my entire body focuses on the feel of the place.

Cold.

The sensation skitters over my skin, prickling tiny goose bumps and eliciting a shiver.

A shiver.

Shivers and goose bumps aren't for people like me with a constant fire sitting just below the surface of my skin. But here, in this ice cream shop, I experience the sensation of being chilly for the first time in my life.

The bell chiming over my head alerts me to my sisters' arrival.

I whirl around to clutch Harley's shoulders. "This is amazing! I didn't think you could control the fire this much!" I'm so moved that I rise on my toes to press a kiss to her cheek.

She stares at me with eyebrows scrunched together and her lips pursed in a confused smile. "What?"

"Oh my gosh. I've never ... this place is so cool!" Cat's exclamation as she dodges around us breaks into my out-of-character thank-you.

Moving past my first experience with the sensation of cold, I finally take in my surroundings. No wonder I was never able to spy much from outside the window.

Most ice cream parlors are all bright colors and delicate furniture. Cute little shops that bring to mind quirky sprinkles or fragile ice sculptures.

Land of Ice Cream and Snow crushes the idea of delicacy under the heel of its heavy boot. This place resembles the homestead of some rugged mountain man or the headquarters of a Viking clan. Solid wooden furniture stretches the length of each wall, and the floor is dark oak. Lights hang from the ceiling, giving off a low glow—small areas of warmth in the stark terrain of the shop. I'm not even sure *shop* is the right word.

More like cabin. A cabin that sells ice cream.

A handful of people sit, talking and eating. I expect, if we came a couple of hours later, after dinnertime, this place would be overrun with sugar hungry customers. A granite slab serves as a counter in the back of the shop, next to it the one familiar item all ice cream parlors possess—a glass container to view the offered flavors.

I take a single step before realizing the danger behind the counter.

A man.

But not just a man. This man is ... well ... a *man*.

I think I've found the Viking who pillaged and plundered and built this cabin of a shop with his bare hands. A black T-shirt stretches over shoulders wide enough for me to perch on one side and Cat on the other. His strong, ivory face belongs in a superhero movie. Sculpted cheekbones, square jaw, and enough golden stubble to leave a delicious burn on the inside of my thighs.

Oh shit.

The wonderful cold sensation drifts away as my inner fire senses a rising lust. Heat trails just underneath my skin, pulsing with a life of its own.

"I was right. This is a horrible idea."

But, as I turn back toward the door, Harley wraps an arm around my waist. To onlookers, the embrace probably appears friendly and innocent. But, in truth, her hold is stronger than steel as she drags me to my doom.

"Focus on the ice cream. Ignore the beautiful man."

"Ignore him? By gouging out my eyes?" I mutter, fighting an onslaught of lust and panic.

The ice cream god steps forward, his frosty gaze locked on the three of us. I watch with fascination as he slips a blue apron, the same shade of his eyes, over his head. The muscles in his biceps flex as he reaches to tie the strings behind his back.

At the display of his glorious muscles, I brace myself for another surge of heat. Instead, my fire remains stoked. The embers are there, teasing me, but they don't burst forth, causing mass chaos.

I guess Harley is as good as her word.

"How can I help you?" The ice cream god's words rumble out like tires across gravel as he watches us.

Not us, I realize. *Me.*

Being the middle child, I've often silently longed for a little bit more attention. But, right now, I'm considering hiding behind my curvy older sister or picking up Cat to use as a human shield. All in the name of self-preservation.

As if sensing my cowardly plans, Harley gives me a shove forward, so I end up stumbling into the granite counter. My hands land flat on the surface to steady myself.

Cold shocks through my palms, racing over my skin, practically extinguishing my fire, if not my lust. To my utter embarrassment, my nipples tighten with a shiver, and my bralette does nothing to hide the reaction.

When ice cream god's eyes drop to my chest, I'm torn between crossing my arms over my boobs and attempting another escape or ripping my shirt off and asking if he has a bed in the back room.

I settle on the happy medium of staring up at his gorgeous face and losing the ability to form a coherent sentence.

Maybe, if he were a creepy perv, I'd be able to collect myself. Unfortunately, ice cream god almost immediately removes his stare from my overly excited nipples to look me in the eye again.

"Do you know what flavor you'd like?"

I begin to thaw with a shake of my head. The Viking man turns his back. Steady again, I drag my hands off the frigid counter, rubbing my palms on the sides of my jean shorts.

Not that I mind the cold. In fact, I find the sensation fascinating.

I'm never cold. I was beginning to think I'd have to be dropped in glacial waters or launched into space to truly experience such a low temperature.

But, apparently, I just needed my big sister to crave ice cream. Despite her borderline bitchiness earlier, I throw a grateful smile over my shoulder.

In classic Harley fashion, she pokes me in the back. "Stop ogling the man candy and figure out what you want."

Feeling less generous, I stick my tongue out at her and then glance forward, attempting to kick my brain into gear, so I can remember what flavors I like.

But I'm thrown off track again when I find a mini wooden spoon in my face.

"Flavor of the day: blueberry pie." Grumbly-voiced ice cream god holds out the offering.

On pure instinct, I reach for the spoon. The tip of my finger brushes the edge of his thumb.

At the brief contact with the gorgeous man, I fully expect the utensil to burst into flames, forcing me to pretend I'm a street magician and my sisters are my camera crew and that everything has a weird but still plausible explanation.

But, instead of heat, there's another trickle of coolness.

Harley is going to be exhausted after tamping me down. She'll probably pass out in the car on the way home.

Ice cream god continues to watch me, and I realize I'm just standing, holding the sample, and staring at his expansive chest. To my amazement, the sample hasn't melted. However, it's headed in that direction with one and then two drips falling from the spoon onto the counter.

Desperate not to reveal my detrimental effect on frozen treats, I shove the flavor of the day into my mouth.

When I smelled waffle cones outside the shop, I kept my composure. When I set sights on the mountain of sexy behind the counter, I had a brief internal freak-out, but overall, I held it together. When cold visited my nerve endings for the first time, I kept my reactions on lock.

But this? It's too much.

"Oh, fuck me," I groan, not caring if there are children around, being corrupted by my involuntary reaction. In my opinion, no one under eighteen should be allowed in this shop. This ice cream is too sinful for young innocents.

I want to fashion a man out of this ice cream, marry him, and then devour him for as long as we both shall live.

The Viking ice cream man clears his throat in a glorious deep rumble as he crosses his arms over his chest, all the while watching me. The pressure of his eyes sits cool and heavy like the chilled treat currently melting on my tongue.

Would he taste just as delicious?

Keep reading Fire Magic & Ice Cream!

NEWSLETTER SIGN UP

Get another Folk Haven romance for FREE! Sign up for my newsletter to receive *A Selkie's Secret,* a novella that tells the story of Isla, a selkie, and Finn, the human she refuses to fall in love with...

ALSO BY LAUREN CONNOLLY

Paranormal

Folk Haven

A Selkie's Secret (Book 0.5)

Seduced by a Selkie (Book 1)

Sucker for a Siren (Book 2)

Swearing at a Sea Monster (Book 3)

Shelter for a Shifter (Book 4)

Casual Magic

Fire Magic & Ice Cream (Book 1)

Seasonal Magic

Holding a Witch (Book 1)

Remembering a Witch (Book 2)

Wanting a Witch (Book 3)

Contemporary

Forget the Past

Rescue Me (Book 1)

Read Me (Book 2)

Resist Me (Book 3)

Standalone Novel

You Only Need One

ABOUT THE AUTHOR

Lauren Connolly is a Colorado Book Awards and HOLT Medallion Finalist. She is an author of contemporary and paranormal romance stories. She has lived among mountains, next to lakes, and in imaginary worlds. Lauren can never seem to stay in one place for too long, but trust that wherever she's residing there is a dog who thinks he's a troll, twin cats hiding in the couch, and bookshelves bursting with the stories written by the authors she loves.

www.ingramcontent.com/pod-product-compliance
Lightning Source LLC
Chambersburg PA
CBHW060903190726
48286CB00002B/348